Title:	Second Chance Garden
Author:	A.J. Pine
Agent:	Emily Sylvan Kim Prospect Agency
Publication date:	9/5/2023
Category:	Romance
Format:	Mass Market Paperback Original
ISBN:	978-1-7282-5384-8
Price:	$8.99 U.S.
Pages:	384 pages

The Second Chance Garden

A. J. PINE

Published by Sourcebooks Casablanca, an imprint of Sourcebooks
P.O. Box 4410, Naperville, Illinois 60567–4410
(630) 961-3900
sourcebooks.com

Printed and bound in [Country of Origin—confirm when printer is selected].
XX 10 9 8 7 6 5 4 3 2 1

To second chances… It's never too late to try again.

Chapter 1

Emma tapped open the music app on her phone before putting the car in drive.

"Okay, Pancake. You pick the playlist," she said to the gray and white cat perched between her neck and the headrest behind her. His fur was warm and comforting on her neck, and his tail occasionally swished over her shoulder. The extra allergy pill, hit from her inhaler, *and* stiff neck would be worth it to keep Pancake from yowling the entire three hours from her apartment in Chicago to her hometown of Summertown. She held the phone up to her shoulder. A few seconds later, "Summer of '69" by Bryan Adams streamed through her speakers, and Emma bopped her head to the Canadian crooner's opening guitar riffs. "Eighties," she said with a grin. "Nice choice."

And that was how the two of them chased the final hours of summer daylight, cruising along the interstate to the soundtrack of synthesizers and saxophones, everything from the Go-Go's to Depeche Mode to OMD to Wham!

But when she hit the outskirts of town, Emma killed the music altogether as she slowed to a stop. The Welcome to Summertown sign lay toppled on the side of the road in what used to be a bed of blue wildflowers. She stared at the torn-up dirt and shreds of unrecognizable plants, and for a moment she was paralyzed, terrified of what she might find if she drove any further. Her throat tightened, and she blinked.

"What are we walking into?" she asked Pancake, who'd jumped down onto the passenger seat to peer out the window.

Summertown had weathered plenty of storms. It was par for the course in farm town, Illinois, but Emma had the feeling what she was about to see was worse than anything she'd witnessed growing up. What about her parents' inn? The gardens that were Summertown's biggest tourist draw and the town's livelihood?

The gardens. *Shit.*

She grabbed her phone and fired off a text.

Emma: Long story, but I'm in Summertown. Water my plants while I'm gone?

The three dots appeared almost immediately, and Emma winced, waiting for her best friend Haddie's reply.

Haddie: You left TOWN? Without telling ME?
Emma: Tornado. Will call tomorrow. The plants? PLEASE?
Haddie: K. Not my strong suit. Actually killed my gran's plastic fern. You've been warned.

Emma blinked and made a mental note to dig deeper on this when she had more time.

Emma: THANK YOU. Talk tomorrow.
Haddie: TONIGHT.
Emma: Marshmallow
Haddie: Only for you.

A smile still lingered on Emma's face as she rolled down her window and breathed in the warm, humid air. Even if Summertown didn't look the same, it still smelled like home, and that at least buoyed her spirits for what lay beyond the welcome sign.

That was when a white pickup sped past her, honking twice before water sprayed up through the open window and into the driver's seat, soaking her T-shirt, shorts, and *phone* with warm, muddy water. *Not* that it stayed warm for long.

"Shit!" she hissed as she spat silt from her lips and her phone screen went black. Pancake scurried onto the floor and under the passenger seat.

"Shit! Shit! Shit!"

Emma grabbed a napkin from her glove box

and made a futile effort to dry herself off. Now her clammy T-shirt was clinging to her skin, but at least there was no more water dripping down her legs. She eased her foot off the brake.

"Nice driving, asshole!" she called out her window to the truck that was already out of sight. Then she rolled past the broken sign and into town.

"Oh thank goodness!" she blurted through something between a laugh and a sob.

Lights glowed inside the inn, and Emma could hear the sounds of laughter and music and the chaos of the Woods Family Inn, the best chaos around.

She loaded a reluctant tabby into her pet duffel and zipped him in, leaving her small suitcase for after she got the cat settled.

"This is a good sign, P-cakes. A *really* good sign."

If the inn had guests, that meant the town wasn't as bad off as it seemed from the outskirts. It meant she'd worried the whole drive down for nothing. It *meant* she could spend some quality time with her parents for a few days and then head back to Chicago and rescue her plants from Haddie's murderous hands.

She laughed as she took the stairs to the porch two at a time, not letting the splintered banister bother her because everything was *fine*. She ignored the window shutter torn from its hinges, lying on a smashed Adirondack chair. The inn buzzed with warmth and excitement. So what if her clothes were soaked and her phone possibly destroyed if her parents' livelihood was still intact.

Emma wrapped her palm around the door handle, pressed her thumb against the latch, and strode inside.

She ducked as a bird dive-bombed her head, shrieked as something that might have been a guinea pig, *might* have been a rat scurried over her flip-flopped feet, and threw herself back against the door as a child whizzed by on a Razor scooter.

"What the actual f—"

"Ems!" her father cried as the guinea pig/possible rat scrambled back toward her as he chased it with an open box.

He stopped to catch his breath and plant a hurried kiss on her cheek.

"Watch the front desk, will you?" he asked. "I have to catch Goose for Mrs. Pinkney. He got out of his cage again."

"Goose?" Emma's head swam. "Mrs. Pinkney?" The weather had settled, but the inn felt like a cyclone of its own.

"You know Mrs. Pinkney's chinchilla, Goose." He threw his hands in the air, the box still in one. "I'll be *right* back, sweetheart. Promise!"

He took off again, but not before she could yell, "But why are Mrs. Pinkney and Goose *here*?"

"Whole town is!" her dad called over his

shoulder. "Most of it, at least. I'll explain everything as soon as I… Hey!" His voice grew further away, but Emma could still hear him shout. "You get back here you pain-in-the-ass fur ball!"

Emma moved slowly past the reception area and into the small lounge, wading through a sea of welcoming neighbors, their children, and apparently their pets.

The inn *was* alive and kicking. But the tornado had seemingly broken her town.

She stood amid the din, Pancake's carrier slung over her shoulder, the moisture from her wet clothes seeping into her skin, her family's inn now a surrogate for the town.

Welcome home, indeed.

Chapter 2

Matteo Rourke had only planned to go back to Summertown for a week—a month at the most—to keep his father's business afloat after a back injury laid him up. Matteo's brother, Levi, couldn't leave his job in Indiana. He didn't have the same flexibility Matteo did, *not* that Matteo was bragging about the flexibility of only being able to work odd jobs any place someone would hire a convicted felon.

Wrongful accusation or not, he had a record. Pleading his case to potential employers or the neighbors who used to feel like family didn't matter when a court of law said otherwise. So, he'd weathered being fodder for the rumor mill for a good month before the talk about Mayor Green's wife leaving him for the mayor of Middlebrook graciously took over the spotlight and allowed Matteo to settle into what should have been a temporary existence.

One month turned into two, and two into three.

Now here he was a year later, donning a Rourke Pest Control Carhartt shirt and driving his dad's old-but-still-running white pickup to and from calls to do everything from setting mouse traps to removing birds from oven vents. This evening, though, he'd spent the waning daylight hours clearing debris from the town square, cutting branches off of mangled trees, and hosing tattered rose petals off of walkways. Scratches covered his forearms and his shoulders ached, but none of that mattered when he knew he'd have to do it all again tomorrow. He wondered if everything would look better in the light of day or if dawn would only shed light on how bad things truly were. The town would have to forfeit the Garden Fest this year, a year when the prize money was needed more than ever.

"I don't get the point of competing with *gardens*," he'd complained the summer before he turned thirteen when he'd wanted to ride dirt bikes with his friends rather than prune bushes and scrape his hands on rose thorns. "What do we even *win*?"

"Someday you'll get it, sweetheart," his mother had said. "There's a lot of satisfaction to be had out of working for something bigger than yourself. We have to give back to our community, not just be takers. Lottie Green put our town on the map with her garden designs. She's the reason we get all those tourists every summer." Then she'd buried her face in his hair, kissing the top of his head as he rolled his eyes and wriggled away. "And we win *money* for our town." She ambushed him with a kiss on the cheek after that, making him groan before getting back to work.

"The animal ones creep me out," Matteo once again argued when he was a teen. "When I go for a morning run, I feel like the dragon in the Duboses' lawn is watching me. I swear it has those eyes that follow you no matter which way you go."

She'd snort-laughed at this one. "I don't know what's funnier, the fact that they put googly eyes on a plant or that you think those googly eyes can follow you."

His mom was right about one thing. Lottie Green *had* put Summertown on the map—turning the town hall lawn into a scene from *Edward Scissorhands,* trimming the overgrown shrubbery in front of the building into the likenesses of her cavapoos, Zeus, Apollo, and Hermes. Soon she was called upon by homeowners and business owners alike to transform their hedges into sculptures. Only now she'd taken her talents across the border to Middlebrook, leaving her husband and any chance of Summertown winning the fest again in her rearview mirror.

Matteo's chest ached. He'd take back the eye rolling, the groaning, *and* the complaining to feel the press of his mother's lips to his head or hear that snort laugh again. Instead he was making his final drive back into Summertown after helping rake up what once was the Duboses' dragon and hauling it—along with other debris—out to the woods on the outskirts of town. He squeezed the steering wheel tight, focusing on the feel of the rough, worn leather against his palms rather than on his regret.

His one saving grace for tonight was that his father's house was one of the few that had sustained minimal damage.

He was tired and hot; his shoulder ached; and he was ready for a shower. He yawned and then shook his head, attempting to shake some energy back into his being when he hit a pothole he swore wasn't there twenty minutes ago. The truck jerked to the left and into the oncoming lane, and he overcorrected by swerving right and nearly hitting a small car that had stopped in front of the Summertown welcome sign. Or what *had been* the Summertown welcome sign. He could fix it, but what would be the point? It would only be a Band-Aid on a wound that right now felt beyond healing.

He honked to let the driver know they were asking for trouble and then hightailed it back into town. Power wasn't up yet, so he enjoyed a cold shower. He didn't have high hopes of staying cool with nothing more than a box fan to move the air around the garage apartment he now called home, but the cool water sluicing down the tired muscles of his back gave him renewed energy and maybe even a little hope. The storm *had* devastated the town, but little by little, Summertown would rebuild. He conjured his mother's words that she'd told him so often about *the importance of working together for something bigger than yourself,* and for the first time, he was suddenly happy that he'd come home. Despite what anyone thought about the things he'd done in his past, he was here when the town needed him. There was nowhere he'd rather be.

"We have to eat everything in the fridge," his father said when Matteo strode into the kitchen in a pair of running shorts and a Paramore concert T-shirt that fit snugly against his lean, muscled frame and was worn so thin you could see through it. He didn't care; it felt soft and comforting against his skin. The tightness almost felt like an embrace. If he closed his eyes, he could almost conjure a face—*her* face—as her arms wrapped him tight.

Matteo sighed. "I mean, I *am* hungry, Dad. Don't get me wrong. But that seems a little extreme, doesn't it?"

Denny Rourke ran a hand through his thick salt-and-pepper hair as he stood with one hand on the refrigerator door, the salt and pepper the only part about the man that betrayed his fifty-five years. Okay that *and* the back spasms that had brought Matteo back to Summertown last year and still laid his father up every now and again. But aside from a bad back, the man was trim and tall, just like his son, and Matteo certainly appreciated the possible look into his own future. If he had enough of his father's genetic makeup, it hopefully meant his hair not thinning and his midsection not thickening.

He laughed softly and shook his head, wondering what purpose there was to any sort of vanity when he kept so much to himself.

"Holy hell," Matteo said under his breath, but considering the lack of any other sound in the room from a blowing air conditioner or a refrigerator's hum, his father heard him loud and clear.

"Having some sort of light-bulb moment?" the older man asked.

Matteo scratched the back of his neck and shook his head. "Just realizing I'm already living my future," he said. "Dad, do you…" He cleared his throat. "Um…ever go on dates?" He winced as soon as the last word passed his lips.

"Course not," his father said. "Your mama was the love of my life. What would be the point of inviting someone else to compete with her ghost?"

Matteo swallowed. "And you're not…lonely?"

He wasn't sure where this was coming from or why he was all of a sudden thinking of the years his father had spent alone in Matteo's boyhood home. He'd simply come downstairs to grab something to eat and check on the electricity situation. Matteo and his dad were great housemates—especially since Matteo technically had his own space above the garage. But they didn't do heart-to-hearts. Maybe it was the storm or the unrelenting summer heat, but he felt off-kilter this evening, and he needed something or someone to set him straight again.

His father let go of the fridge handle and stood straight, crossing one arm over his chest and scratching the stubble on his jaw.

"I was for a while, especially when you and your brother grew up and left home."

Guilt socked Matteo in the gut, but his father waved a hand at him before he could respond.

"I don't blame you, Son. There's no rule that says you have to live your whole life in the place you were born. I love this town and the people are like family, always have been. I never wanted to leave. For you and Levi it was different." He shook his head and scratched the back of his neck, then let out a soft chuckle. "If you're ready to head back out on the road and live your nomad life again, I'll be okay, Son."

Matteo opened his mouth, but his father turned back and opened the freezer door.

"We should start with the ice cream, don't you think? It'll be the first to go." He grabbed a pint of salted caramel pretzel crunch from Sweet, one of the oldest and most loved shops in town that sold pretty much anything that included sugar as an ingredient, all made fresh in-house. His father raised his brows in question, but Matteo suddenly wasn't hungry anymore. He needed to clear his head.

"Actually, Dad, I think I'm going to head out for a run first." He pointed at the pint. "If that's a full pint, though, you better save me some."

Denny Rourke shrugged. "Can't make any promises. If the power's still out, I have to do what's necessary so it doesn't go to waste."

The screen door off the kitchen that led to the backyard squeaked open, and in walked Tilly Higginson with a perspiring pitcher of sun tea.

"Evening, Tilly," Denny said.

"Hey there, Tilly," Matteo added.

She set the pitcher of tea on the counter and clapped her hands together, her side-swept silver bangs bouncing on her forehead as she grinned. She was an attractive woman, younger than his father but "embracing my gray!" as she often liked to say when anyone complimented her hair.

She turned her gaze to his father, and Matteo bit back a grin. Denny Rourke might not be looking for a companion, but Tilly Higginson was certainly looking at *him*.

"I'm going to head out on that run now," Matteo said, suddenly feeling like a third wheel. "Feel free to share that ice cream with Tilly so it doesn't go to waste," he added, winking at his father.

"Ice cream?" Tilly raised her brows. "How about we wash it down with some tea?"

Denny Rourke stared wide-eyed at his son for a long moment until Tilly nudged him with her elbow. "Hello? Den? Ya there?"

"Yeah, *Den*," Matteo repeated, teasing his oblivious father. "Ya there?" Then he waved to them both as he headed out of the kitchen. "I'll be back in an hour!" he called over his shoulder as he slipped on his running shoes, which he left conveniently on the rug just inside the front door. He'd need another cold shower when he got back, he thought. Right now he needed to run, but his usual route through town would probably still be a mess of debris, so he hopped in his truck and headed straight for Summertown High School and the track that had been his home away from home for four years of his life.

While Levi Rourke ran passes on the field, Matteo ran the track. When their mother first got sick, Levi dove into the game, becoming the most scouted athlete in Summertown's history. Matteo dove into the more solitary nature of running. He was part of the track and cross-country teams, but when his feet hit the pavement, it was him and him alone until he crossed the finish line.

Five miles and forty-five minutes later, Matteo lay on the home team bleachers staring up at the clear sky speckled with so many stars. It was hard to believe that only a few hours ago the same sky had been a mess of wind and rain and anything the storm could pick up and toss around.

He took several gulps from his water bottle, then squirted the remaining liquid on his neck and forehead, cleaning off the sweat and allowing his body temperature to cool. He closed his eyes and let the unexpected breeze finish the job. He wasn't in a rush to get back home and interrupt whatever might be happening between his father and Tilly—even if it was only harmless flirting—so he let himself relax, the magnitude of the day finally hitting him.

His phone buzzed in his pocket, and he pulled it out to see his dad's number on the other end of the call.

"Yeah, Dad, what's up?" he asked groggily.

"Matteo? Hi. It's Tilly."

Matteo slowly sat up and gave his head a shake, waking himself up.

"Hi, Tilly. Is my dad okay?" His stomach dropped.

"It's a back spasm. He got a call about a squirrel chasing a cat or something at the inn? Or maybe it was the cat chasing the squirrel? I'm not sure. The person calling seemed a bit frantic from what I could hear. We were just sitting at the table eating ice cream. Have you tried this new flavor? It's to die for. I'd save you some, but..."

The lights over the field suddenly switched on, and Matteo—whose eyes had grown used to the moonlight—had to shield himself from the glare.

"Oh, look at that!" Tilly exclaimed. "Power's back on. I'll put what's left of the pint in the freezer for you. See, Denny?" Her voice sounded further away as she turned to address his father. "We don't have to finish it. Okay," she said back into the phone. "So there's a squirrel and a cat situation, and all your father did was get up from his chair, and his back said *Not today, Denny Rourke*. Do you think you could take the call while I get your dad situated on the couch and run to the pharmacy to get him some pain medication, and ice packs, and maybe a heating pad? How you boys live without the basic first-aid necessities is beyond me. Anyway, can you take the call?"

Matteo blew out a long breath. Nothing in Summertown ever actually closed. If it was midnight and Tilly Higginson needed to run out for pain meds and ice packs, good old Solomon Grant would crawl out of bed and open up shop so she could get what she needed. Or he'd simply give her the key code to the door and tell her to pay him in the morning.

His father was right. The people of Summertown were indeed family—to Denny Rourke, at least. Once upon a time, they'd been Matteo's family too, but everyone looked at him differently now, some with pity and some with accusation. Even if Lottie Green fed the party line of gossip these days, Matteo had been branded.

Ex-con.

Addict.

Thief.

Despite the battle of truth vs. fabrication, his story had been rewritten in the span of an evening nearly eight years ago, the week after he'd lost his mom. Grief had a way of turning you into someone you weren't. He couldn't change the decisions or mistakes he'd made when he was in the thick of it or what happened to him because of it. And he certainly couldn't change the way everyone saw him now—the kid who let that grief ruin his future. Except he wasn't a kid anymore. He was a man living each day in the aftermath of those mistakes, doing the best he could to get by.

"Yeah," he finally said. "I have traps in the truck. I can take the call. Thanks for taking care of my dad, Tilly. Maybe you can talk him into finally seeing a specialist once this episode is over."

"Will do," she said. "I can be very convincing, you know."

Matteo had no doubt she could. "Thanks again," he said. "And if you need to head back home before I get there—"

"I'll stay until you're done," she assured him. "Now that the power's back on, I might even fix us a proper meal. Oh no," she added. "The inn's calling again. You better get there as soon as humanly possible to deal with the—well—the *non*-humans."

Matteo was already exiting the stadium and on his way to his truck when he ended the call. Less than five minutes later, he was parking in front of the Woods Family Inn, the one place in Summertown he used to know almost as well as his boyhood home. Now it felt like a stranger's home, despite him knowing every nook and cranny of the space inside.

In a town this size, he hadn't been able to avoid Mr. and Mrs. Woods entirely since his return, but there'd never been cause to *enter* the inn.

His jaw clenched as he steeled himself. Then he hopped out of the truck and grabbed a trap from the cargo bed. He hesitated for one final moment—noting the upturned dirt where the bushes used to be and the splintered rails heading up the stairs—before striding onto the porch, pushing open the door, and stepping inside to find *Emma* Woods standing on the registration desk holding a thrashing cat in her arms as she yelled, "No, Pancake! Hold still!"

She glanced down at Matteo as he stood momentarily frozen in the open doorway. Her eyes widened, and the cat thrashed again.

"Ow!" she cried. "Dammit, Pancake!"

Then he noticed the scratches on her arms, neck, and cheek.

"The squirrel just ran back into the fireplace. Do you think you can catch it before this guy turns me into ground beef?"

Shit. Had he still not moved or spoken?

"Right," he finally said. "Fireplace."

Matteo strode past the desk and into the small yet cozy reception lounge. He guessed the squirrel had likely entered from the chimney. The pesky rodent was lucky it wasn't winter, or he'd have had a much less friendly welcome at the other end of the flue.

"It's a humane trap!" he called over his shoulder. "In case you were wondering."

"The only thing I'm wondering is if you can get the rodent out of the hotel before any guests find out that we *have* rodents! Not sure if you noticed the tornado damage throughout town, but anyone whose house isn't livable is living *here*!"

"Doesn't care about humane traps," he mumbled under his breath. "Noted."

Something flew past his ear, and he swatted the already empty air.

"What the hell was *that*?" he called over his shoulder.

The cat in Emma's arms yowled in response before she chimed in.

"That would be Harmony Sapperstein's parakeet, Pikachu, who Pancake is desperate to eat, so if you could expedite the process of whatever it is you're doing over there, that would be great."

Sure. He'd just scurry up the fireplace and catch the little bugger with his bare hands. The only issues were him being a human-sized human and his inability to crawl up walls like Spider-Man. So he did the next best and *logical* thing.

Matteo squatted in front of the fireplace, set the trap on the floor next to him, then pulled his phone out of his pocket so he could shine his flashlight up the chimney.

"I don't see it!" he shouted back toward Emma at the desk. "Probably crawled back up to where he was hiding before popping out to say hello. I'll leave the trap at the bottom." He set the baited cage in the center of the fireplace, then crawled out and stood up, brushing his hands on his running shorts.

"Do you have a screen or a grate for the fireplace?" he asked when he made it back to Emma and her slowly calming cat.

"I don't know!" she exclaimed, her eyes darting from him to the fireplace and back. "I *just* got here a couple of hours ago and said I'd take the night shift, and now there is a *squirrel* loose in the inn!"

He held his hands up in an effort to appease. "It's okay. Really. As soon as he smells the bait, he'll head right in the cage, and then I'll relocate him to Wilton's Farm." He crossed his arms over his chest and stared up at her.

His instinct was actually to run rather than reach a hand for the woman he hadn't spoken to in eight years, but he couldn't just leave her up there. Could he? No. He couldn't, not now that she'd actually seen him.

Matteo sighed. "Can I give you a hand getting down off that desk, or is that your new home?"

Chapter 3

Was Pancake purring, or was Emma shaking? She tried to calm herself down enough to confirm, but she couldn't listen for her cat's reassuring purr when her heart was beating in her ears.

"Emma?"

Somehow, Matteo's voice registered amid the din.

"Huh?" she asked, then noticed his extended arm. "Oh. Right. Okay." She swallowed. "Are you sure Pancake's not going to get rabied by a rodent if we come down?"

He laughed, then cleared his throat. "*Rabied*?"

Emma groaned. "You know what I mean. And I can make a noun a verb if I want to. . Also I'm—I'm flustered, okay?"

Ha! Understatement of the year, the decade even.

Matteo. Rourke.

Matteo Rourke. Right there, standing in front of the desk reaching out to grab her hand.

"Are you sure it was a squirrel and not one of Mrs. Pinkney's chinchillas?" he asked.

"*One* of?"

He nodded. "Maverick and Goose. Goose is always getting out of his cage."

Maverick and Goose. Now the name made more sense.

"I'm sure," she insisted. "I saw my dad catch Goose earlier this evening. And chinchillas have those big floppy ears. This thing had the little pointy ones and a long bushy tail. He even stopped to give me the stink eye with that beady little eye of his like he *knew* he could give me rabies if he wanted."

"It's okay," Matteo told her for the second time, biting back another laugh, which only agitated her more. "Pancake is safe. I promise. Unless he—or *she*—tastes like sunflower seeds buried in peanut butter. In that case, yes. He might get rabied."

The corner of his mouth twitched into an almost-grin.

His voice was deeper than she remembered, his tone more reserved, but even after all these years, a warm flow of reassurance pumped through her veins.

She believed him. She *trusted* him—about the squirrel, at least. But the twenty-one-year-old boy who said he loved her eight years ago and then cut her out of his life when she thought he needed her most? That guy sat on the biggest throne of lies.

"He's a *he*. Pancake, I mean." Emma carefully lowered Pancake to the desk and set him down, her eyes now level with Matteo's. The cat scurried to the floor and took off, hopefully not into the squirrel trap himself. "Don't eat Pikachu!" she called after the blur of gray and white fur.

"I, um, got myself up here," she assured him. "I can get myself down."

His barely there grin faded, and the muscle in his jaw pulsed.

He nodded as she climbed down with as much grace as she could muster. Once she was standing on the floor with the desk providing a safety buffer between them, she brushed her hands off on her T-shirt and squared her shoulders.

"You're…um…*home*." Her skin prickled with goose bumps.

He nodded, his expression impassive. "So are you."

"I meant…" she continued, but he interrupted her.

"Good behavior," he told her. "Turns out I was a model prisoner. Only had to serve eighteen months of a two-year sentence. Lucky me, right?" he added drily. "But I only came back to Summertown last year to help out my dad." He scratched the back of his neck. "Anyway, about this squirrel situation…"

Right. Subject change. Why would he want to talk to her about where he'd been the six and a half years—or about the eighteen months prior—when they could talk about rodents?

Her eyes finally registered on the man-who-was-now-a-stranger standing in front of her. "That's *mine*," she declared, pointing at the garment she only now realized he was wearing.

He glanced down at the threadbare cotton hugging his chest—a chest that was much more filled out on this almost thirty-year-old version of the boy she once knew.

"This is *my* shirt," he insisted. "We both bought one at the concert."

Emma cleared her throat. "I remember. But that one is *mine*. I got the pink one, and you got the black one. Plus, look how tight it is on you. Even in high school, you weren't small enough to fit into that shirt. I thought I lost it, but it turns out you stole it."

He flinched, and she realized what she'd just said, opening her mouth to… What? Take it back? Rephrase the accusation when it was the truth?

"It's fine," he said, reading her thoughts and painting on a smile that was about as genuine as Monopoly money. "Once a thief, always a thief, right?"

"I didn't…" she stammered. "You're twisting my words."

Matteo shrugged, and the goose bumps that had peppered her flesh moments ago vanished.

"This is the only Paramore shirt I have. You must have the black one *somewhere*, if it even exists. I guess when you find it, we'll compare sizes and solve the mystery."

It was just a *shirt*. It didn't mean anything that he still had it, especially when he didn't even remember it was hers.

She tried to plaster on her own mask of a smile but winced. She gingerly touched her cheek with the tips of her fingers, and they came away with tiny streaks of blood. That was when she saw the puffy, livid scratches on her forearms, some of them bleeding as well.

Emma's stomach churned, and she swallowed the threat of nausea as she tried to casually cross her arms behind her back so the blood was out of sight.

"Looks like Pancake got you pretty good. You should clean those cuts and put some antibacterial ointment on them. You have a first aid kit, right?"

"Mom had one under the front desk, but I don't see it there now. She might have taken it to the office to restock it or something..."

Matteo scrubbed a hand across his jaw, the light catching on his ginger stubble. Then he sighed. "I have a kit in my car. Is it okay if I...? I mean, I could help you... You should clean the wounds, okay? I know they're just scratches, but they'll heal a lot quicker and hurt a lot less if you take care of them now."

Now that the adrenaline was subsiding, Emma could feel the hot sting of each and every cut and knew once she looked at the wounds again, she might actually lose her lunch this time.

"Okay," she relented. "I guess you can get your kit."

He nodded once and then headed out the door.

For several seconds, Emma wondered if what had just happened had really happened.

Matteo Rourke, after shutting her out of his life eight years ago, *here*. In her family's inn. Wearing *her* Paramore T-shirt and fetching a first aid kit from his truck to treat *her* wounds.

"Thanks for giving me a heads-up he was back in town, Mom and Dad," she mumbled bitterly to herself as she plopped onto the stool behind the registration desk, forcing herself *not* to look down at her arms again. And okay, a tornado ripping through Summertown *maybe* was enough to give her parents a pass for not offering such pertinent information, but it didn't make tonight's run-in an easier pill to swallow. She reminded herself that her emotional wounds were more than healed after so many years, but no one liked being caught off guard.

The bell over the inn's door tinkled as Matteo strode back in, a soft red case with a white cross on it in his hand.

"So that's, like, a legit kit, huh?" she asked, then groaned at her own awkwardness. She stood and held a hand out over the desk. "You can just give me what I need, and I'll take care of it," she added coolly, hoping to save face, but she caught sight of a bloodied scratch out of the corner of her eye and wavered, catching herself with both hands on the desk.

Matteo narrowed his eyes at her. "You never could stand the sight of blood."

Emma opened her mouth to protest, then threw her hand over it as her stomach threatened to speak for her instead.

Matteo quickly rounded the desk and grabbed her hand. "Come on." He tugged her arm with gentle insistence and pulled her into the lounge, seating her on the sofa that sat opposite the fireplace before kneeling in front of her.

She froze, her hand still in his, as a familiar jolt of electricity passed through her.

Muscle memory. That was all it was.

"Close your eyes," he commanded, and she complied. Anything not to see even the tiniest speck of blood again. Or Matteo Rourke's brown eyes this close to hers.

"I'm going to clean you up first," he continued. "And not gonna lie, but the antiseptic wipes'll sting."

She nodded. "Just tell me when you're going to do it so I can—" She hissed in a breath as the cold swipe across her forearm was followed not by a sting but by *fire*. Actual. Fire.

"Sorry," he offered.

She sucked in another sharp breath as he cleaned the top of her hand, her other arm, and then her cheek.

A soft breeze cooled the sting on her skin, and Emma popped an eye open to see Matteo softly blowing on her wounds.

Her stomach tightened, and she quickly squeezed her eyes shut again.

She felt his rough fingertips slide along her skin as he spread the ointment over each scratch, and she finally exhaled, realizing the hard part was over. Except the hairs on the back of her neck still stood on end, and though the nausea had subsided, her head swam with an unexpected dizziness.

She heard a ripping sound and winced.

"It's just the medical tape for the gauze," he told her. "All done, by the way. It's safe to open your eyes."

She hesitated, then cracked one eye open and then the other.

Her forearms were wrapped in gauze, and there was a butterfly bandage over one of her knuckles. She gingerly touched her cheek and felt the small Band-Aid.

When her eyes finally met his, she swallowed. "Um… Thank you. I'm going to have a stern conversation with Pancake about his reaction to squirrels so this doesn't happen again."

He didn't move. Just stayed there on his knees, his brown eyes locked on hers for several seconds.

"Was there something you wanted to say?" she asked.

Something maybe like *I'm sorry I didn't think of telling you I got out early.*

Or *I* wanted *to tell you I was back but didn't think you'd care after all this time.*

Which she shouldn't, right? So why was she traveling down this mental road?

She'd even be open to something along the lines of *So, you're never going to believe this, but the second I stepped foot outside the prison property line, I was in an accident, and when I woke up, I had amnesia, and I only just remembered who I was today and came rushing to the inn to tell you I was back. I can't tell you how happy I am that you're here.*

But instead he shook his head, standing back up to his full height so that now she was staring at his running shorts and his lean, muscled thighs.

"You know the whole story now that you know I'm back. Not much else to report."

She stood as well so she wasn't continuing the conversation with his shorts, her eyes traveling up as she rose.

"Wait!" She grabbed his wrist and studied scabbed scratches traveling up his warm, freckled skin. "What happened to *you*?"

He glanced down to where Emma held him, and she yanked her hand away as if she'd been burned.

"Tornado cleanup," he responded without

incident. "Every rose has its thorn, right? Imagine cleaning full, uprooted bushes. It gets a little prickly." He gave her a dry laugh.

Emma felt like she was still catching her breath, and *he* was cracking dad jokes.

For a second she wondered if she needed another hit from her asthma inhaler, but she wasn't wheezing. She felt more like the wind had been knocked from her lungs and she was waiting for them to fill again.

"Call me—or, I mean, my dad—if you find our little friend in the trap. Otherwise, I—or my dad if he's feeling better—will pop back over tomorrow during daylight to do a full inspection of the place and determine if the inn needs repairs to seal up any holes."

He took a step back, the increased distance finally making it easier for her to breathe. Pancake reappeared, making a figure eight between her feet as he rubbed his head against her ankles.

Emma crossed her bandaged arms and glared down at him. "Just because you're cute doesn't excuse what you did." She turned her attention back to Matteo. "Yeah. Okay. Thanks," she said. "For setting the trap and for cleaning me up."

He pressed his lips together and nodded. "You should take the bandages off in the morning and let the wounds breathe. It should all look a little better by then too." He checked his watch and then gave her one final glance. "Good to see you, Emma."

Then he pivoted back toward the entrance, striding through the door and out of sight.

Except the image of him was burned into her brain now—his dark-brown eyes, stubbled jaw, and the way *her* T-shirt clung to the adult man's torso beneath.

Emma had locked her memories of him far into the recesses of her mind where they'd stayed for years. But the practiced art of avoidance meant nothing when your past walked into your family's inn, saving you not only from a likely rabid rodent but also from a long-standing physiological reaction to the sight of blood.

"Good to see you too," she said absently as she bent down to scratch her attacker under the chin.

It was a lie, of course. But she'd been lying to herself for years, so why would she stop now?

When he got home that night, Matteo stripped out of his running gear and took an extra-long shower to clear his head.

Wearing only a towel, he strode to his dresser where he grabbed a pair of clean boxer briefs from one drawer—and then a black Paramore T-shirt from another. He stepped into the briefs and pulled the shirt over his head, the ghost of a smile pulling at the corner of his mouth as he crawled into bed.

It was the first twinge of something resembling happiness he'd felt in years.

Chapter 4

SWEAT SOAKED MATTEO'S CARHARTT—AND THE white T-shirt he wore underneath—after two hours of crawling through the attic and along the roof of the Woods Family Inn. With electricity restored, the air-conditioning was back up and running inside the inn proper, but the attic and the great outdoors were another story.

"I think I found your problem," he commented as he strode through the inn's back door that led to the owners' private quarters—a couple of bedrooms, a bathroom, a small kitchen, and an office where Lynette Woods looked up at Matteo from her desk.

"Let's hear it," the older woman replied, then dipped her head back toward the laptop she'd been staring at when Matteo had left her in the very same spot two hours before.

He swiped his arm across his forehead, and it came away wet. Then he held up the metal clipboard with the carbon copy Rourke Pest Control forms.

"You've got a hole in your chimney right at attic level. The critter..." He cleared his throat. "Or... uh...*critters* got in that way and had a bit of a party in your attic tearing apart the insulation and scratching at the wood. The damage inside is minimal. I can probably take care of that in less than a day. But the chimney, since it's a wood casing, is going to need a rebuild."

There was more, but he paused, waiting for some sort of reaction from Mrs. Woods. For several seconds she said nothing, so he opened his mouth to continue, but right as he was about to tell her the best—or actually *worst*—part, her head shot up, her gray chin-length waves bouncing from the movement.

"What's your estimate, Matty? I'm knee-deep in what it's already going to cost us to replant the shrubs in front, fix the porch rails and a couple loose steps Hank found this morning, and don't get me started on the zinnias on the front walkway and the garden out back. Plus, I can't charge for rooms when every occupant has a home of their own to rebuild. Now you're telling me that after a tornado left my inn standing, I gotta worry about rodents in my attic?" She groaned. "I'm sorry. I know none of this is your fault. I'm already talking to the bank about a line of credit. We could really use that prize money from the festival right now, but we sure aren't the belle of the ball."

She finger quoted *belle of the ball* as Matteo simply stared. He was pretty sure he'd heard every word, yet he was still stuck on that one—*Matty*. No one other than Emma's mother had ever called him that. Not his own mother, not even Emma, unless you counted her version of it, Matty Matt, a name she was never allowed to call him in public but that he secretly loved. In all the years this inn had been like his second home, he'd always found comfort in the way Emma's mom had talked to him like he was family, and the nicknames… Everyone had multiple nicknames, and thinking about them warmed his heart.

"Hello?" she added, waving her hand in Matteo's direction. "You still there?"

"What?" He coughed. "I mean, yes. *Yes.* I'm… uh…I'm here. And yes, you do have rodents in your attic, but also…"

He let his voice trail off, afraid this last bit would be too much for her to deal with.

She sighed. "No use sugarcoating it."

Matteo felt an involuntary quirk at the corner of his mouth as he suppressed a grin. It was like something in the air had shifted somewhere between the tornado touching down and a squirrel showing up in the inn's lobby last night, something that filled his chest with a lightness he didn't recognize.

"Of course," he finally answered. "So while there wasn't too much damage on the inside, there is the situation with the nest."

"The nest?" she asked.

He nodded. "The nest."

"The *nest*," she repeated.

Matteo nodded again. "The nest. Of baby squirrels. Just inside the chimney where it meets the attic."

Lynette Woods's eyes widened. "You can move it, right? The nest?"

Matteo sighed. "The babies would probably die." He winced.

Her mouth fell open. "I can't *murder* baby squirrels."

"Technically," he started, "it wouldn't be *you*…"

She gasped. "Well I can't *hire* someone to do it either! Matteo, I would *never* ask you to do such a thing. Your dad's always been so proud of his company's humane treatment of animals."

"'Whether squirrel or skunk, we'll protect *your* home and theirs too,'" a voice chimed in over Matteo's shoulder.

He cringed at his dad's cheesy slogan, then spun to find Emma Woods standing in the doorframe with her arms behind her back so he was able to read the entirety of the red tee that hugged her curves: *Challenge Accepted* in white, framed by a white line above and below the words.

That was his Emma. Always up to the task and ready to prove she could go one step further.

Correction.

That was *Emma*. At least the Emma he once

knew. But she most certainly wasn't *his*, and Matteo wanted to pinch—or better yet—throat punch himself to snap himself out of the nostalgia that kept muddling his thoughts.

"It's a bit clunky but sweet, don't you think?" Emma asked, referring to the motto.

Matteo stared.

Emma's brows furrowed as she grabbed a hair tie from her wrist and piled her loose brunette waves into a wild bun on top of her head.

"You there, McFly?"

"Right?" Emma's mom added from the other side of the room. "Our pest control expert seems a little out of sorts today."

He pivoted to face Mrs. Woods. Then he spun back toward Emma.

"I'm not out of sorts," he grumbled. "It's just *hot*. And I'm *hot*. And there are baby squirrels in the attic." And Emma looked *hot* with those words stretched across her chest, and Matteo was too old to think the word *hot* like that. But it would have been nice if he'd had some sort of warning she was coming home. Or that the first time he saw her, he'd have to nurse her damned wounds. Or that she was even more beautiful now than she was almost a decade ago.

Fine. Maybe Matteo was out of sorts, but there was no way in hell he was going to admit they were right or *why*.

"Oh goodness!" Lynette exclaimed. "What kind of an innkeeper am I, not offering you something cold to drink after all the work you've been doing in the heat?" She pushed her chair back and sprang up as she rounded the corner of her desk and hooked her elbow with Matteo's. "Let's get you lemonade or tea while you lay out all the details about our furry friends and what it will cost to repair the damage they've already done. Or maybe one of Hank's fancy IPA beers he saves for his nights off?"

"It's just IPA, Mom," Emma replied. "The A stands for 'ale,' so the beer part is redundant."

Lynette waved her off. "What do I care? I'm not a fan, but Hank seems to like them, so maybe you do too?" She raised her brows in question as she set her eyes on Matteo.

He cleared his throat. "No thank you. I'm technically still on the clock, so I really shouldn't." Which was *technically* the truth. The fact that he hadn't had a drink in nearly eight years was another story that he didn't need to get into now.

Lynette shrugged. "Suit yourself. The lemonade is better, anyway. I infuse it with fresh strawberries." But as soon as she made a motion to leave, her desk phone rang. "I have to get that, Em." She directed her attention to her daughter. "Can you take Matteo to the kitchen and grab him a drink? He can give you the estimate, and you can relay the information to me later. Then maybe you can check in on the dining room, make sure I put out enough food for whoever needs it." She unhooked her arm from Matteo's and was already heading back to her chair before Emma had a chance to answer.

A second later, Lynette Woods was on the phone and quietly shooing the two of them out of her office.

Once in the hallway, Matteo closed the office door behind him.

"I can come back," he told Emma just as she blurted out, "You don't have to stay."

He swallowed.

Emma did the same.

He could leave and come back later, but what were the odds he would catch Emma's mother at a good time and not get pawned off on her daughter then as well?

"Your mom seems super busy," he began. "And a line of credit is a pretty big deal."

Emma's eyes widened. "Line of credit? My mom said she's taking out a line of credit? Why did she tell you and not me? Are things that bad? What else did she say?"

Shit. He didn't know *she* didn't know. "Sorry. I didn't mean to make you worry. She just sort of mentioned it but didn't make it sound like a big deal. Just a possible option to help the town," he lied. It wasn't his place to get involved. "The estimate for repairs and plan for the nest shouldn't take long. And I'm sure we can work out a payment plan. Probably best to just get it out of the way. Should we head to the public kitchen so it's not—I don't know—just us?" He figured he'd acknowledge the elephant in the room.

Emma fidgeted with the hem of her T-shirt and shuffled her feet. He glanced down to see her lean legs extending from the bottom of her cotton shorts. But instead of shoes, she wore fluffy, orange cat slippers.

"Hey, Rourke. My eyes are up here," she teased.

When his head shot up from her feet, she was staring at him with brows raised.

He raised his right back. "You can't wear something like *that* on your feet and not expect people to stare."

She pressed a hand to her chest and gasped. "Do you mean to tell me these are not on the cusp of feline couture?"

"I'm sorry to say I was unaware of feline couture all together," he countered, giving himself a mental pat on the back for keeping up with her banter after years of being out of practice.

"It's a thing," she insisted. "It might only be *my* thing, but it's a thing nonetheless."

"Plus, the slippers are safer than the actual animal. *They* can't turn you into ground beef." He bit back a grin as he lobbed her words from last night back at her.

Emma threw her hands in the air with mock exasperation. "I should have gotten *slippers* as a pet. Why didn't I think of that?"

He barked out a laugh, the sound of it catching him off guard, then finally noticed the scabbing cuts on her knuckles, forearms, and chin. "Your wounds look a lot better."

Her cheeks reddened. "I took the bandages off this morning and let them breathe like you said. Still stings a little, but I think I'm through the worst of it."

"Glad to hear."

"It was touch and go there for a bit," Emma teased. "But after making it through the night, doctors think I'll not only make a full recovery but be back on my laptop scheduling social media posts in as little as days, *maybe* even hours." She bit her bottom lip as she smiled.

The gesture was too familiar yet at the same time so foreign.

Matteo tapped his fingers against the clipboard he was now holding against his torso. "So, I'll take that cold drink if it's okay. I'll just finish filling out your estimate and abatement plan, and then your mom can call me with any questions."

"Okay," Emma replied. "Let's go to the private kitchen."

She spun to face him as she rounded the corner into the quaint yet roomy personal kitchen. "Did you say something?"

Matteo was so caught up in overthinking their banter that he kept walking straight into her, dropping his clipboard in just enough time to catch her as she toppled toward the ceramic tiled floor.

He held her there, arms wrapped around her waist as she stared up at him like they'd just struck their final, dramatic pose in *Dancing with the Stars*. Her chest heaved, and he could see her pulse throbbing in her neck. His own heart beat in the same frantic rhythm as he stared into the emerald pools of her wide-open eyes.

If this had been a romance novel—and yes, he'd read one or two—this would have been one of those climactic moments where the hero and heroine might have shared their first kiss. But this was no story. It was real life, and Matteo and Emma's first—and *last*—kiss was long behind them, now punctuated by eight years of silence.

She'd moved on with her life, and he'd given her the freedom to do so. End of story.

Emma has a life of her own now, and I'm not going to mess with that.

That would be his mantra now that their worlds had unexpectedly collided.

So, no. There would be no dramatic kiss after their unexpected reunion. He was here to catch rodents and to tell the once love of his life how much that would cost.

"Sorry," he finally said, straightening to his full height and pulling her back to standing.

"Yeah," she squeaked, then cleared her throat. "I mean, watch where you're going next time, okay?" She let out a nervous laugh.

His hands were still wrapped around her, and they stood close enough that he could feel her breath on his neck, could hear the slight tremble in the sound of it.

He let her go and all but pushed her away, then bent down to grab his clipboard.

"Also...thank you," Emma added when his eyes met hers again. "After Pancake's freak-out last night, I'd really prefer not to add a concussion to my list of injuries."

"You're welcome," he replied, the memory of her warmth against his palm seared into his skin like a brand. How, after so many years, could a simple touch be charged with memories and emotions he'd long since locked away? He was over her. Happy that she seemed happy. This was nothing more than his body remembering what his heart had already laid to rest. "Where is that assailant of yours, anyway?"

As if on cue, the tabby meowed from somewhere in the kitchen and then appeared at Emma's slippered feet, rubbing his head against the fluffy, stuffed cats that made Matteo perspire even more imagining how warm they must be on a scorcher like today.

Or maybe the extra perspiration was because of getting a little too up close and personal with the woman who still occasionally visited his dreams.

"I forgave him," Emma said, dropping to a squat to scratch the purring feline behind his ear. "Hard to stay mad at someone I love so much. Isn't that right, Mr. Pancake?"

Pancake dropped to his side and then kicked all four paws in the air as Emma gave his furry belly a rub.

Matteo knew those were throwaway words meant only for the cat. But he couldn't help but wonder what it might be like if maybe, someday, Emma Woods forgave *him*.

"I have another appointment before I can close out my day," he lied. "So I should finish up here and get going. I'll call your mom to set up a schedule for repairs and abatement as long as you're able to sign off on the paperwork. And as long as you haven't found any new friends in the fireplace trap."

Emma stood and shook her head. "Not yet, and thankfully the trap is well hidden behind that metal panel thingy, so no one knows we're overrun with pests." She stared up at him, quiet for a moment. "Lemonade, right?"

"How long are you in town?" he blurted out.

Emma's mouth fell open. "I...um...I don't know. A week, maybe? Just to make sure my parents and the inn are doing okay with all the unexpected guests. Why? Did you—"

"Actually, I'll take a rain check on the lemonade," he interrupted. "Just your signature if that's okay. I've got water in the truck." He handed her the clipboard as his heart hammered in his chest.

Her eyes widened, but she took the paperwork, looked it over, and signed. She opened her mouth to say something else as she handed it back to him, but Matteo didn't give her a chance.

"Great. Perfect," he added as he backed away. "I'll be in touch."

Then he spun on his heel and strode toward the back door, his feet picking up the pace with every step.

One week. He could survive one week avoiding her. Then everything would be back to normal, and she'd be back to her happy life in Chicago.

Matteo didn't deserve her forgiveness, and in a week, once she was gone, he'd stop wishing he did.

Chapter 5

"Yes. Thank you. Sounds perfect. I just need twenty-four hours' notice before an in-person meeting if that's okay. Excellent. Thanks again. I really appreciate it."

Emma ended the call with her boss and gently slammed her phone down on the commercial kitchen's counter. Her father's eyes widened.

"Ems, honey, I can't ask you to stay."

She shrugged. "You didn't. *I* offered. I can work on my current accounts from here, set my hours around helping out at the inn, and use the paid time off I have by the end of the year that I'll just end up losing anyway. It's not like I take big, extravagant vacations."

Emma heard a screech and hiss. She ran to the door to peek out into the dining room only to find Pancake leaping from table to table—an arc of gray fur every time he moved—trying to catch Pikachu the parakeet as those who'd been enjoying their breakfast went right on enjoying it as if a cat chasing a bird was an everyday occurrence.

Actually, since she and Pancake had set foot in the inn, it *had* been.

"That has to be violating *so* many health codes," Emma mumbled under her breath.

"Not now that Mayor Green has officially declared the inn an emergency shelter," Hank Woods commented from right behind his daughter's shoulder.

Emma yelped, then spun to face her sneak of a father.

He shrugged and held his hands up, eyes wide with mock innocence. "What? I wasn't going to miss the Pancake and Pikachu show."

Emma gave him a pointed look. "Face it." She nodded back toward the dining room. "You and Mom need the help, and with the free room and board you're giving everyone, you can't *pay* someone to do it. So let *me*."

Neither of her parents had breathed a word about the line of credit to her, and she was too afraid to tell them she knew. Were things that bad already? Or were they just planning ahead, making sure there was a cushion to fall back on?

"Okay," he finally answered. "We need help. The kind that will work for no more than room and board." He gave her a weak smile.

"You and Mom are okay, though, right?" She fidgeted with the hem of her T-shirt, focusing on the fraying edges of the cotton between her fingers rather than the possibility that her parents were sugarcoating their current situation.

He sighed. "We're short on almost every produce item this week, and one of the clothes dryers stopped working, which means we might be looking into a clothesline until we can figure out the problem. Not to mention the inn is now only *part* inn and also part petting zoo. Other than that, though, we're right as rain. *As* long as it doesn't actually rain again this week."

He laughed despite the tinge of worry in his voice he wasn't able to hide.

Emma's heart squeezed. She didn't know *how* she was going to give them all the help they truly needed, but the thought of leaving now to go back to the city felt like desertion.

She blew a frizzy strand of hair out of her face and silently cursed the summer humidity.

"I want to help Summertown too," she told him.

"How?" he asked.

She turned back to the window separating them from the microcosm that *was* Summertown just on the other side.

"I'm still figuring that part out," she admitted. "But I'm in social media marketing. As soon as I find my angle, I'm going to put a campaign together to get paying customers through the door not just at the inn but in every door to every store that's still standing. Either we figure out a way to still win that prize money and get Summertown back on its feet, or we come up with a plan B. I mean, look at this town, right here in our dining room. Who wouldn't want to be a part of a place where Old Man Wilton goes table to table with the coffee carafe. Or where Delilah Palmer happily rests her bowl of cereal on her pregnant belly as the town pediatrician gives her a free consult. And over there at the corner table? See what those kids are doing?"

Her father squinted through the window and then back at her.

"It looks like little Jimmy Webster is stirring a drink. Oh hell. Did I leave the tequila bottle in the dining room last night?"

Emma laughed. "They're fifth graders, Dad. I'm not standing by and watching a bunch of ten-year-olds get drunk. They're making betchyas."

Jimmy passed the glass to the boy on his left, and Emma watched as the not-so-lucky recipient first sniffed what was inside.

"*Betchyas*?" her father asked, repeating the word.

Emma sighed. "It's when one person loads his or her water glass with *everything* they can find on their table. Then he offers it to a friend and says, 'Betchya won't drink this without throwing up.' And you know what? Now that I'm saying this out loud, we should maybe put the kibosh on the game before we *really* start violating some health codes."

"And you know about this game because...?" her father asked.

"Because I was a kid, Dad. Pretty sure you were too once." She laughed and grabbed him by the wrist and gave him a gentle tug. "Come on."

She stormed through the door, her father right behind, and strode through the room. She made a beeline for the kids' table, getting there just as Madison Templeman slowly raised the glass toward her lips.

"Wait!" Emma said, waving her hands overhead like she was a referee calling a play. "No betchyas in the inn!"

The young girl looked at the cloudy liquid in her glass, then glanced up at Emma with a diabolical grin. "Betchya *you* can't drink this without hurling."

Emma stopped short, catching herself before she reverted to her ten-year-old self.

"Emma," her father implored.

"Don't worry, Dad. I'm not a kid anymore. I like to think I make better choices than I did back then." Her stomach churned as she relived the memory of ten-year-old Emma finding out *after* she downed Mabel Beckman's concoction that the girl had blown her *nose* into it when Emma wasn't looking. She spun to face the chef of the betchya himself.

Emma glared at Jimmy Webster so hard and so long that he flinched when she raised her arm to point to the glass still in Madison's hand.

"You'll be taking that to the kitchen and cleaning it. *Twice.*"

He opened his mouth to protest, but Emma didn't give him a chance.

"Or should I run over to the general store and tell your parents that on top of the free room and board you're getting, you're wasting clean water and a perfectly good canister of sugar—"

"And ketchup!" Madison added.

Emma raised her brows. "*And* ketchup."

Jimmy's shoulders sagged. "No, ma'am."

"Okay, then," Emma continued. "Kitchen. All of you. Come to think of it, we could use some help with the dishes, so how about I put you four to work? If you do a good job, you get first pick at whatever we've got for dessert tonight."

In a matter of seconds, they scrambled from their seats, dirty dishes and glasses full of who-knows-what in hand, and scurried to the kitchen, smiles stretching from ear to ear.

Emma bowed dramatically as her father gave her a round of applause.

"Nicely done…*ma'am,*" he said with a smirk.

She grimaced. "You heard that too, huh? That definitely stung."

She laughed and then shrugged. "Hey, are you and Mom okay holding down the fort for a few hours? I'd like to spend the morning getting reacquainted with the town outside the inn. Maybe that will help me figure out my angle." She ran her teeth over her bottom lip. "There's nothing in the…uh… fireplace trap yet, right?"

"Not yet." Her father cleared his throat. "I think your mother has someone coming out tomorrow to work in the attic to figure out how to keep the babies safe while also keeping the mother *out* of the inn proper." He scrubbed a hand across the salt-and-pepper stubble on his jaw. "How's that for your angle? Tornado leaves inn standing but overrun by family of rodents. Book your room today!"

"I think I can do better," Emma teased with a grin. "And about the…uh…*someone* coming out to do that attic work. How's Denny Rourke's back doing?"

"Is that your way of asking if Denny's *son* is the one coming or if Denny's actually back on the clock?"

She brushed the tips of her fingers over the nearly healed scabs on her forearm, recalling Matteo's featherlight touch as he patched her up. "Guess I need to work on the fine art of subtlety, huh?"

Her father set a gentle hand on her shoulder.

"You have no idea how much your mom and I appreciate you dropping everything and coming home to help us this past week. But we also appreciate that you came home to a bit of a surprise with…with…"

"Dad," Emma interrupted. "You can say his

name. It's not like that time you said *Macbeth* at the theater-in-the-park rehearsal of *Cats*."

He stifled a laugh, then had the decency to look chagrinned. Everyone who ever went anywhere near a theater production knew that you *never* said the name of Shakespeare's play *Macbeth* out loud while the play was in production. It was cursed, and something bad was bound to happen.

"Denny Rourke had no business climbing that tree, even when he *was* ten years younger and ten pounds lighter. He's *not* an actual cat, and *you* were studying *Mac*—" He cut himself off, then squared his shoulders. "The *Scottish* play. You were studying the Scottish play. I was just asking you how your midterm went. I did *not* make that branch snap. Besides, he walked away without a scratch."

"And now has chronic back issues that—" She drew a circle in the air with her index finger. "Circling back to He-who-shall-not-be-named. You could have told me he got out early—and also that he was back in Summertown."

Her father nodded, his eyes apologetic. "As much as your mom and I were thrilled to hear you were coming back last week, we thought it would be a short visit. And we certainly didn't anticipate the squirrels."

Emma opened her mouth to respond, but her father continued.

"We get it, sweetheart. Chicago is your present,

and Summertown is in your rearview mirror. I guess we just figured you'd be heading back to the city after a day or two and we wouldn't have to tell you about Matteo coming back last year."

"Last *year*?" Emma threw her hands in the air. "He's been home for a year? I know it's been a while since I've been back, but work's been… And I wanted you to see Michigan Avenue and State Street during the holidays…" She groaned. "I didn't mean to stay away so long."

He nodded. "And we didn't mean *not* to tell you."

Emma had spent years protecting herself from her own memories, and it looked like her parents had been doing the same.

She wrapped her arms around her father and squeezed him hard, burying her head in his shoulder. She breathed in the familiar scent of kitchen cleanser and pine, sighing as he hugged her back.

"I love you, Daddy," she whispered.

He laughed softly. "Oh, Ems. We love you so much. Your mom and I just want you to be happy." He leaned away and tilted his head down so his eyes met hers. "You're happy in Chicago, right?"

She pressed her lips together and smiled, nodding her head.

"I am," she told him. "Great job where I don't have to worry about office politics or what to wear. Great apartment." Small apartment. Tiny, even. But the location was perfect. She could see the river from her tiny balcony if she turned her chair exactly at the right angle and craned her neck. She'd even made a small garden in her window seat—the reason she'd taken the apartment in the first place despite its minor shortcomings. She'd managed to bring a small part of Summertown to the big city. And it was all *hers*. Plus she had an amazing best friend.

Without Haddie, Emma would never know which neighbor was having an affair with the UPS guy—6B—or why last winter she could *never* call the super for repairs on a Wednesday night, the night Netflix dropped a new episode of his favorite drama. Haddie would be right at home in Summertown, where the gossip wire was always humming. And she couldn't forget Pancake. Despite learning of her cat allergy only after she'd adopted him, she'd take itchy eyes and the occasional asthma attack over a home without his lovey, furry snuggles.

The list was short, true. But every item on it *did* bring her joy. Though she wasn't entirely sure if that was the same as being happy. If you added up all the parts of your life that brought you happiness, the sum should *be* happiness, shouldn't it? Everyone felt lonely *sometimes,* like those random days she'd walk down Michigan Avenue surrounded by people, yet not knowing a single one. In those moments she missed Summertown and the ability to simply open the front door, take a seat on the wraparound porch of the inn, and within five minutes have someone join her to chat about the latest scandal in their tiny town.

But those moments were fleeting. Chicago was home now.

Her father stepped back, then pressed a kiss onto her forehead.

"Well then, let's get this social-media marketing circus going, I guess, so we can get you back where you belong." His voice sounded hoarse where she thought he'd meant to lighten the mood.

"I miss you too, Dad," she admitted. "I promise not to stay away so long next time."

Chapter 6

Emma stood across the counter from Harmony Sapperstein, co-owner of Wicks and Wax, marveling at the array of beautifully crafted scented candles the other woman placed in her shopping tote.

"Promise you'll mention our classes on your social channels," Harmony requested with a soft smile. "They're after hours, and it's BYO."

Emma's brows furrowed. "Bring your own what? Wine?"

Harmony shrugged, her loose white waves bouncing on her shoulder. "Sure. Wine or—whatever. Aurora and I say that as long as *it's* legal, *you're* legal. And if it doesn't impede our wick-dipping abilities, BYO." She slid the brown paper tote across the counter to Emma.

Emma gave her a nervous laugh. "Yeah. Okay. Thank you, Ms. Sapperstein." It didn't matter how desperately she wanted to know if *wick-dipping abilities* was a euphemism for something else or if it simply referred to candle making. It didn't seem appropriate to ask since it was her first time in the shop since—since she couldn't remember when.

Harmony leaned over the counter, bringing her face almost nose to nose with Emma's.

"Did you *hear*?" the older woman whisper-shouted.

Emma had heard a lot in her week back in town, but she hadn't lost her knack for tuning out the gossip and turning it into white noise.

"Heard *what*?" she whispered back.

"About Lottie Green switching her allegiance to Middlebrook."

Emma shook her head. "Afraid I haven't. In between keeping my cat from eating your bird, making sure Mrs. Pinkney's chinchillas stay in her room, and protecting our town's youth from drinking the inn clean out of ketchup and sugar, I think I've missed out on all the gossip."

Harmony straightened and pressed her hands to her hips. "I hope Pikachu hasn't been too much trouble. Your folks are truly the best. I don't know what we'd do without them. Store's still standing, but our house is missing half its roof!"

Emma pressed her lips into a smile. "Of course he's no trouble. It's just been a busy week."

"It *has*," Harmony agreed, straightening and slapping her palms on the counter. She sighed and stared wistfully into the distance.

Emma glanced over her shoulder to see what she was missing, but there was nothing.

"Harmony?" she asked, turning back to face the other woman.

"Yes?"

"You were saying something about Lottie Green and Middlebrook?" Emma couldn't believe she was perpetuating the gossip mill, but this was the mayor's wife. She had to admit her interest was piqued.

"Yes!" the other woman declared. "Right. Right. Lottie Green. I can't believe you haven't heard! She left the mayor early last year for Mayor Munson of Middlebrook."

Emma snorted, then covered her mouth.

Harmony raised her brows.

"I'm sorry," Emma coughed, trying to cover up her giggle. "But that is *not* his real name."

Harmony let out a full-on belly laugh, and Emma finally gave herself permission to join in.

"Oh but poor Mayor Green," Harmony added through fits of laughter. "I swear I'm not laughing at what happened to him. I guess it's been a while since I've heard anyone say, 'Mayor Munson of Middle…'" She giggled again. "'Mayor Munson of *Middlebrook,*'" she finally got out. But then an invisible switch flipped, and Harmony Sapperstein's laughs turned into sobs.

"Oh god," Emma started, rounding the front counter so she was standing before the other woman. "Are you okay? Do I need to call someone?" She grabbed Harmony's hand and gave her a gentle squeeze. The other woman squeezed back, her soft skin belying her years. Then she surprised Emma once more by pulling her into a hug, enveloping her in the soft cotton of her peasant blouse, in her comforting scent of lavender and rosemary.

Emma closed her eyes and breathed it in, the faint familiarity of it all—this store, her scent, the way someone could simply surprise you with a small dose of affection you never realized you needed until you had it.

"I'm sorry," Harmony began. She straightened but kept her outstretched arms on Emma's shoulders. "We're all so lucky no one got hurt, but our homes, Emma. Our *gardens*. This town and its traditions probably seem so silly to you now that you're a city girl, but Lottie Green was our ace in the hole for winning that prize money. It'd be one thing if she simply wasn't on our team anymore, but she's playing for our rivals. I'm not sure how we can beat that."

Harmony dropped her hands.

Emma's throat tightened. Her eyes roamed the small shop, scanning the white wooden shelves of tea lights and votives, of scented soy candles in mason jars with labels that read Warm Hug, Rumor Mill, or—the one Emma just bought—Rosé All Day. Scent? Self-explanatory.

"Any bar reservations?" she asked with a nervous smile as she nodded toward what looked like a small café—a dark wooden counter with high-backed stools—but was actually the DIY candle station.

Harmony shook her head. "All our bookings canceled after the storm. Same with the inn, though I guess your folks have their hands full with half the town living there."

Emma tapped her index finger against her lips, an idea taking root.

"Do you mind if I take some photos of the shop on my phone?"

Harmony shrugged. "The place is yours. I'll be back in the workroom if you need me."

"Harmony?" Emma called as the other woman turned to leave.

"Yeah?" she answered, spinning back to face her.

"I've never once thought Summertown was silly," Emma told her.

Harmony gave her a sad smile and then disappeared through strings of colorful beads that hung from the doorway to the back of the shop.

Emma grabbed a stool from behind the checkout counter and carried it to the front of the shop. She placed it up against the door, hoping she could get the whole store in the shot from her vantage point. Grabbing the door handle for purchase, she climbed up, wobbling slightly as she let go and stood to her full height.

She spread her arms wide, regained her balance, and let out a sigh. Except—she was facing the door and not the shop. She looked down at her flip-flopped feet that covered most of wooden stool's seat.

Just pivot like a dancer, she told herself, despite having never taken a dance class in her life.

The door creaked as it fell open against the stool. She must have loosened it on her ascent. Or maybe it was simply mocking her for perching precariously for a photo op before thinking the entire situation through. Either way, it was time to pivot. Along with the door's taunt, she could hear Ross Gellar yelling *Pivot!* in her head, so she planted her toes and attempted to spin, realizing too late she'd stepped on the heel of her flip-flop.

Emma rocked forward, arms flailing as the stool and her shoes fell out from under her. She caught the top of the door, her body slamming against it as it swung further open, trapping her behind it as the stool came to rest under her dangling feet.

"Ow?" she said to herself, only loud enough for her own ears. Then she looked down. How freaking tall was the door? It looked like there was at least three feet to where the toppled stool lay on the floor. If she let go, she'd have no choice but to land on or between the legs, which made her pretty sure she'd break one of her own. And as far as she could see, Matteo Rourke wasn't hiding around the corner to catch her this time. *Not* that she was thinking about Matteo Rourke and their moment earlier that morning when she was clearly in physical peril.

It was a moment, wasn't it?

She fell. *He* caught her. She couldn't help but stare into those deep, inscrutable brown eyes of his for what felt like an eternity but had barely been a second or two.

Oh. My. God, Emma. FOCUS. This was ridiculous. It had been *eight* years. Emma was past the past. She'd started over, made a life for herself. But Summertown was a like a time machine, transporting her back not to a place but to a feeling she didn't want to feel ever again. She felt trapped. She *was* trapped—hanging from a door.

"Harmony?" she tried to call, but her palms hurt, and her voice was strained, so it came out more like a squeak that started with the letter H.

Her palms were sweating. And *slipping*. Welp, this was it. She headed out this morning to find a way to help the town and wouldn't make it past her first stop without a broken toe or ankle or possibly worse.

Through the door's window she saw him stride over the threshold, his khaki uniform snug against his muscled torso.

He tipped his campaign hat and pulled off his aviators, sticking them in his shirt pocket as a grin spread across his face.

"Little Emmy Woods, as I live and breathe," the man said. "Need a hand?"

Before she could answer, he kicked the stool out of the way and positioned himself beneath her dangling body.

"I got ya," he said, and Emma finally gave her aching, slipping fingers permission to let go.

She could have landed on her feet, but he caught her under and freaking *pivoted* away from a nearby shelf so she wouldn't knock anything down.

Her palm braced against the wall of muscle that was his chest as dark-blue eyes stared at her from under the brim of his hat.

"Dawson Hayes?" she croaked.

He set her down gingerly, and it was all she could do to keep from fanning herself.

He crossed his arms, and Emma swallowed as his biceps stretched the short sleeve of his uniform shirt. The sun streaming in through the door backlit him so he looked almost otherworldly. Except once her eyes adjusted, she wasn't looking at the deputy anymore but past him and out into the square.

"What the…?" Emma's mouth couldn't form the rest of the words.

Because the gardenless, dirt-filled square she'd been walking through all week was not exactly gardenless anymore.

Crawling up what was left of the trunk of a

mostly destroyed tree were three giant, vibrant, beautiful metal sunflowers.

"Vandalism," Dawson replied in answer to her half-asked question. "That's why I'm here. Mayor Green wants me to arrest whoever's responsible, and who better to question than the eyes and ears of Summertown, Ms. Harmony Sapperstein."

Chapter 7

Matteo did what he promised himself he'd do. He stayed away for the duration of a week. When he finally called the inn to follow up, he knew he was in the clear… Or so he thought.

"Hello, Mr. Woods. I was hoping we could talk about the estimate and the abatement plan I gave to Emma last week. I can come over at your convenience."

"Estimate? Abatement plan? I'm sorry, Matteo. We've been so slammed with guests—well, you know, not the paying kind—that I haven't had a chance to look. I'm pretty sure Emma still has all the information, so it might be better to ask her."

"I thought she was on her way back to Chicago," Matteo responded. Had he counted the days wrong?

"Should have been," Emma's father remarked. "But that girl of ours… She arranged it with her boss so that she can stay indefinitely. At least until we've got things under control here. Heck, she might even stay until the festival—if Summertown can still participate. We're all planting as much as we can as fast as we can, but..." His voice trailed off. "I'm sorry, Matteo. I lost my train of thought. What did you need? Oh! The estimate and abatement. Right. Right. I'll have Emma give you a call when she gets back. She's out doing a little research. Said she's going to start up one of those accounts for Summertown and help get the word out that we're still up and running."

"A social media account?" Matteo asked, confused. "For the town?"

"Yeah! That's it. I never really saw the need to get involved in all of that seeing as how everyone I might want to be social with is only a stone's throw from the inn. But apparently people pay my daughter to be social for them, and now she wants to be social for the town. I'm not going to argue, especially if it means having my girl home for a little while longer."

Matteo cleared his throat. "So, Emma's *not* going back to Chicago." Apparently, that was all he'd gotten out of the exchange.

"Not for the foreseeable future," the other man replied, and Matteo could hear the joy in his voice. "I'll make sure she gets back to you about all that squirrel nonsense," he added.

"Right," Matteo responded absently as he tried to reconcile what all of this meant. "Thank you, Mr.

Woods. I, um, I need to head out for a run and to pick up a prescription for my dad."

"Tell Denny to rest up." Emma's father chuckled. "We're bringing poker night to his place so I can win back what he took from me last week." He paused for a long moment. "You're a good son for taking care of him like you've been," he added. "He's lucky to have you around."

Matteo swallowed but didn't respond. Saying thank you felt like agreeing with the other man's assessment. Arguing against it meant opening up old wounds, especially the one he'd caused Mr. Woods's daughter.

"You take care of yourself, Matteo," Hank Woods added.

Matteo ended the call before Emma's father could be any nicer to him.

It was funny how he could waffle between resentment of the town's judgment of his past and regret for the one part of that past he wished he could undo—hurting Emma.

You don't deserve nice, and certainly not from Emma's father.

Emma was staying. And *she* was the one heading up the squirrel situation at the inn. Unless his father was suddenly running laps around the house when he returned with the prescription, Matteo would *have* to see her again.

How they would manage working together after

eight years of silence was all he could think about now as he found her in the crowd gawking at the sculpture in the town square.

He cleared his throat. "That's...odd," he said over her shoulder.

She whirled around to face him. Her cheeks were flushed from the heat, and her hair sat atop her head in a crazy, messy, bun-nest sort of thing. She looked like the girl he fell in love with in high school, unassuming and unaware of how beautiful she was. At least that was how he'd always seen her.

"Odd?" she asked, incredulous. "*Odd*? It's... it's...it's..." She squinted, even though the sun was behind her. "Can you please put your shirt on so I can concentrate," She motioned at his bare torso.

Matteo laughed, thankful for the levity after trying—and failing—to run hard enough and long enough that he would forget that Emma hadn't gone back to Chicago.

"Thank you." She jutted her chin out and dropped her phone into the fanny pack around her waist. Then she stared at him with her hands on her hips, giving him the chance to appreciate her attire: a gray T-shirt that read *Um* in white, the letters in a box so it looked as if it came straight off the periodic table. Below the box, it said, *The element of confusion.*

He laughed again, opening his mouth to comment on the tee, but she didn't give him a chance.

"Come on! We have to figure out who did it!" She grabbed his wrist and yanked him toward the uniformed deputy who was kneeling to repaint one of the square's park benches that had been damaged in the storm.

"Deputy!" Emma called, her hand still wrapped around Matteo's wrist.

Matteo knew he could simply stop moving, forcing her to lose her grip. But the stupid sense memory of her skin on his—one that caused a smile to play involuntarily at his lips—made him soldier on, continuing as if he truly was being dragged.

"Deputy!" she repeated, and the man squatting in front of the bench stood, then pivoted to face her. He stood a full head taller than Emma, his eyes meeting Matteo's first before dipping to meet hers.

"Deputy, do you—?" Emma suddenly dropped Matteo's wrist, and he instinctively took one more step forward so he was next to her and able to see her mouth fall open.

"*Lemmy,*" said the uniformed man with a dark, quizzical look. "I promise it's okay if you just call me Dawson."

"I know." Emma bounced on her toes. "But deputy sheriff is a big deal! I'm so happy for you!"

The tall, dark, and broad-shouldered man pointed at her with his paint-soaked brush. "And *I'm* happy I was on duty this morning so I could rescue Summertown's visiting damsel in distress."

He winked at her, and Matteo clenched his teeth and felt a muscle tick in his jaw. Then the words finally registered.

"Damsel in distress?" Matteo asked Emma. "Did something happen? Are you okay?"

Emma looked from Dawson to him and blushed, but Matteo was pretty sure it had nothing to do with the heat this time.

"Matteo, you remember Dawson, right? He was a senior when we were freshmen. He graduated with Levi, I think." She turned back to the deputy, not waiting for Matteo to respond. "You were in Levi's class, right?"

Dawson grinned. "You've got a good memory, Lemmy. And how is that brother of yours, Rourke?"

Lemmy? Who the hell was Lemmy? And why did Emma seem to bite back a grin every time Dawson said it?

"Rourke?" the deputy said again. "Where'd you go?"

Matteo blinked. "What? Sorry. Did you ask me something?"

"Yeah. I did." Dawson laughed. "Off in our own little world, I guess. I asked how your brother was doing. Levi. You remember the guy, don't you?"

Matteo shoved his hands in his pockets and nodded, fully back in the present now. But this was twice, he realized, that some sort of Emma-related interaction had taken him out of the moment. First it was her mom calling him *Matty,* and now it was this guy calling her *Lemmy*.

"He's doing it again," Matteo heard Dawson mumble to Emma. "Does he know he's doing it? Like, do you think he can hear me right now?"

Matteo groaned. "I can *hear* you," he said, crossing his arms over his chest. "Levi's good. He's still coaching over in Indiana. Just finished his second year with varsity."

Dawson nodded. "Heard he took those kids to a couple of bowl games last year."

"Won 'em, too," Matteo added. "But remind me who *Lemmy* is?" It wasn't that Matteo lacked pride in his older brother's accomplishments. There were just more pressing matters at hand.

He watched Emma's cheeks turn pink again, and felt his palms itch to clench into fists.

Dawson pointed at Emma with his paintbrush again. "Little Emma here had freshman bio right after I had chem in the same room. After a few times of saying, 'Hey, li'l Emmy,' it just sorta turned into Lemmy. I'm sure you heard me say it a thousand times."

Matteo cleared his throat. "Right. I'm sure I did," he lied.

"So, Dawson…" Emma began, rocking back and forth from her heels to her toes. "Did Harmony have any information about the sunflowers? Looks like they're painted hubcaps or something." She let out a nervous laugh. "You're not really going to arrest the artist, are you?"

The deputy tilted his head in the direction from which Emma and Matteo had just come and raised his brows.

"Harmony didn't see anyone and swears she heard nothing about it. No one's reported any missing hubcaps, so we can rule out theft. And look, I'm not complaining. Actually improves the view, if you ask me. But if the mayor says it's vandalism, it's vandalism." He shrugged.

"*Vandalism*?" Matteo asked. "That doesn't make any sense. Isn't it, like, art or something? You just said it improved the view."

Dawson dropped the paintbrush into the bucket of paint next to the bench and crossed his arms. "That *art* is nailed to public property. Without a permit. And if that tree hadn't already been destroyed by the storm, driving those nails into the trunk might have done the trick. The fact no one's owning up to it tells me the culprit knows on some level that they've broken the law. If you ask me, their time would be better spent helping rebuild the square and the town's surrounding gardens in order to give us a fighting chance at the garden festival, especially with Middlebrook stealing our ringer."

"Middlebrook," Matteo and Dawson replied at the same time.

Emma raised her brows, her eyes volleying back and forth between the two men.

"We're tied nine to nine," Dawson explained.

"As far as who takes home the golden topiary," Matteo added.

"And fifty *thousand* dollars." The deputy waggled his brows.

"Okay, I know I've been gone for a while and a little out of the loop," Emma chimed in. "But that only adds up to eighteen. How does that make this year the twentieth anniversary? And I'm sorry, but fifty *thousand* dollars?"

"The scandal," both men said in unison again.

Matteo narrowed his eyes at Deputy Hayes, but the other man didn't seem to notice. This only made Matteo narrow his eyes to mere slits, willing Dawson to *loosen* his focus on the girl standing between them.

"Okay, did you two plan that?" Emma teased, wagging a finger between them. "Or do you just have some sort of bromance I don't know about?"

"No," both men responded, and Dawson finally glanced at Matteo with something that felt like understanding.

Emma shook her head. "Okay, fine. Lottie Green switches sides so they postponed?"

Dawson nodded. "It was Mayor Munson's consolation prize, a one-year reprieve."

"That doesn't explain the *money*," Emma added.

"I thought that came from raffle ticket sales. The biggest prize I remember was less than five grand."

"Rumor has it..." Oh god, did those words just come out of Matteo's mouth?

"Rumor has it *what*?" Emma asked, backhanding him on the shoulder.

He shook his head, resigning himself to playing into the one aspect of small-town life he couldn't stand, the rumor mill, all in the name of what was starting to feel like a pissing contest in front of a girl who wanted nothing to do with him other than ridding her parents' inn of squirrels and getting to the bottom of the art/vandalism in the square.

"Rumor *has* it," Matteo continued, "that Lottie Green made a pretty penny in some of her out-of-state gigs, but in order to keep the money from getting into *Mayor* Green's hands, she 'donated' it to the contest kitty."

"Which she plans to get back by winning the golden topiary for Middlebrook," Dawson concluded.

Emma shook her head with a laugh. "Guess I've missed more than I thought in the past year." For a second her eyes met Matteo's, but then they darted away.

Despite having always found his town's claim to fame slightly silly and a little more than odd, in the years he'd avoided coming home, he found himself developing an unexpected sense of pride whenever anyone asked where he was from. Brows would furrow when he uttered the word *Summertown*. But when he added that it was home to the now famous landscape designer Lottie Green, every now and then he'd see a spark of recognition.

"Isn't that the place where all the bushes are carved into animal sculptures?" some would ask, and Matteo would laugh and nod his head.

Not much had made him laugh in the years following his mother's death and the fallout that came after. But the memories of Summertown's town hall guarded by the Mayor and First Lady's cavapoo topiaries, the tulip maze in the middle of the town square, and the zinnia garden behind the Woods Family Inn had become a secret comfort while he was gone, and now that he was back, he'd started looking at the *silliness* with a nostalgia he hadn't expected.

Except the cavapoos were gone now, as were the tulips and zinnias.

"Then the *vandal*—I mean *artist*—is our key!" Emma exclaimed, bringing Matteo out of his reverie.

"What do you mean?" he asked.

"Look!" she added, pointing back toward the brightly painted metal on the mostly destroyed tree. Locals were gathering with their phones raised as they took photos. "If that small act of defiance is garnering this much attention among those of us who *live* here, imagine what tourists might think."

Matteo squinted toward the small crowd. "A few scraps of metal is not going to jump-start summer tourism," he claimed.

Emma raised her brows. "It will if we make it a game—trying to uncover the mystery gardener of Summertown. I've got some connections with marketing managers at Yelp and Trip Advisor. If I use our mystery artist as the jumping-off point for Summertown's social media presence, they can share to their audiences, and voilà! The Summertown curiosity is awakened, and they can see we're still open for business. And who knows? Maybe the publicity will tempt our anonymous criminal to add to their display."

Dawson scratched the back of his neck. "I don't know, Lemmy. If the mayor wants us to do a proper investigation, that might get in the way."

Matteo said, "And if we're considering this—I don't know, artist?—a criminal, bringing him/her into the public eye is hardly doing them a favor. We should probably just let it lie and work on the *actual* planting and rebuilding of the living gardens to maybe give us a chance against Middlebrook."

"I'm with Rourke on this one, Lemmy," Dawson added, clapping Matteo on the shoulder. "The storm barely even touched Middlebrook. If the festival was today, there'd be no contest. The golden topiary would go to them, and then where's the upholding of our legacy?"

Emma groaned and placed her hands on her hips. "Is it illegal for me to share a couple of photos on social media even if you're investigating?"

Dawson's mouth fell open, and Matteo stifled a grin at Emma's defiance of the deputy.

"Well, no," Dawson admitted. "It's a public square, which means it's open to public viewing whether in person or virtually. But—"

"Then it's settled," Emma interrupted. "We still have seven weeks until the festival, which gives us plenty of time to plant and rebuild. I hope. In the meantime, I can get us noticed, which will help bring more revenue to the town, and revenue means more money to put toward the festival and beating Lottie Green at her own game!"

She grinned as her excitement grew, and Matteo found himself getting caught up despite himself.

"Might actually help your investigation," Matteo told Dawson. "Maybe your *vandal* is an attention seeker. They might strike again just to taunt you."

Deputy Dawson Hayes rolled his eyes, clearly annoyed at Matteo now joining Emma's cause. This only spurred Matteo to continue, which made him realize that while he was not competitive by nature, something in the deputy's familiarity with Emma had flipped a switch inside him.

The deputy sighed. "At least give me a heads-up before you—I don't know—approach the person *if* you figure out who it is. Just in case they're dangerous."

Emma nodded, but the deputy didn't so much as pull out his phone. Instead he grabbed the paintbrush again, squatted down at the bench, and went back to what he'd been doing before they'd interrupted him.

"You're not going to enter me as a contact?" she asked.

"I will eventually, when my hands aren't full of paint. For now just lay it on me. I'll remember it—just like I remember your nickname."

"That only *you* called her," Matteo mumbled under his breath.

"What was that?" Emma asked, briefly turning to him.

"Nothing," he said. "I mean, *not* nothing. I… uh…I have a camera you can borrow if you want to get something a little better than a phone," he told her.

What the hell was he doing? *Shut up, Matteo. Just stop talking.*

"Really? Oh my god, that is *amazing*!" She rattled off her number to Deputy Hayes and then clapped her hands together as she bounced on her toes.

Emma wasn't simply smiling. She beamed, and Matteo tried not to let the wind get knocked from his lungs. She wasn't smiling at *him*, only at his offer of help, which he never should have blurted out in the first place.

"Can we go get it now?" she asked.

She grabbed Matteo's wrist again, and he was powerless to say anything other than, "Yes."

"Be careful, Lemmy," Dawson warned. "You don't know who you're dealing with."

Matteo shot Dawson a look, but the deputy was only looking at Emma.

Emma laughed off his comment. "It's art, Deputy Hayes. You can't really think this person is a vandal. Especially if they might be able to help the town."

She tugged at Matteo's arm. "Thank you for offering to help. I can't wait to get started!"

And with that, Matteo did what he never thought he'd have the opportunity to do again. He ushered Emma Woods from the Summertown square to the path that led home.

Chapter 8

Emma stopped at nearly every driveway along the residential street, snapping photos with her phone despite being on her way to getting her hands on an actual camera.

She dropped to a squat on the cobblestone walkway that led to Harmony and Aurora's home, hand brushing over the brittle ruined petals of what was once a path of purple, orange, and pink peonies guiding visitors to their front door.

"I have a pot of these at home," she said softly.

Matteo dropped down next to her, his nearness adding a layer of heat to the air that wasn't there before.

"You do?" he asked, picking up a torn and faded petal, cradling it gently in his palm.

She nodded. "I work from home, mostly. Filling the apartment with flowers makes it feel like I'm not so far away from *this* home."

He looked up at her, and she could see his dark eyes swimming with questions. But he only asked one.

"You miss this place, huh?"

She turned her gaze back to the ground. Of *course* she missed this place. She grew up in Summertown. She fell in love in Summertown. She might have moved away, but some roots held fast, too strong to tear from the ground. No matter where she was, this town would always be a part of her.

"Of course," she admitted.

Didn't you? she wanted to ask. If he was out after eighteen months, why didn't he come back? Where did he go?

Why, once he was able to, had he never reached out to see how she was?

But she couldn't ask him any of this, not when he'd made it clear the first time she brought up the past that it wasn't up for discussion.

"But you still left," Matteo finally replied. It wasn't a question but a simple observation.

"I needed a fresh start." She brushed her hands clean of the dirt and petals and stood, looking out on the half-remaining roof of the house next door. "Mrs. Dubose's house is next, isn't it?" He wasn't the only master of the subject change.

She stepped back onto the sidewalk and headed for the next house, but she could hear Matteo's footsteps right behind her.

"Don't you want to wait?" he asked when she captured what was left of the topiary dragon alongside the Duboses' driveway. "You can grab all your photos on the way back to the inn. Unless you want a ride. I'm happy to give you a lift."

She shook her head, then realized he'd asked her more than one question. "I can walk back, but the natural lighting is so good right now. I don't want to chance losing it. Plus, I have to get to know the camera and how to use it and all that fun stuff. Might as well grab some key pieces of Summertown—or remnants of what it used to be—while I can."

And might as well busy herself with anything to avoid small talk. She'd been so caught up in the excitement of not only figuring out her marketing angle for Summertown's inaugural social media campaign but also the thrill of what might be Summertown's first actual town *mystery*.

But now here they were. At his house. *Matteo's* house. What she wouldn't give to be able to call Haddie right now and ask her what the hell to do.

But Haddie wasn't here, and Emma was an adult fully capable of making her own decisions about whether or not to go into her estranged ex's house where she lost her virginity in his childhood bedroom three years before he disappeared off the face of the earth. Well—*her* earth, at least.

Matteo stood on the porch, his hand gripping the front doorknob, ready to enter. But Emma's feet were still planted three steps down on the cement walkway.

Thank you, universe, for at least leaving the Rourke

house intact. What would she have done if *he'd* been forced to stay at the inn too?

As if sensing her hesitation—or maybe realizing she wasn't standing next to him, Matteo turned around.

"Hey," he began. "I can just run in and get the camera. You don't have to come in."

Emma *heard* his words. She even understood them. Yet her mouth wasn't moving. Zero sound came out of it other than the quiet exhale of her shaky breath.

He let go of the door and slowly walked back down the steps, dropping down to sit on the middle one.

"Em," he said, and everything inside her contracted to one sharp, tiny pinpoint, pricking her in the heart.

She was past this. Past him. A shattered heart certainly healed itself after *eight* years. Yet one word, one *tiny* syllable had the ability to bring it all back.

"Em?" This time it came out as a question. "Are you...okay?"

He rose and took a step toward her, the movement enough to spur her to action.

"Fine!" she blurted out. "I'm fine. Sorry. Totally fine. Fine-a-*rooney*."

He stopped and held up his hands as if to promise a feral cat that he meant no harm.

"I shouldn't have suggested you come here. I'm sorry. I don't know what I was thinking."

She saw the genuine pain in his brown eyes, heard it in his voice.

She shook her head. "I'm actually the guilty party," she replied, raising her hand. "I guess I just got caught off guard with the familiarity of it all."

He lowered his hands and paused for a few beats before responding.

"Look. I'm not suggesting that you have any residual feelings about how things ended between us. It's been almost a decade. But I should have realized it would be weird to bring you here. It's weird for me too, if that makes any difference."

Weird? It was a hell of a lot more than weird. It was déjà vu but with a side of nausea and heartache—echoes of what she felt the night before his sentencing when he'd told her they were done.

Just like that.

"No residual feelings," she told him, willing the words to be true. "Just weird. Like you said."

Matteo's jaw tightened as he nodded. "If it's *too* weird, I can just drop the camera by the inn later. I'll even do what I can moving forward to make sure our paths cross as little as possible while you're in town. Aside from the squirrel situation at the inn, of course."

She forced a laugh. "Quite the confident guy assuming you have that much of an effect on me, aren't you?" She'd meant to add some levity to the situation but instead seemed only to add credence to his assumption. "You know what? Don't respond to that," she added. Then she squared her shoulders and looked straight into his deep-brown puppy dog eyes and used every ounce of her mental strength *not* to fall under their spell.

"Considering I bumped into you within the first two hours of my arrival, I think it's safe to say this town is too small to keep our run-ins to a minimum. You're doing well. *I'm* doing well. We're both trucking along and living our lives, you know? Plus, like you said, I'm out of here once the festival hits, so what's the point in trying to avoid one another when we both know we'll fail miserably. So how about if we just start fresh as two adults who once knew each other a long time ago and happen to be in the same vicinity for a while? No steering clear necessary."

She wasn't so sure about that last bit, but he was right. Summertown *was* a small town. The only way they were going to be able to avoid each other was if Matteo never set foot in the inn again and Emma never left it.

He shoved his hands in the pockets of his running shorts and rocked back on his heels.

"Are you sure about this, Em? It's your choice. Your pace. I'll follow your lead."

She nodded, then shook her head. "I'm sure. Yes. With *one* little caveat. It's…Emma. *Just* Emma."

His brows furrowed at first, but then his eyes

widened with recognition. He cleared his throat and squared his shoulders, then held out his right hand.

"Hi…Emma, right? I'm Matteo. Matteo Rourke. I think we went to the same high school."

He gave her a tentative smile.

She could do this—coexist in the same town as him for the next six to seven weeks. She didn't need to prove to herself that she was over him. That ship had sailed years ago. It was the sense memory of this town—the place where they'd fallen in love—that she'd been avoiding.

Finally, she offered him her hand and gave his a good, hearty shake.

"Yes. Emma Woods. And you're Matteo… Matteo Rourke? Hmm…sounds familiar," she teased despite the electric charge she felt pulsing between his palm and hers. "It's nice to make your acquaintance again."

His nervous smile bloomed into a full-fledged grin.

Emma ignored the butterflies in her belly, biting her lip as she smiled back at him, their hands still clasped even though the handshake itself had ended.

"I was wondering if maybe you had a camera I could borrow?" she asked innocently. "It's for a project I'm working on."

He raised his brows. "What sort of project? I'd

love to loan you my camera, but I want to make sure it's being used for non-nefarious purposes."

"Hmm," Emma mused. "That might be tough because my purposes are almost always of the nefarious kind."

Matteo bit back a laugh. "You know what? I like your honesty. I'm going to let you borrow that camera. Would you like to come inside, or should I just go grab it for you?"

And there was the million-dollar question again. Maybe she *was* ready to rip the bandage off, but she could do it in baby steps, right? Her choice. Her pace.

"I think maybe it's best if you grab it and I wait here," she told him.

Matteo nodded, but before he could drop her hand, the front door to the Rourke residence flew open, and Denny Rourke stepped onto the porch.

"Emma Woods as I live and breathe," the older man said, opening his arms. "Goodness you are a sight for sore eyes."

Emma hadn't spent any real time with Denny Rourke since the last time she'd seen Matteo—at his wife's funeral. She'd seen him in passing, but it was always an awkward *hello* or a wave from across the street. It was as if both of them knew distance was easier than acknowledging the elephant in the room—Matteo. Self-preservation was tricky like that. It kept you from doing things you knew you should for the sheer aspect of escaping any semblance of pain. But Emma felt no pain upon seeing that man who, at one point in her life, was like a second father.

She dropped Matteo's hand and, without thinking twice, bounded up the steps and into the other man's embrace.

"I don't think I realized how much I missed you until this very moment," she whispered as she squeezed him tight. "I'm sorry it took me so long to come see you."

He squeezed her back, and she felt him let out a sigh.

"You made it here," he replied. "And that's all that really matters." Then he stepped back, his arms on her shoulders as he gave her a good once-over. "Welcome home, Emma. I'm so glad you're back."

Emma, Denny, and the Rourkes' next-door neighbor Tilly Higginson sat at the kitchen table drinking Arnold Palmers—the only way Emma could stand to drink iced tea—and playing Jenga while Matteo disappeared to his garage apartment to retrieve the camera.

"Make sure you don't sit for too long a stretch, Denny," Tilly warned as she deftly slid a center block from one of the lower rows of the Jenga tower. "The doctor said you need to get up and walk around every half hour so there's not too much compression on your bulging discs."

"Sounds like you have some good home care going on over here, Denny," Emma teased with a grin.

The older man nodded his head toward Tilly. "She threatened to report me to the nice back specialist we met at the hospital if I don't follow the doctor's orders."

"Dr. Dorothea Geiger," Tilly added without missing a beat. "We're having coffee tomorrow morning before she opens her practice. Love that she has Saturday hours. Anyway, it's sort of a new friend thing since she's still getting to know the area. Just moved here last year after finishing her residency at a hospital out in Denver. Got her fellowship in Summertown, and the rest is history. Poor girl works so much, though, that she barely knows anyone here. Told her I'd buy her a cup of coffee and show her around town."

Emma squinted at the tower of blocks, strategizing her next move. This all felt so…normal. Like she was seventeen again and it was her and the whole Rourke family crowded around the very same game. The only difference was the absence of Levi and Mrs. Rourke—and no Matteo sitting next to her tickling her ribs every time she tried to remove a block in the hopes of making her knock the tower down.

"Found it."

They all turned toward the sound of Matteo's voice.

Emma flinched, sending the tower spilling over onto the tabletop.

The corner of Matteo's mouth twitched. "Can't blame me," he said, holding his hands in the air while the camera in question hung in its case around his neck.

Emma narrowed her eyes at him. "Oh no?" she asked. "That felt like a very deliberate entrance, Rourke."

He shrugged. "Physics is also pretty deliberate." Then he lifted the camera from around his neck and held it out toward her. "Want me to show you how it works?"

Excitement bubbled inside of her as she nodded eagerly and stood from the table. "Game's all yours," she said to the other two at the table. "Although maybe this is a good time for you to get up and walk around, Denny."

Denny Rourke groaned, but a smile played at his lips. "Great. Now I've got two of you nagging me to take care of myself."

"Make that three of us, Dad," Matteo added. "The more you take care of yourself, the sooner you'll be back at work so I don't have to be on call twenty-four hours a day."

The older man laughed as he stood up and gingerly

straightened his back. "I see you've got your own selfish motivation to get me back up and running."

Emma rounded the table toward Matteo, but not before catching a glimpse of Tilly gently holding Denny's elbow as she guided him up.

Good, she thought. *It's about time he found some happiness again.*

"*That* and I'd like to keep you around for as long as possible," Matteo replied.

Denny gave his son a perceptive nod, and Emma swallowed the unexpected knot in her throat.

Emma reminded herself that whatever happened eight years ago, it began with Matteo, his brother, and his father suffering immeasurable loss.

Matteo turned his attention from his father to her, his smile masking the hint of pain she'd just heard in his voice.

"Outside?" he asked. "Since that's where the bulk of your photos will be taken."

"Yes. Perfect," Emma replied, noting that not only had Matteo changed into a heather-gray T-shirt and faded jeans but that his hair was damp, and he smelled like sandalwood and summer.

"Did you shower?" she asked as he led her toward the front door.

"I always shower after a run," he called over his shoulder as he pulled open the door and motioned for her to take the first step onto the porch.

"Right," she said, striding past him and

inadvertently breathing in the scent of him again. "That makes sense."

She laughed at herself for thinking even for a second that he'd wanted to clean up for her. Not that she *wanted* him to want to clean up for her because that would be ridiculous since they'd agreed to be nothing more than newly acquainted locals who knew each other way back when.

He just smelled good and *looked* good with that thin cotton T-shirt clinging to his lean-muscled torso and… *Stop thinking things you have no business thinking, brain.* Just because the man looks good doesn't change anything.

"You okay?" Matteo asked, and Emma realized she had her hands braced on the porch railing as she stared into space while trying to reconcile her thoughts with reality.

"Yes!" she exclaimed. "I mean, *yes*." She repeated the word with measured calm. "I am ready to learn all about this high-tech-looking camera that I did not expect you to own."

She scrunched her nose as she scrutinized the item in his hands.

"Since when are you into photography?" she asked, then wished she could shove the words back into her mouth. The *since when* implied she knew even the slightest detail about the man standing in front of her when for all intents and purposes, they were strangers now.

"Since…a while," he answered, not thrown by the hint of accusation in her tone. "I've traveled a lot over the years, picking up new hobbies and interests along the way. I guess I'm into a lot of things now I might not have been when…" He cleared his throat. "When you knew me before."

"Right," she said, letting go of the porch rail and wiping her damp palms on her legs. "Right. Of course. That makes total sense. I've picked up a lot of new interests too over the years."

He raised his brows. "Like what?"

Like what? Like…what?

She was sure there was an answer, but of course her brain was still stuck on sandalwood and muscles, and did she mention the low-slung jeans? Yeah. Low-slung jeans.

"Cat!" she blurted. "I have a cat now. I like cats." Oh god. She not only *was* a crazy cat lady, but she sounded like one.

Matteo bit back a laugh. "I gathered that."

"And—and running!" she lied. What was she doing? *Haddie* loved running. Emma loved standing on the sidelines with the other spectators drinking spiked cocoa during the Chicago Marathon or a mimosa if it was a summer race. Haddie had tried time and again to teach Emma to love the sport like she did, but Emma's couch-to-5K attempts always consisted of a lot more couch than they were supposed to.

"I like my VR workouts," she always protested when Emma would cancel a race Haddie signed her up for. "If it's a game, I don't realize it's actually exercise."

"I just worry about you only existing behind a screen," Haddie always said. "You're only going to meet someone if you get out there and *do* things with other people."

But Emma liked the security of working on a screen or exercising inside a VR headset. She was safe there. No one could get too close, and no one could let her down.

"Basically," she told Haddie, "I need to be tricked into doing it. If you can trick me into running by having some fast zombies chase me or something, then maybe I'll reconsider."

Yeah, *that* challenge resulted in Emma's worst Halloween to date. At least now she was certain that when the zombie apocalypse came, she would be the first one eaten.

"I'm just not a runner," she'd finally said after crossing the finish line long *after* the rest of the racers *and* the hired zombies.

"Fine," Haddie acquiesced. "Then you're my permanent cheerleader."

Except apparently *now* Emma Woods—in some feeble attempt to what, sound interesting to Matteo?—*was* a runner.

"You run now?" Matteo asked.

Emma straightened her shoulders and jutted out her chin. "Yes."

"*You* run," he repeated.

She scoffed. "*Yes,* Matteo Rourke. *I* run. I didn't realize you held a monopoly on the sport."

He raised his brows. "I don't. It's just, you always turned me down when I tried to get you to come with me. I'm pretty sure the words 'I hate running unless something is chasing me' came out of your mouth at least once or twice."

She shrugged. "I guess we've both changed since we knew each other. You like photography, and I like running." Her pulse sped up, and she could feel it kicking in—her fight-or-flight response. It was definitely dialed to flight.

She glanced up at the sky, then back at Matteo and his furrowed auburn brow. "It's a little overcast right now, don't you think?" She didn't wait for him to respond. "Probably best to do the photo lesson with better sun. Plus, I'm really in the mood for a run right now. Pick this up later?"

She hopped down the steps and started a slow shuffle down the driveway, picking up speed when she reached the sidewalk separating the Rourke family home's yard from the street. Then Emma did what even zombies couldn't force her to do. She ran.

In the distance she heard Matteo call out, "But you're wearing flip-flops!"

She most definitely was, and her shins and ankles both screamed in protest as her feet pounded the pavement. But Emma didn't stop. Because focusing on putting one foot in front of the other—despite the pain in her lower extremities and the tightening in her lungs—was oddly soothing. The thoughts swirling like a tornado in her head all fell away until the only sound she heard was the slap of her flip-flops against her heels.

Forgetting her troubles? Great. But Emma also forgot one very important detail when embarking on the very first run of her life—her inhaler.

Chapter 9

Matteo found her on the sidewalk halfway between his house and the inn, collapsed on all fours and wheezing.

"Emma! Oh my god!" He threw the truck in park and flew out of the driver's side door without even turning the vehicle off. "I'm taking you to the hospital!" he cried, placing one arm around her back and the other under her knees.

She shook her head. "Inn is closer," she mumbled between gasps for breath. "Inhaler behind front desk."

The rest was a blur—carrying her to the truck, driving at breakneck speed to the inn, and somehow getting her inside and onto the couch by the fireplace as he watched her lips turn blue.

He found the rescue inhaler right where she said it would be. She was so weak from loss of oxygen that he had to hold the damned thing to her lips and administer one puff and then another.

Once her color returned and her inhales and

exhales slowed to a respectable rhythm, Matteo threw his hands in the air. He paced back and forth in front of the fireplace, swearing at himself for letting her run off in the first place.

He stopped abruptly, pointing a finger at his patient who straightened where she sat, eyeing him warily.

"What if I hadn't gone after you, Emma? Huh? And what if I'd gone on foot instead of taking the truck? What if…?" He paced again, growling as he mumbled to himself. He tugged at his hair as his own breathing grew more and more erratic. "Dammit, Emma!" he exclaimed, stopping to face her again. "You scared the shit out of me!"

She raised her hand meekly. "Um—remember me? The girl who almost died out there? Was pretty scared myself."

He was too angry to sympathize, especially when she obviously *knew* she was asthmatic and ran without her inhaler anyway.

"And—and your feet!" he sputtered.

"My feet?" she responded, looking down at the appendages in question. Her eyes widened when she noticed the bloodied cuts and scrapes adorning her skin like confetti. "Oh," she added. "My *feet*."

He crossed his arms and nodded at her. "You're *not* a runner." It was a statement, not a question.

She huffed out a laugh. "What gave me away? The willingness to destroy my feet, ankles, and shins—because *ouch*—or the gasping for air mere minutes into my sprint?"

He dropped to squat so his eyes met hers. He didn't want to admonish her, didn't want to feel this aching sense of loss every time he looked at her, especially after having just witnessed how easy it would be to lose her in a way he hadn't fathomed before now.

He placed his hands on her knees. She flinched but didn't push him away.

"Just because we aren't a—a *we* anymore doesn't mean I stopped caring about you, Emma. Despite what you might have thought of me all these years, it always made me happy knowing that *you* still existed somewhere in this world. So even though you owe me *nothing,* I need you to promise me you will never do anything like this again."

The admission hung frozen in the air between them. Emma's wide green stare rooted him in place. If she wanted to start fresh, fine. He could do that. But at the very least, he needed her to know that even though he might have ended their relationship, he hadn't erased her from his memory. Painful as it might have been, all he wanted was to know she was happy and doing okay.

She opened her mouth to say something, but instead he heard a voice call from farther away.

"Emmy Bear, is that you?"

She held his gaze for a moment longer before

finally looking over her head to where her mother stood in dirt-caked coveralls, a sun hat, and gardening gloves.

"Hey, Mom," she replied, and Matteo could hear a slight tremor in her voice. "Need help out back? Maybe in the kitchen?"

The older woman waved her off. "Nah. Most of the residents are tending to work on their homes or businesses or the square. Your father and I have everything under control for now. We were listening to an audio narration of *The Hound of the Baskervilles*—personally I prefer music, but your father was in a Holmes sort of mood. We just heard voices that weren't the dreadfully dry reading of the book and came to see who needed what. Did I mention I prefer to garden to music?"

Emma laughed, then spun around on the couch to her knees so she was fully facing her mother.

"I think you mentioned it once or twice in the past fifteen seconds," she teased.

Matteo sighed at the cuts and scrapes on her ankles and heels that were even more visible now. She'd wanted to get away from him so badly that she'd chosen actual physical pain *and* loss of oxygen to escape.

His chest ached, and his throat tightened. Why did he think they could just start over like nothing ever happened?

"Anyway," Emma's mother continued, "Just wanted

to pop in and make sure it wasn't a*nother* guest," her mother added with what looked like forced smile, but then her expression perked up. "But did you hear about the mysterious sculpture thingy?"

Matteo stood and rounded the sofa so he could see both women head-on.

Emma grinned. "In the square? Yes! Matteo and I saw it this morning, and Deputy Hayes… Did you know Dawson Hayes was a deputy? Of course you did. You live here. Well he says it's vandalism and that whoever is doing it could be arrested. But it's also art, and it's beautiful, and I think this little mystery might be the key to my social campaign for Summertown."

Her mother shook her head. "There's a sculpture in the square? I was talking about the one at the town line. The deputy's vandal not only *fixed* the Welcome to Summertown sign, but they also framed it with these beautiful painted metal flowers made from—"

"Hubcaps!" Emma interrupted. Then she glanced up at Matteo with a nervous smile.

He sighed. "*You* want me to take you there. After the stunt you just pulled."

"What stunt?" her mother asked.

Emma raised her brows, pleading with those green eyes of hers that got him *Every. Single. Time.*

"It's nothing," Matteo replied. "Just a sneaky Jenga move she pulled on my dad and Mrs. Higginson."

Emma's mom beamed. "Oh, Emmy Bear, I'm so glad you went to see Denny. He asks about you all the time. And that Tilly Higginson," she added. "Sounds like she's taking quite a liking to your dad. I think she might have a little crush."

The hairs on the back of Matteo's neck stood on end. It had been one thing for him to tease his dad about Tilly's attention. But it was just harmless flirting, wasn't it? Tilly just finalized her divorce, and his father clearly said he didn't date. But if other people were noticing… "What? No. Crush?" he stammered. "You don't think it's anything serious, right? She's just being a helpful neighbor."

"Mom," Emma protested. "Come on. Just because we're all adults now does *not* mean we are mature enough to think of our parents as actual people with lives of their own. And certainly not *love* lives of their own."

"Right," Matteo responded. "Thank you, Emma." Except she was looking at him with a knowing grin. "Oh. I get it. You're mocking me. Well, I guess my work here is done." He pointed at Emma with both index fingers. "You've got your own car, right? You can go see your mystery *vandal's* work on your own?"

Emma winced. "Okay! Okay! Sorry! I take it back. I'm not mocking you. I mean, I was, but I'm not now. I would go on my own, but I'm really spent after the…uh…Jenga stunt. So if you could please drive me to the town line? And maybe still show me how to use your camera?"

He sighed. One of them had to put a stop to the disappearing acts already. They had seven more weeks to get through. So he figured it might as well be him.

"Fine," he acquiesced. "But there's a lot of debris out there still. I'm not taking you unless you put on proper shoes."

She nodded with a grin. "Deal." Then she turned her attention to her mom. "I guess we're heading out to check on mystery sculpture number two!"

Emma's mother clapped her dirt-covered gloves together. "Well, I guess if we don't have any new guests to worry about, it's back to working in the garden with your father and Sir Arthur Conan Doyle. Let me know if you solve your mystery before Mr. Holmes solves his."

She waved goodbye with both her gloved hands and headed back in the direction from which she came.

Emma slid off the couch and approached him, stopping only inches from where he stood.

"I'm sorry for the…uh…Jenga stunt. I don't know what I was trying to prove. I guess I didn't want you thinking I hadn't grown or changed after so long. How boring and predictable, right?" She let out a breathy laugh.

He nodded and opened his mouth to respond, but she held up a finger.

"I'm not done yet," she continued. "I also need to thank you for not bailing on me *after* the ridiculous Jenga stunt. You saved my life." She glanced down at her scraped-up feet, then patted him on the chest. "You're a good egg, Matteo Rourke. Do you mind waiting a few minutes? I'd like to hop in the shower and rinse off."

He nodded, unable to come up with any actual words while her hands were on him.

"Good." She grinned. "Then don't go anywhere."

She bounded toward the back of the inn and left him standing there, all the air knocked from his lungs.

Matteo reached into the pocket of his jeans and found her inhaler, a nervous laugh escaping his lips as he considered administering his own rescue puff, but he knew it wouldn't have the desired effect. Apparently, there was no remedy for the things Emma Woods could still do to him.

"Did the cat have to come with?" Matteo asked. He rolled to a stop at the town entrance, but before he could pull the keys from the ignition, he heard a curious sniffing noise from over his shoulder. "He's, like, right behind me, isn't he?"

Emma laughed. "He was getting bored being cooped up in the back of the inn all the time. Until we catch that squirrel—and its babies, ohmygod—I don't want him roaming freely. What if he gets bitten, you know? Plus there are the chinchillas and the bird. If he ate Pikachu?" She pressed her hand to her chest and gasped dramatically.

Matteo groaned. "What if he shreds the leather of the truck's back seat?"

Emma unbuckled her seat belt and leaned between the two front seats to give Pancake a scratch behind his ear and, thankfully, peel him away from where he was aggressively sniffing *Matteo's* ear.

"The back seat that is twenty years old and covered in duct tape? Does your dad have some sort of sentimental attachment to this truck?"

"If it ain't broke, don't fix it. That's the Denny Rourke way. The man does *not* like change." Which was why Matteo was confident that the Tilly thing was just flirting. "Also, why do I smell apples?" he asked, then wished he hadn't actually spoken aloud because he knew as soon as the words left his mouth that he was smelling *her*.

"Sorry," she said, sliding back to the front but stopping when her eyes met his. "My hair's still damp, so it's probably my shampoo. If it bothers you, I can pull my hair back into a bun. It just dries faster this way."

He leaned back against his window, trying to put at least another inch or two between them.

"It's fine," he said. "I was just caught off guard. It, um, doesn't usually smell so good in the truck. Not that *you* smell good. Er…you *do* obviously. I just mean with all the wild animals we deal with, it tends to get a little gamier in here. You know, like… Actually, I'm just going to stop talking because I took it somewhere gross."

What was his problem? So she showered and smelled good after. Wasn't that the point of a shower? Everyone smelled better after a shower. He just wasn't in the habit of *smelling* Emma Woods—showered or not, yet suddenly all he *wanted* to do was bury his face in her still- damp hair and breathe.

Shit.

She quirked a brow, then finally sat back in her seat, giving Matteo room to breathe again.

He nodded toward her window. "There it is, by the way. Should we get out and take a look? I can leave the AC running for the cat."

Emma pivoted toward her window and pressed her nose to the glass.

"Whoa," she whispered, incredulous. "Yeah. Yeah, let's go take a look."

She gave the cat specific directions not to touch anything he shouldn't and then hopped out. Matteo chuckled as he exited the vehicle himself. This Emma—the cat-whispering, smelling-like-apples mystery solver—was someone he no longer knew. That was his doing, and he owned that. He never fathomed he'd have a chance to get to know her again, so he was trying to savor every little moment since he knew eventually it would come to an end.

His sneakers squished into the mud in front of the Welcome to Summertown sign, and he was happy to see that although also caked in mud, Emma wore sneakers too.

"Careful," she told him, her eyes fixed on the sign. "The mud is slick."

"I'm used to it." He shrugged. "It's always like a swamp around here." Then he took another step toward her, and his heel slid out from under him. "Shit!" he hissed, then caught his balance before he launched himself straight into Emma and took them both down.

She spun to face him and snorted, then covered her mouth with her hand.

"Like I said, the mud is slick." Her words came out with muffled laughter.

Matteo stifled a grin and held up the camera that hung from his neck.

"Laugh all you want, but if I go down, you're back to running your big campaign with your phone."

"Here." She held out her hand. "I'm pretty steady. You can hold on to me for purchase if you need."

He hesitated for a second, then grabbed her wrist and took a long stride over a particularly muddy spot. He dropped her hand as soon as he found his footing, and both of them simply stared.

"Looks like our *vandal* got even more creative with this one," she whispered.

"What do you mean?" he whispered back. "And why are we whispering?"

She reached a hand to gently touch a rusted metal flower petal, flinching at the sharp point before skimming her finger over a flatter part of the surface.

"The pistil is a hubcap, but the petals are fashioned from a thinner metal. Look at how the bright copper contrasts with the polished silver of the hubcap."

She was right. Where the sunflowers had been painted right onto the hubcaps in the square, this sculpture was more intricate, more detailed.

"Look at you, remembering your flower parts," he mused.

She hummed. "I wasn't lying about my small garden at home. But even if I was, you don't grow up in a town like Summertown and forget, no matter how long you've been gone."

Home. Every time she said that word in relation to the place that wasn't *here,* it reminded Matteo that this reacquaintance between the two of them would be over almost as quickly as it had started.

"No," he finally responded, his wistful tone matching hers. "I guess you don't." He ran his own fingertips over the Chevy symbol stamped onto one of the hubcaps, and for a stretch of silence they simply stood there, hands touching the same surface, feet rooted in the mud. If he could capture the moment on film, he would. Instead he closed his eyes and breathed in the damp, earthy scent that carried with it a hint of apples. He took a mental picture and placed it in a long-concealed compartment in his mind, the one with memories of her. "They're lotus flowers, right?" he asked.

Emma nodded. "The lotus is famous for growing in the mud—no mud, no flowers. It's a revered symbol of self-regeneration and rebirth in yoga traditions, I think." She pressed her hand to her chest and turned her gaze to him. "The flowers…This sculpture…" There were seven flowers in all. "It's *Summertown*." Her voice cracked on the second syllable of the town name. "Sorry. I don't know why this is making me so emotional."

Matteo swallowed. "Because it's *not* just the town. It's any of us. Or *all* of us. Who doesn't want to rise up from the dregs or their mistakes or whatever and be able to start again?"

She nodded with a smile, and her brows rose as she swiped at a tear leaking from the corner of her eye. "Will you snap some photos? I'm not exactly in the right frame of mind to learn how to use the camera right now." She laughed and sniffled at the same time.

Matteo obliged, and the repeated click of the shutter matched the quickening of his pulse.

He moved deftly around the sign, the mud behaving or at least calling it a truce while he captured the sculpture from every angle as Emma stared. He maybe, possibly, took the slightest advantage of how transfixed she was by including *her* in some of the photos as well.

Now transfixed himself, Matteo forgot about the truce between himself and the mud. Or, more likely, the mud decided it was time to snap him back to reality.

The last thing he saw through the camera's lens before his legs went out from under him was Emma's wide-open eyes and her mouth rounded into an O.

He hugged the camera tightly to his chest as he crashed to the ground, landing flat on his back with a harsh squish. He gasped for air, the wind knocked from his chest. Pain shot through his shoulder, an old injury rearing its ugly head. But his breath returned and with it a welcome distraction from the unfortunate situation he was currently in… the sweet hint of apples along with the pungent scent of earth. His vision cleared—his head having gotten knocked almost as hard as his lungs—so that he saw Emma mere inches above him, braced on all fours over his chest.

"I tried to grab you." Her words came out between panting breaths.

"I tried to save the camera." He tilted his head to

see he was still hugging the device against his chest and sighed with relief.

She swallowed, then licked her lips, and Matteo forgot all about the ache in the back of his head.

"Are you okay?" she asked, still not moving from her perch above him.

No. I'm not okay. I'm caked in mud, possibly concussed, and if you lick your lips again, things are going to start happening below the belt that make me really grateful I swapped the running shorts for jeans.

"I think so," he lied.

He dropped his hands from the camera and made a move to push himself up, but Emma shook her head.

"Wait," she pleaded. "Can I…? Will you let me try something?"

"Okay," he said softly, his heart hammering against his chest. "But I need to tell you something first."

Emma nodded.

"Just so you know, you have *nothing* to prove to me. Even if you were the same exact person you were eight years ago—which, be*lieve* me, you are not—you could never…not for a single second… be boring or predictable."

He heard her breath catch. Then she dipped her head and brushed her lips against his, the kiss soft and tentative. She lingered for a few seconds and began to tilt away. But like a magnet unable to escape her pull, he rose to meet her once more, his mouth colliding with hers.

She pulled him up to sitting and collapsed into his lap, her legs wrapping around his hips and muddy palms cupping his cheeks. He didn't care. She could turn into an actual swamp monster at this point, and he'd be powerless against her spell.

Because she was *Emma*.

Despite the camera and years of estrangement between them, they found a rhythm of touching and tasting, of remembering and reacquainting, until finally they had no choice but to breathe.

They sat staring at each other for a long moment until Emma finally spoke.

"Bet you weren't predicting that."

Her palms were still on his cheeks, and Matteo swore he would stay right here, caked in mud, if she never let go.

"Not in a million years," he told her. He would never have hoped for a second chance because he knew he didn't deserve one. Yet here they were, muddy limbs draped over muddy limbs and lips swollen with evidence of a mutual hunger and need.

"I needed to see if *we* were meant to rise up and start again."

He nodded slowly. "And what's your verdict?"

She skimmed her teeth over her bottom lip and let out a long, slow sigh.

"I–I don't know."

Chapter 10

HADDIE SAT ON EMMA'S LAPTOP SCREEN, FACING her from the dresser as she changed the linens in one of the upstairs guest rooms.

"Tell me again why I'm watching you short-sheet one of your poor neighbors who came to the inn for refuge and not to stub their toes on their linens."

Emma looked over her shoulder and glared at her friend.

"Hospital corners is *not* short-sheeting. It's a way to turn an unfitted sheet into a fitted sheet. And I think my *neighbors* like getting treated like guests. Hopefully makes their stay feel more like a vacation rather than a necessity because their homes aren't livable at the moment." Emma shrugged. "Also keeps me busy." *Not* that there was a shortage of anything to do at the inn, but any idle time brought with it idle thoughts, and right now those thoughts were on a one-way street to Matteo Rourke.

"Why not just use fitted sheets?" Haddie

continued. "Then you wouldn't have to break a sweat trying to make one from scratch."

Emma groaned. How did her friend know she was sweating?

She finished the corner she was on, then collapsed onto the floor at the foot of the bed so she could face her laptop.

"It's all about wear and tear, really. If we order all the same kind of sheet, it's easier to replace one when it's seen its last tight corner."

Haddie was facing the screen but wasn't exactly making eye contact as she bounced softly on her treadmill.

"Are you still listening to me, or have I finally bored you to the extent of sleeping with your eyes open *while* jogging? I'd like to remind you that *you're* the one who asked about the sheets."

Haddie slowed to a stop and took a few hearty swigs from her water bottle. Then she finally looked up.

"*Ems...*" She leaned in close. "If you really only called to talk about sheets, then I'm all in. But I'm thinking this goes *deeper* than sheets." She waggled her brows.

Was she *that* obvious? The idle thoughts she *thought* she was avoiding seemed instead to be oozing from her pores, visible even via shitty, small-town Wi-Fi.

"Fine... I didn't call to talk about sheets."

"You called because you missed me terribly?"

"Always," Emma replied. "But also because there was a, um, a kiss."

Here was the thing. Telling Haddie about the kiss wasn't just telling her about a *kiss*. It meant opening a can of worms that had stayed tightly closed since before she'd even met her now best friend.

Haddie's eyes widened. "One in which *you* were involved?"

Emma gave her a pointed look.

"Well, I wasn't sure. People kiss all the time. I mean, people who *date* do. People who hole up in their apartments with their cats don't seem to do it as much, so you can understand my need for clarification."

"Ouch," Emma replied. She rested her head on her knees with a pout. "I *date*."

Haddie nodded. "I will hand it to you that you are the *queen* of first dates. But you always find an excuse to put the kibosh on the whole thing before it gets to the fun stuff like kissing. Like that guy Toby you went out with last month. He was cute, employed, owned his own condo—"

"Wore mismatched socks..." Emma interrupted.

Haddie barked out a laugh. "And for that he never made it to date number two?"

Emma threw her hands in the air. "If a man doesn't even put the effort in to match his socks before tossing them in the drawer, think of all the other corners he'll cut in life. That was just me being proactive."

"What about Keith from the New Year's Eve party last year? You gave him the cheek at midnight when he was more than willing to play a little tonsil hockey."

Emma grimaced. "He'd just eaten a full plate of chips and guacamole."

"So had most everyone else at the party!"

"Yeah," Emma added. "But it was full of cilantro, and you know how much I hate cilantro. It's genetic. I googled it. Something like four to fourteen percent of the population has this genetic mutation that makes cilantro taste like soap. I'm one of the four to fourteen. So, yeah, a man who wants to kiss me with a soapy cilantro mouth is a no for me."

Haddie sighed. "You *look* for reasons not to give anyone a fighting chance, yet you wonder why I question whether this supposed kiss that took place involved you." She pressed her lips into a sad smile. "I love you, Ems. You know I do. But I worry about this little cocoon that you've formed, you know? If our mail hadn't gotten mixed up in the mail room that one time all those years ago, we might never have even met. And then where would either of us be?"

Emma huffed out a mirthless laugh. "You'd still be living your best life with all your face-to-face interactions, and I'd probably have two more cats."

"At *least* two more cats," Haddie added. She paused for a beat before continuing. "Tell me about the kiss. You've been gone for over a week, and I didn't even know you'd met anyone with kiss potential, so there is obviously a story here."

Emma nodded. "His name is Matteo. Matteo Rourke. And eight years ago, he broke my heart."

High School, Junior Year...

"What if I bomb the test and don't get into college and I have to live in the inn and never find my true purpose?" Emma asked Matteo before they took the school-administered SAT.

He kissed her on the forehead and backed through the gymnasium door, holding it open for her as they entered to find their assigned seats at the testing tables.

"You won't bomb it," he assured her without so much as a tremor in his voice. "And neither will I."

"How do you *know*, Matteo? Did you forget to tell me about your psychic abilities? Because it's really important for a girl to know up front if her boyfriend can predict the future." She rummaged through her pencil case to make sure her number-two pencils were sharpened and that she hadn't forgotten her school ID.

"I *know*..." He kissed her again, then ushered her through the door so she wouldn't hold up the growing crowd of fellow classmates also heading into the test. "Because you're you, Em. And I'm me. We're *us*. And we didn't sign up for a life of animal trapping or innkeeping. You're going to find *your* thing, and I'll find mine. We'll graduate with all sorts of ridiculous honors, backpack across Europe, and then find our dream jobs—"

"In the same town," she interrupted.

"I go where you go," he said with a grin as they searched the name cards on the testing tables to find their spots.

"Promise?" she asked when he found his spot first.

"I go where *you* go," he told her again, this time his jaw set with conviction.

Her nerves calmed, and when she found her own name card, she settled into her chair with renewed confidence and twenty-four sharpened number-two pencils.

"I'm going to *ace* this," she mouthed to Matteo when he glanced back at her.

She hadn't, of course. Emma was smart, but she wasn't a test-taking savant. Although she did score high enough to get into her safety school. The *second* time, though, she got the score she needed for her dream school in Michigan. Matteo had too. But no sooner had they gotten their acceptance letters than Matteo's family received other news as well.

"My mom is sick," he told her, showing up on the inn's porch late one January night their senior year of high school. "I'm going to stay home for the first year and go to community college…just until she's done with treatment. Levi has his scholarship, and the team needs him. But my dad can't keep the company going *and* take care of my mom by himself. Michigan is letting me defer for the first year, and then sophomore year I'm there. With you. Like we planned."

She hugged him, and he buried his face in her neck. She felt his warm, trembling breath on her skin.

"I'm so sorry, Matty-Matt. I love you."

They lowered themselves to the inn's top step as snow flurried down from the night sky.

"I love you too," he told her.

He didn't say anything else as she held him for what might have been minutes or might have been hours. Time seemed to bleed into itself from that point on.

The rock for both his father and his brother, Matteo didn't cry then or at his mother's funeral less than three years later.

And he never made it to Michigan.

"Prison?" Haddie blurted out. "As in *jail.* Locked up. Behind bars." She blinked.

Emma nodded. "It still doesn't make sense. The guy barely even drank in high school, and then he's pulled over and arrested for driving under the influence of a controlled substance and later charged with possession and intent to sell. It was on the front page of the *Town Crier,* Summertown's local paper, which is the only way I found out."

Emma's chest tightened as she relived her own shock and grief—and the betrayal of finding out what happened to Matteo the same way everyone else did.

"And that was it? He dumped you, and then yada yada yada, it's yesterday and you're kissing him in the mud at the town entrance?"

Emma winced.

"Sorry," Haddie added. "This is just *not* the story I expected, and also *how* have you never told me any of this before?"

"I visited him. Once." She felt the threat—or maybe it was just the memory—of hot tears pricking her eyes.

"I'm not going to let you put any part of your future on hold for a guy who doesn't have one anymore," he'd told her.

"What happened to 'I go where you go'?" she asked via an old-school telephone, a pane of glass separating her from the boy she'd thought *was* her future.

He let out a mirthless laugh. "I'm not *going* anywhere, Emma. Not for the next two years, at least." Silence stretched out between them for several seconds before he spoke again. "You believe the charges, right?"

Emma hesitated, and it was in that moment of doubt, contemplation, or whatever it was that she believed he truly made his choice.

"Live your life, Emma. Okay? Be…happy." She heard the tiniest falter in his voice, and for a second she thought he was going to take it all back and ask her to wait. Instead, he added, "And please don't visit me again." Then he pushed his chair back and stood.

It all seemed to happen in slow motion. She opened her mouth to say something—to say the *right* thing—but the words she needed wouldn't come. Matteo looked at her one more time and then pivoted toward the guard, telling him the visit was done.

When Emma finally finished, Haddie's mouth hung open.

It surprisingly felt like an invisible weight had been lifted from her chest. "Wow," she added. "I don't think I've said that all out loud before. It felt…good?" Not the reliving of it, but the unburdening herself.

"So…let me make sure I understand," Haddie began, regaining her seldom-lost composure.

"Mismatched socks and cilantro are deal-breakers, but your high school sweetheart breaks up with you from the other side of a prison partition, and almost a decade later, you tackle him in the mud and plant one right on his heartbreaking lips?"

Emma worried her bottom lip between her teeth and nodded.

"Yeah," she admitted. "That about sums it up."

Chapter 11

"You really don't need to be up here with me," Matteo told Emma, looking over his shoulder and then squinting as the flashlight beam hit him square in the eye.

"I wasn't going to let you hold the flashlight in your teeth." She waved the light at his gloved hands that were well enough equipped to handle a rogue squirrel but not so much a mini Maglite. Actually, the thick, *hopefully* impenetrable-by-rodent-claws-and-teeth accessories went all the way up to his elbows.

He crossed his gloved arms and narrowed his eyes at her. "You know, if you had called me sooner to get the abatement plan going, our furry friend would already be confined to the area with her nest, and you wouldn't hear scurrying in the ceiling."

Emma's stomach *and* tongue tied themselves in knots. He was right. But calling him would have meant seeing him, which would have totally gotten in the way of her plan to *avoid, avoid, avoid* what happened in the mud. What if when she saw him again she wanted to *devour* him again? She needed to be logical and not let her libido make decisions her brain and *heart* didn't approve of.

"I've been busy helping out at the inn and doing my *real* job. Speaking of helping out at the inn, I can't get the Instagram account going until you send me the photos. I texted you my email."

Matteo huffed out a laugh. "The text that had nothing *but* your email address?"

She shrugged. "I didn't think it needed further explanation."

Something scuffled across the floor to her right, and Emma yelped.

"Is it on me? I feel like it's on me!" She squeezed her eyes shut and frantically pointed the flashlight at all appendages, her torso, her head.

Something touched her hand, and she yelped again, then heard the clank and roll of the flashlight hitting the floor.

"It touched me!" she cried.

"It did *not* touch you, Emma. That was my hand! I was trying to get the flashlight from you so I could find the squirrel while you freaked out!"

She opened her eyes, indignant and ready to let him have it except that it was now pitch-black in the attic.

"Um…Matteo? What happened to the *light* from the flashlight?"

She heard him groan, but whether he was right beside her or several feet away, she couldn't tell.

"You probably *broke* it, which means you owe me thirty-five bucks."

It sounded like a joke, but she could hear the irritation in his voice. Not that it mattered because all she could focus on was the fact that she couldn't see her own hand when she waved it in front of her face. She swayed and grappled in the dark until she touched something.

"Is that you?" she squeaked. "Oh god, please tell me it's you before my imagination gets the best of me and I start down a rabbit hole of serial killers or ghosts or—"

"It's me, Emma," he said, his voice rough.

She fisted her hands in his shirt and let out a shaky exhale.

"Sorry. I got dizzy. I think the dark is messing with my equilibrium, and I needed to grab on to something. I'm just really glad you're not a ghost or a serial killer or a giant squirrel."

He laughed, and she felt his warm breath on her cheek. "That *you* know of," he teased.

Okay. Good. Her little avoidance scheme hadn't disrupted their rhythm. Not that she *wanted* to have a rhythm with him. Did she? Either way, she figured she had a little leeway when it came to fleeing the scene of the kiss the other day.

Another scuffle sounded on the floor. Matteo

covered her mouth with his palm before she could cry out again.

"Sorry," he whispered. "But I don't want to scare it away. My eyes are starting to adjust, and I think..." His voice trailed off, and then he pressed his lips directly on the skin next to her earlobe.

Emma shivered, and her belly tightened.

"Don't...move." His words were so quiet, she barely heard them. But she felt them in her bones and at the tip of every nerve.

He dropped his hand and pried her fists from his shirt.

Then he darted—*somewhere*.

She heard scratching on wood, heavy breathing, something like metal rolling, and a long beat of silence.

Then a high-pitched screech pierced the air, and she dropped to a squat to keep from pitching forward as she covered her ears and squeezed her eyes shut.

Emma reconsidered her thoughts on ghosts, realizing apparitions most likely were *not* rabid. Come to think of it, neither were serial killers. Okay, fine, the latter was maybe more dangerous than the squirrel that could be chewing off Matteo's face at this very moment.

She gasped. What if it was a serial-killing *squirrel*?

Emma snorted, obviously losing her grip with reality, when her face was hit by a light so bright that she had to squint even though her eyes were already closed.

"Did someone just open a portal to the sun?" she asked, shielding her eyes with her hands as she blinked one open and then the other.

A tall shadow loomed over her.

"Got her." She could hear Matteo but couldn't make out his features.

"Do you think you might be able to remove the flashlight beam from my retinas so I can get my bearings?"

"What? Oh. Sorry!" he said, turning the flashlight on himself instead.

Emma pushed herself to her feet and waited for the spots of color to dissipate from her vision. Her mouth fell open when Matteo came into focus, a small and very frightened-looking squirrel held carefully in his gloved hand.

"That's her?" she asked, gingerly taking a step toward him.

"That's close enough," he warned. "She's really scared and probably thinks we're here to harm her babies. I need you to grab the cage I left by the attic door and set it on the floor a couple feet away from me. Do you think you can do that? I'll light your path."

Emma nodded and followed the beam of light toward the opening in the floor.

"Guess I didn't break it, huh?" she whisper-shouted over her shoulder.

Matteo chuckled. "No. Just knocked the power off."

She grabbed the cage and pivoted back toward the wildlife trapper and his prey. Well, not really *prey* because he was saving the pest.

She set the cage down a few feet from where Matteo stood, then stepped back another few feet for good measure.

Seconds later, the squirrel was in the cage happily nibbling at a glob of sunflower seeds and peanut butter with Matteo squatting beside it.

"That was amazing," Emma told him. "*You* were amazing. I'm over here screaming and jumping, and then there's you—calm, cool, and more collected than I think I've ever been in my entire life." Her chest tightened. That was one of the reasons she'd fallen for him. But it was also what made it seem so easy for him to end things and then simply walk away.

Steady, unflappable Matteo Rourke. How much had she really known him at all?

"Did you hear me, Em?"

The nickname jolted her out of the daydream, and she was staring at adult Matteo again.

"What?" she asked, too confused to call him out on the *Em* thing.

"I'm going to head down and get my work light and supplies to install the temporary cover on the hole and put our mama back in her nest. Then she and her babies won't be able to get back into the attic or the rest of the inn. I'll leave the outside open so the mother can forage but…" He paused, scratching at the stubble on his jaw.

"But what?" she asked.

"She's obviously been making use of the inn either for nesting purposes or food. Sine we're cutting her off from the inside, I'm probably going to need to come by a few times a week to make sure she's still finding what she needs to take care of her young and to make sure partially trapping them doesn't actually scare her away. Just until the babies are old enough to leave the nest, of course."

Emma nodded absently at him. Sure. Matteo at the inn a few times a week. That should make it easy to avoid planting one on his heartbreaking lips again. "How long will that be?"

He shined the flashlight on her, careful to avoid her eyes. "About twelve weeks."

So…the whole summer. Emma swallowed.

"You look a little shaken," Matteo added. "Maybe you should head back downstairs until I'm done. Should only be another twenty minutes or so."

Shaken, sure, but she wasn't sure how much it actually had to do with squirrels.

"And the email with the photos from the other day is in my drafts. I, uh, I was just assuming we might talk first about…" His voice trailed off, and Emma wasn't ready to fill in the blank. "Anyway, I can send the email from my phone, and when I'm done, maybe you can tell me what you think."

About the photos? About whether or not she wanted the two of them to *rise up and start again*?

"Yeah," she finally replied. "That would be great."

Emma grabbed her laptop and parked herself at the registration desk. With her mother working in the office and her father out back in the garden, the quiet reception area was oddly the place with the most privacy.

She opened her email and refreshed it once. Twice. But still nothing from Matteo. So she responded to a client about SEO metrics and doing an A/B test of two differently worded Instagram ads. Still, her inbox hadn't changed. So she made a new tab, placed her cursor in the URL bar, and typed.

Metal flower art.

Infinite results stared back at her from the screen.

Hubcap flower art.

The second search offered almost as many.

She sighed. Her mysterious painted flower gardener would not be unmasked so easily.

Painted. Flower. Gardener.

The *Gardener*. That was what she would call her. Or him. Or them. Whoever it was, they were responsible for—so far—*two* unique and unexpected gardens sprouting up in a town whose earth had been churned and overturned.

Movement flickered in her periphery, and Emma's eyes darted to the inbox number on her other open tab, now one number higher than it was before.

Emma sucked in a breath and clicked back to her email.

She wasn't sure what she was expecting. Some eloquently worded explanation for the flurry of emotions that rushed through her every time she tried to reconcile the man she'd kissed with the boy she'd loved?

Instead, the topmost message in her inbox boasted the words ROURKE PEST CONTROL in bold letters as the sender. The subject line was blank, and the message itself held nothing but image files. No text.

"Touché, Mr. Rourke," she mumbled to herself. After sending him nothing but her email address in her last text, she guessed she deserved that.

So she opened the first image and began clicking through each one.

The lighting, the angles, the detail—everything from the droplets of morning dew that had been preserved in the coolness of the shade to the copper rust patterns on the lotus petals—her phone never could have taken photos like this, nor could the camera she'd left behind in her apartment. In fact, Emma was certain that had *she* been the one handling the thirty-five-millimeter back at the Summertown town entrance, she never would have produced photos with such insight and care—or so many that included *her* as the snapshots' focus.

Just because he'd sent her an email without text didn't mean Matteo had nothing to say.

Emma had already set up the Instagram account for the Gardener, which was what she decided to call the mystery artist. All she needed was the right photo to get it started, and Matteo had sent her all that and more.

She crafted the first post, a reel of all of the photos that didn't contain *her*, with "Here Comes the Sun" by the Beatles playing underneath. Summertown, Illinois, in one way or another, was in bloom again.

She tagged the Twin Town Garden Fest, local press and government affiliates, her connections at Yelp and Trip Advisor, and even set up a paid boost. One way or another, Summertown was making a comeback.

Only after tweaking her wording for the seventh time did Emma finally post, then slamming her laptop shut and running up the stairs to the top floor until she reached the storage closet that led to the attic.

She found Matteo climbing down the ladder, having just closed the attic's trapdoor.

"Emma?" He startled to see her when he spun toward the open door.

She heaved a breath in and out. In and out.

"What's wrong? Do you need your inhaler? Did you pretend you were a runner again?"

She scoffed.

"I'm *thinking*," she told him. "Give me a minute."

"Okay." He set his toolbox on the floor and dropped his trapped gloves on top of the box. "Take all the time you need."

Her pulse raced, and the hairs on the back of her neck stood on end.

"I saw the photos," she finally said. "They were perfect and beautiful, and I don't know what I was expecting, but you exceeded my wildest fantasies. Your *photos*, I mean!" She let loose a shaky breath. "Even the ones of *me*," she added. "Though I wasn't expecting those."

He nodded slowly.

She still wasn't sure what she was trying to reconcile in her brain. All she knew was that Matteo was thinking about her as much as she was thinking about him. It was all there in the photos. He didn't have to send them all. He could have left the ones with her out of the email. But he didn't.

He wanted her to see. And she wanted…

Eight years ago, she'd stood by while *he* chose their fate. But he wasn't turning away from her now. He was looking her square in the eyes and *waiting*.

The ball was in her court, and he was letting her decide what she wanted to do with it.

What the hell did she want?

"If we're going to keep bumping into each other, we might as well *work* together to track down the Gardener. That's what I'm calling him. Or her. Or them. Anyway, I'm going to use social media to publicize Summertown and what our mystery artist is doing to help beautify the town. I'd like you to be my photographer. I could pay you for your time if—"

"Okay," he interrupted. "I'll help you. But I don't want your money, Emma."

She bounced on her toes, rising as far as she could toward his height.

"What *do* you want, Matteo? Because the last time we saw each other, you didn't—"

"Please," he whispered, and she knew what came next.

Don't bring up the past. Don't talk about what happened then.

But instead he said, "Don't ask me about what I want when I don't deserve to want *anything* from you."

Her breath caught in her throat, and Matteo's brows furrowed.

"Does it surprise you to know I have regrets about that day you came to see me?"

His voice was barely above a whisper, but she

could still detect the unexpected hint of pain in his voice.

"Yes," she admitted, hearth thrumming in her chest.

"Then you never really knew me, Emma." He dipped his forehead so it rested against hers. "Because there is *nothing* I regret more than how I hurt you."

Her lips parted as his approached, but he didn't kiss her.

"So please don't ask me what I want," he continued. "Because for eight fucking years, all I've ever wanted was *you*."

Chapter 12

MATTEO PADDED DOWN THE STAIRS FROM HIS garage apartment. Sure, he could make his own coffee in the small kitchenette he and his father had built, but somehow it always tasted better when someone else brewed it. Plus, not that he'd ever admit it aloud, but the fact his father hadn't changed anything about the interior of the house since he was a kid helped him remember his mother—and what life was like *before*.

Sometimes it took several seconds or even minutes to conjure the image of her in his head without the familiarity of home to remind him. For the years he was away, he thought it was a comfort. It took coming back to Summertown for him to realize that no matter how painful the memories, he didn't want to forget.

He scratched his bare chest and yawned as he made his way into the kitchen from the mudroom, not having bothered to put anything on over his boxer briefs.

"How'd you sleep, Dad?" he asked, his eyes closing as he paused to inhale the aroma of fresh-brewed coffee and… Was that bacon?

"Shhh," a clearly *female* voice whispered. "He's not up yet, and I want to surprise him with breakfast in bed."

Matteo's eyes shot open to find Tilly Higginson standing at the stove folding an omelet in a pan.

"Tilly!" He glanced down at his unmistakable morning wood. "Holy shit." He cupped his palms over the front of his briefs.

"Oh, honey." She waved him off with the spatula. "I raised two boys of my own and once had a Pomeranian who woke up happy every morning too."

Matteo squeezed his eyes shut and shook his head. "I don't think I ever needed to know that about Kong."

"Let me pour you some coffee," Tilly continued, unfazed.

"Um… How did you…? I mean, did you sleep…? Like, does my dad know…?" Matteo stammered.

She grinned, then turned the burner off and slid the omelet onto a plate.

"About that coffee…" she began again, grabbing the fresh pot in one hand and a mug in the other.

He held his hands up in protest, remembered his erection, and immediately dropped his palms back over it.

"No!" he exclaimed. "Thank you. I should go back upstairs and—"

"Tilly, are you up already?" Denny Rourke called from around the corner to the kitchen's entrance. "I thought you were going to stay in bed until I had a chance to talk to Matteo about—"

He stopped short as he came into Matteo's view, hands fumbling to tie his robe as his eyes locked on his son's.

"Matteo!" Denny Rourke glanced from his son to the clock on the stove and then back. "It's six in the morning on Sunday. What are you doing up?"

A muscle ticked in Matteo's jaw. "I didn't sleep much last night." Or any night for that matter, but that wasn't the issue right now. "From the looks of it, neither did you."

His issue in his nether region subsided, but the sudden ache in his chest made his knees threaten to give out. "I should go," he croaked, then spun back toward the direction from which he came. He braced his palm on the wall to steady himself, sucked in a deep breath, and then disappeared back up the stairs.

The second he clicked the door to his apartment shut, a knock sounded on the door.

"Jesus, Dad. Not now, okay? Go eat your eggs and give me a minute." Or an hour. Maybe a lifetime.

"Son…we need to talk. Open the door. Please?"

Matteo grabbed his jeans from where he'd

kicked them off the night before and slid them on, then did the same with the T-shirt still draped over the foot of his bed. He sucked in a steadying breath and headed to the door, hesitating before he turned the handle because the second he let his father in, *everything* was going to change.

"*Teo*," his father pleaded, using the nickname his mother had given him when he was a toddler, too young to successfully pronounce his whole name.

Matteo opened the door and sighed. "That's not playing fair, Dad."

His father shrugged, only looking mildly chagrined. "Does that mean I can come in?"

Matteo pulled the door open the rest of the way and held out an open arm, welcoming his father inside.

"You didn't sleep again, did you?" the older man accused as he nodded at the photography books and camera accessories strewn across Matteo's untouched bed.

He cleared his throat. "I dozed off for an hour, I think. Maybe two."

His father scrubbed a hand across his unshaven jaw. "You could talk to the doctor about a prescription," he started, but Matteo shook his head.

"*You* know that's not an option."

"I could ration them… Only give you one when you need it," his dad continued.

"I'll babysit myself, thanks," Matteo grumbled.

"I've been doing it for almost a decade and haven't slipped up yet."

Denny opened his mouth but hesitated. Then he approached his son and clapped him on the shoulder. "I should have been there for you more when we lost your mom."

Matteo let out a bitter laugh. "We're going to have a heart-to-heart about this now? I'm good, Dad. Really." His words came out crueler than he'd intended. But if there was one thing Matteo Rourke knew all too well, it was regret and how much it didn't matter. Didn't change a damned thing. No matter how much Matteo wished he could have done something differently, the past and all the mistakes he'd made had still happened. The people he'd hurt were still hurt.

The same went for his father. Yes, the man was grieving the loss of his wife and taking care of his injured older son at the same time. He had a lot on his plate, which meant some things had to fall by the wayside. Matteo just happened to be one of those things.

His father lowered his hand.

"Okay… But about Tilly…"

Matteo held up his hands. "You don't need to explain. I get it. That whole thing about not wanting anyone to compete with Mom's ghost was—"

"True," the older man interrupted. "Every word

was *true*." He strode toward Matteo's unused bed and gingerly lowered himself onto the foot of it. "Tilly's not trying to compete. She's just…I don't know…making me realize that I don't *have* to be alone. I like her, and she likes me. Is that so bad? You even winked at me and told me to share my ice cream with her the night of the storm."

"Yeah, well that was when I thought she was harmlessly flirting with a guy too clueless to notice. I didn't think you actually liked her like *that*." He groaned. "It just happened so fast. I'm gonna need some time to wrap my head around it."

"That's fair." His father shifted his weight on the bed and winced.

"How's your back?" Matteo asked, choosing to keep his distance from the subject *and* from his dad. He backed up toward the breakfast bar of the kitchenette and leaned on a stool.

His father slapped his palms on his thighs. "The physical therapy is helping, and the doctor said I can manage living with the injury if I keep up the exercises. But…"

"But what?" Matteo asked.

"But if I want to alleviate the pain, I'll need surgery." His father added.

Matteo cleared his throat. "*Spine* surgery?"

Denny Rourke laughed. "That is usually how they correct injuries to the spine."

"But that's dangerous, isn't it?" Matteo crossed

his arms. "If you can manage without it, why would you take the risk?"

His father pushed himself up with a grimace. Then he untied and retied his robe. "I think it's time I did better than *manage*. And yes, there's risk with any surgery, but this is fairly routine. At least as spinal surgeries go." He took a couple of steps toward his son, but stopped when Matteo leaned further against the counter. "I've got a lot of good years left in me, you know? The thought of being able to live them without pain? That's gotta be worth the risk."

"Are we still talking about the surgery?" Matteo asked.

"For now," his father replied. "But we should talk more, don't you think?"

"Yeah. Sure," Matteo answered absently. "You should get back down to your guest."

Denny Rourke nodded. "I don't suppose you'll join us?"

Matteo was already eyeing his running shoes at the other corner of the room. "I'm going to go for a run. Clear my head. There are no scheduled appointments today, are there?"

"No," his father shook his head. "But keep your phone on you just in case. You know, if I do the surgery, I'll be able to get back to work eventually. Then maybe you can focus more on what *you* want."

Matteo closed his eyes and shook his head. "Who would hire me other than you?"

His father looked past him, eyeing something on the bed as he moved closer to it.

"This isn't photography," the older man mumbled, picking up the articles Matteo had printed from his laptop. "Wrongful incarceration," he read softly. "Statute of limitations…" Denny Rourke rifled through the papers, only pivoting to face his son after he'd gotten through the pile.

"It's nothing," Matteo told him.

His father's brows furrowed. "I thought it was too late to do anything about this."

Matteo pinched the bridge of his nose. "Legally, yes. But there are other ways to unbury the truth, whatever it is."

His father took a few steps closer and placed a hand on his son's shoulder, giving him what should have been a reassuring squeeze, but all Matteo felt was pity.

"You know I'm here for you regardless of what happened, right?"

Matteo closed his eyes and took a step back, forcing Denny Rourke to drop his hand.

"You really think I not only got behind the wheel high but also decided to go back to school and start a new *business*?"

The other man sighed. "I'm saying that it was a shitty time for all of us, and I was too caught up in my own grief to see how you were handling yours."

Matteo shook his head. "I committed a

misdemeanor, Dad. And I was charged with a felony. I get that no one else believes that, but it doesn't mean *I'm* not going to figure out the truth." He raised his brows. "Are we done here?"

"I guess so." His dad turned toward the door but paused. "Oh, some woman—I think her name was Lauren…something—left a message for you on the landline yesterday. I wrote it down on the message pad. Said she was from Chicago but didn't want to talk on email. Is she a friend of Emma's?"

Matteo's eyes widened. "*No.* No. Not a friend of Emma's, but she left her number? Lauren Monroe?"

The other man nodded with a grin. "Yeah! That sounds about right!"

He'd found her email on her company website and took a shot in the dark. When she'd responded and even agreed to meet for coffee, Matteo had latched on to the first shred of hope in years.

"But it's a dead end," she ended up telling him. "If you really did take the fall for someone else, they covered it up really well. Not super likely in Small Town, USA."

Which meant *she* hadn't believed him either. So what changed in the past month? Matteo couldn't wait to find out.

"I should go," he said, hearing the eagerness in his own voice. "I'll grab that number on the way out."

His dad lifted his hand like he was going to reach for Matteo again, but then he dropped it.

"Have a good run. Probably a good idea to get outside before it gets too hot." He forced a smile and sighed before heading back toward the door, and then his father was gone.

"Hi. It's Lauren. I'm on deadline and will get back to you…um…sometime next week. Leave a message!"

Matteo stood at the foot of his driveway and waited for the beep.

"Lauren. Hi. Matteo Rourke. Hoping you have some good news. This is my cell, so call me back anytime. Thanks."

His feet pounded the pavement as his running playlist blared in his ears. It didn't matter how high he set the volume, though. He couldn't drown out the frenzy of thoughts swirling in his head.

His father and Tilly.

Surgery.

Insomnia.

Lauren from Chicago.

The audacity of his dad to suggest Matteo consider what he *wanted*. Of Emma to ask him the same.

What he *wanted* was…what he *wanted*…

He wanted to know why, when he'd been running toward the high school track, he now found himself at the steps of the Woods Family Inn, the Sunday paper at his feet. Or why when it was barely the crack of dawn, Emma Woods stood on the porch stretching in nothing but an oversize T-shirt of a cat barfing a rainbow and her ridiculous yet adorable cat slippers.

He paused the music on his phone and stared at her, one of the few things he still dared to want that—no matter how many times their lips got close enough to kiss—he knew would always be just out of his reach.

She gasped when she finally realized she wasn't alone, tugging the hem of her shirt over her thighs.

"What are you doing here?" she called down to him.

He shook his head. "I don't know," he admitted. "I don't even remember running here." Then he picked up the paper. "This yours?"

The door to the inn flew open, and a tall blond woman in a sports bra, leggings, and her own running shoes stepped out behind her. She smacked Emma on the ass and grinned.

"I thought you were getting my newspaper!" the stranger teased, then followed Emma's gaze to where Matteo stood, paper in hand. "Ahh," she added. "Wanna introduce me to your paperboy?"

Even from where he stood, he could see Emma's cheeks redden.

"Haddie, this is Matteo Rourke. Matteo, this is

my best friend from Chicago who surprised me with a much needed visit…Haddie."

Matteo waved, a nervous smile on his face.

Haddie waved back, a knowing grin on hers.

The question was, what *did* the woman actually know? What was Emma's version of their story?

"Was there something you needed at the inn?" Emma asked, hands still fumbling with the hem of her T-shirt. "Come to check on the squirrels? Or are you delivering papers now?"

He shook his head.

Why *was* he here? The million-dollar question. The rug had been pulled out from under him first thing this morning, and his feet took him here.

He looked down at the newspaper that was now tucked under his elbow, then back up at Emma and her friend.

Matteo squinted into the morning sun.

"I…uh…I should let you two get on with your morning. I didn't know you had a guest," he finally answered.

"An actual paying one! Not that my parents will let her pay since they're already putting her to work." Emma let go of her shirt and crossed her arms, but this made the shirt ride up her thighs, so she was back to tugging it toward her knees. "Okay…" she added, and he swore he heard hesitation in her voice. Or maybe that was just wishful thinking. "Then I guess we'll just take the paper, and you can finish your run?"

His run. Right. He could get back to his run, the reason why he'd fled his childhood home in the first place. Or was it?

He nodded, then strode up the steps to offer Haddie what she'd come looking for.

"I didn't know people still read these," he said.

Haddie shrugged and happily snatched the thick sheaf of newsprint from him.

"I'm not really into social media or having any online presence. I like my information and interactions to be IRL, as the kids like to say."

Emma laughed. "You're only thirty. I don't think that makes you a true grown-up yet. Does it? Do I have to be a grown-up in less than two years?"

"Absolutely not," Haddie assured her. "But you *do* have to maybe put some pants on if you're going to stay outside for much longer."

"Right! Pants!" Emma exclaimed. "So...I'll see you later?" she asked Matteo.

"Yeah. Later. It was nice to meet you, Haddie."

"You too, Paperboy." Haddie hooked her elbow through Emma's and turned her toward the door.

"So my dad is sleeping with Tilly Higginson," he blurted out, and Emma halted where she stood.

She gently removed her friend's arm from her own, then pivoted back to Matteo.

Her green eyes shone in the early morning sun. Then she grabbed his hand and gave him a reassuring squeeze.

"Do you want to come in for coffee and talk about it?"

Matteo squeezed her hand right back, feeling unexpectedly grounded after the world seemed to be going topsy-turvy.

"Yeah," he said, the surprise in his voice noticeable even to himself. "I think I do."

Emma looked imploringly at Haddie, who didn't skip a beat.

"This sounds even better than the newspaper," she said with a grin. "But you still need pants, Ems."

Emma dropped Matteo's hand and grabbed the hem of her shirt once more. "Pants!" she cried, then scurried inside. "I'll be right back!"

Chapter 13

Emma and Haddie peeked out from the swinging kitchen door into the inn's small dining area. Matteo sat alone at the table, head dipped as he stared into his coffee mug.

"Why do you think he wanted to tell me about his dad?" Emma whispered. "Like…why me when he could have called his brother or—I don't know—a friend?"

Haddie, who stood at least three inches taller than Emma, rested her chin on her friend's shoulder while Emma hugged the insulated coffee carafe to her chest. "Because he only has those sweet little puppy dog eyes for you. *Or* hearing about his dad getting busy made him realize the only person *he* wants to get busy with is *you*." She hummed. "I just said the same thing twice, didn't I?"

Emma shushed her friend and swatted at her face.

"What?" Haddie whisper-shouted. "You *asked* me a question. I was simply using my powers of deductive reasoning—and the way he looks at you with the aforementioned pupper eyes—to come to a conclusion. Come to think of it, it *takes* a puppy dog to stand behind a door and whisper *about* a puppy dog. Methinks I shall start calling you *Lady*."

Emma scoffed, then threw her hand over her mouth when Matteo's head shot up and he glanced toward the door as she quickly pivoted away and it swung closed.

"I'm sorry, my furry little companion, but you've been busted."

Emma's mouth fell open, but she caught herself before uttering another attention-grabbing sound. Instead she narrowed her eyes at her friend and tried to shoot lasers at her. *Not* because she was so certain Haddie was wrong but…what if she was right?

There is nothing *I regret more than how I hurt you.*

Matteo's words had played on a loop in her head ever since they escaped his lips. But if he regretted it, why didn't he reach out? If there hadn't been a tornado and she hadn't come home, would they have lived the rest of their lives as strangers?

Yet here was her stranger, showing up at the crack of dawn because he *needed* someone. And that someone was her?

The dizzying swirl of questions didn't make anything clearer. Instead it kicked up dirt and dust and debris—the remnants of the pain she hadn't completely buried.

"I'm in over my head," Emma mumbled softly.

Haddie's smile fell. "What do you need me to do?" All teasing had left her voice.

Emma. "Keep me from letting Matteo Rourke break my heart again?"

"Tall order," Haddie replied. Then she bowed. "Good thing you've got yourself a tall friend."

"Did you just dad joke yourself into protecting me?"

Haddie raised her brows. "I'm not above a good dad joke when opportunity knocks. But I need you to be clear on what you're asking of me, Ems. Are you looking for a chaperone?"

Emma worried her bottom lip between her teeth. Then she squared her shoulders and nodded.

"I can't go down that road again." She swallowed the lump in her throat. This was a good decision. The *right* decision. Matteo needed a friend right now. She could handle *that*. What she couldn't handle was wanting to reenact the scene in front of the Welcome to Summertown sign.

"Okay!" Haddie clapped her hands together. "Then consider me your cockblocker!"

Emma's mouth fell open.

"Your clam jam?" Haddie amended.

"*Hads*!" Emma shouted, trying not to laugh.

While Emma appreciated the moment of levity, she realized there was *no* way Matteo missed that outburst, which meant her little spying session was over.

"We should get out there," Emma told her friend. Then, carafe cradled in her arms, she barreled backward through the swinging door with more force than she'd meant, and straight into a solid wall.

"*Shit!*" Matteo hissed.

Emma stumbled toward Haddie, who caught her by the shoulders before she *and* the coffee went down.

"Here!" She handed Haddie the coffee and pivoted back toward the door to attempt damage control.

"Matteo?" She gingerly pushed the door open a crack.

"I'm fine," he called back, though the words came out through what sounded like clenched teeth.

"Are you bleeding?" she added warily. "Because I'm really sorry if you are, but if I see it—"

"I'm *fine*," Matteo insisted even though his tone sounded anything but.

"I can handle blood," Haddie assured her. "In my line of work, I deal with bodily fluids almost on a daily basis."

"Where do you *teach*?" Emma asked over her shoulder, but the last word came out as a yelp as Haddie shooed her the rest of the way through the door.

She braced herself for carnage but instead found Matteo simply leaning against the back of a chair, arms crossed over his chest.

"See?" He raised his brows. "Not a scratch."

Haddie set the coffee on the table across from Matteo's. Then she leaned down and whispered in Emma's ear.

"He's *hiding* something."

Emma nodded. "Prove it," she challenged.

He laughed, but she swore she caught a wince beneath the mask of his grin.

"Do you see any scratches? Any blood?" He shook his head ruefully. "I should head back home and check on my dad, make sure he hasn't done anything to cause another back spasm." He buried his face in his palm and groaned. "I can't believe I just said that out loud."

"And there it is," Emma said, pointing at him.

"There *what* is?" Haddie and Matteo asked in unison.

"You're a righty," Emma continued, not taking her eyes off Matteo as he dropped his left hand to his side while very conspicuously keeping his right arm bent over his torso.

She strode toward him, eyes narrowed.

He straightened and let his right arm fall to his other side, and there it was again—an unmistakable wince.

Emma's eyes widened. "You're *hurt*." And worse yet, *she'd* hurt him.

The sound of metal clanging and voices shouting—her parents' version of an early morning chat while preparing to feed a packed inn—emanated from the kitchen.

"Breakfast!" Emma whispered. "Officially starts in thirty minutes!"

She spun toward her friend and gave Haddie a pleading look.

Haddie waved the two of them off. "Go take care of whatever you need to take care of." She raised her brows at Emma, a silent *I'm leaving you unchaperoned but not for long* kind of look.

Emma nodded her understanding.

"I'm gonna take him to the top-floor room. The one by the attic. Meet us up there when you can slip away."

"It's *nothing*," Matteo insisted. "See?" He rolled his right shoulder, and though he avoided the wince this time, Emma wasn't buying it. Not for a second.

"Come on," she said, grabbing him by his left wrist. Her stomach did a small cartwheel as her skin met his.

Not now! she warned her libido.

"Either you let me get you an ice pack, or I'm calling 911. You decide," she added.

Matteo groaned and let her start leading him out of the dining room and around to the employee staircase at the back of the inn. "And then you'll let me leave?"

She stopped at the door to the stairwell and used her master key to unlock it. Then she pivoted to face Matteo.

"You came here because you needed someone to talk to, didn't you?" He opened his mouth to respond, but she didn't give him a chance. "Then you can leave when I make sure you're okay here..." She pressed her palm gently against his right shoulder. "And *here*." This time she lightly tapped her index finger on the center of his forehead.

The corner of his mouth twitched into a brief lopsided smile, and that was all the agreement she needed.

"I remember these stairs," Matteo finally said after they'd made it up two of the four flights.

Emma's stomach tightened. She took these stairs at least once a day and didn't think twice. When every nook and cranny of the inn—of the *town*—held memories she didn't want to relive, it was easy to stuff it all beneath the surface where it had stayed buried for years.

But his seemingly harmless admission brought everything back to the surface.

"That's not why I took this route," she told him when they paused on the landing before the final flight. She yanked her hand away when she realized it was still gripping him by the wrist.

"Whoa..." He held up his hands. "I didn't mean anything by it. I just thought it'd be weird if I pretended *not* to remember."

Was that what she'd been doing all these years? *Pretending* she didn't remember all the nuances of their relationship, like stealing away from the inn's holiday party or a wine tasting to make out with Matteo in this very stairwell?

She stared at him, blinking away the images of *her* Matteo that her brain kept conjuring and trying to focus on the man in front of her now, a man to whom she laid zero claim.

"The room next to the attic, right?" he asked.

She nodded, at least showing proof of life.

"Okay," he said softly. "Looks like you need a minute, so I'll just meet you up there."

He jogged up the stairs and left her standing there with her heart in throat, wondering if she even knew the difference between how she actually felt versus how she pretended to feel.

Emma grabbed the railing at the bottom step, holding on to it like a life preserver.

"I'm not pretending," she told herself and hoped her brain could convince her heart.

She followed Matteo up the last flight and found him waiting outside the lone guest-room door, arms crossed nonchalantly over his chest. Except the slight pulse in his clenched jaw gave him away.

Emma opened the door and nodded toward the room. This was nothing more than one friend helping another. But before either of them could say a word, Pancake came scurrying out and fell purring at *Matteo*'s feet.

Emma's mouth fell open, though she was secretly grateful for the diversion. "You furry little traitor!"

Matteo dropped down to scratch the tabby behind his ears, and Pancake rolled onto his back, purring loud enough to wake the guests on the floor below.

"I'm not usually a cat person," Matteo admitted. "But this little guy obviously has good taste, and I'm not going to argue with that."

Emma scoffed. "I *am*."

She strode into the room where a mini fridge sat next to the bed, under the night table.

"Come here, Pancake," she cooed, patting her knee as she dropped to a squat next to the fridge.

But *her* cat was too busy ramming his head against Matteo's outstretched hand, begging for more pets.

"Matteo...Can you *please* come in here so my cat will follow? Also, the ice pack is in here." She tapped the mini fridge with her elbow.

Matteo laughed, looking a little *too* victorious as he stepped into the room, Pancake scurrying in a figure eight around Matteo's ankles as he tried not to trip over the fair weather feline.

"Why are you staying in here instead of your old room?"

Emma shrugged. "Mini fridge? Privacy from the rest of the guests?" Or no memories in a room that was never hers before.

"Is that Holmes and Watson on a train?" He stepped closer to the canvas print hanging over the dresser.

"Yep. The great compromise between my parents when they bought the place. My father would refinish the hardwood floors—he wanted to carpet them—if he could hang a Sherlock print in every room. Now sit," Emma commanded, pointing at the side of the bed she was happy she'd made this morning before heading down to the porch.

"Me or him?" Matteo asked, still grinning and pointing to himself and then at Pancake.

Emma rolled her eyes. "*You*. Though I'm sure your new friend won't be far behind."

As predicted, as soon as Matteo perched himself on the side of bed, Pancake was in his lap, purring and spinning in circles until finally settling into a blissed-out ball of fur on his thighs.

"Just so you know," she started. "I'm more than a little bitter about this."

She opened the fridge and grabbed the gel-filled ice pack from the small freezer compartment inside.

"Was that meant for me or him?" Matteo asked again with a chuckle.

"*Both* of you," she admitted, then rose to her knees and pulled the neck of his T-shirt to the side, exposing his bare skin and pressing the chilled plastic pack to his shoulder and collarbone.

"What are you doing?" He flinched, but there

was nowhere for him to go. It was enough, though, to send Pancake scurrying *off* the bed and hiding *under* it.

"Making up for hurting you," she replied. But really, it was a test. Could she do this? *Be* this close to him and not let old feelings get in the way?

Matteo closed his eyes and shook his head. "I knew you and Haddie were lurking back there. I should have given you a heads-up instead of trying to catch you in the act."

"We weren't *lurking,*" Emma pouted.

Matteo opened his eyes, but he wouldn't meet hers. "And *you* didn't injure me. It's just an old thing that acts up every now and then."

An *old* injury? As far as she knew, he'd never hurt his shoulder in the time she'd known him.

"You got hurt in..." But the last word got stuck as her throat tightened.

He grabbed her wrist and gently yet convincingly urged her away.

She let go and stood, taking a step back as he held the ice pack to his shoulder himself.

He exhaled and leaned back against the headboard, his focus somewhere beyond the door rather than on her.

"You can't even say the word, Emma."

"Prison!" she blurted out. "There. I said it. I can say it. I just..." She'd wrapped her head around the idea that he'd lived a short stint of his life behind bars, but she never let her mind wander too far into what that life might have been like. Did she worry about him every day for months when it had first happened? Of course she had. But he'd also afforded her an ignorance that, while not exactly blissful, had been bearable at the very least. She strode around to the foot of the bed so he had no choice but to look at her. "I want to know what happened to you," she told him, heart in her throat. "If you're okay with that."

He scrubbed a hand across his face and sighed.

"Please?" she asked.

He nodded.

"I was assigned to the sanitation team, which meant cleaning the dining hall after meals. Our guard wanted complete silence while we worked so he could nod off in his chair until we were done. If you woke him, you finished the job on your own." He gave her a one-shoulder shrug. "So the team hazes the new guy so he does their work for him. Only the new guy doesn't break, not even when he takes a mop handle to the shoulder."

"Oh my god." Emma's voice trembled as she uttered the words. "You told the guard, right?"

Matteo let out a bitter laugh. "No, Em. I didn't tell the guard," he replied dryly. "Then I'd have been mopping the dining hall by myself with a possible torn rotator cuff."

Hot tears pricked her eyes.

He pushed himself up and onto his feet. "See, this is *why* I tried to keep you away from all this."

"Why, Matteo?" Emma asked, anger unexpectedly bubbling up over her sadness, and *not* because he'd called her *Em*. She crossed her arms and strode toward him, not allowing him the safety of the distance he'd had all these years. "Why did *you* decide—without even asking what *I* wanted—to keep me away from all of this?" She motioned to where he still held the perspiring bottle to shoulder.

Because I don't want your pity, she imagined him saying. Or maybe, *Because I don't want you looking at me like I'm some wounded puppy*. But he didn't say either of those things.

"Because..." he started, his voice low and rough.

Silence rang out between them, the air thick with everything he might say, with everything Emma was afraid to hear, and *everything* she pretended didn't matter anymore after all this time.

"Please?" she asked again, her voice this time barely above a whisper.

Matteo cleared his throat, then set his gaze clearly and decidedly on *her*.

"Because...I loved you so much that I couldn't see straight. And I knew that if the cosmic tables were turned, and you were somehow in *my* position with me helpless to do *anything* to make it better for you... It would have killed me, Em. It would have fucking killed me, and hell if I was going to do that to you."

Emma swiped at the tears under her eyes and sniffed. Her chest ached for the boy she loved all those years ago who was too young to know any better. But her fists clenched at her sides, nails digging into her palms as she stared at the man before her who still believed he'd made the right choice.

"Maybe I wouldn't have been strong enough to handle knowing what you went through. Or maybe I was stronger than you ever gave me credit for. But guess what? We'll never know now. Either way, I still loved you. I still felt helpless. And I had to do it all with a broken heart because you decided it was too much for me. I get it, Matteo. We were barely more than kids when you had to become caretaker not only to your mom while she was in treatment, but to your dad who leaned on you personally and professionally. You kept it together for them, but who was keeping it together for you?"

She approached the bed with caution, and when he didn't make a move to push her away, she sat down next to him, pressing her hand over his so they were now both holding the ice pack against his shoulder.

His skin against hers didn't make her want to throw him down on the bed or practically devour him like she had on the outskirts of town. It didn't make her want to pretend he hadn't told her. It made her want to scream and shout at the twenty-one year-old boy who'd been dealt a super-shitty hand. It made her want to hug him and tell him everything would be okay. And it broke her heart all over again to know even a sliver of what he'd endured alone…and to realize that they'd both said the same word. *Loved.* Past tense.

What had she been hoping, for him to have carried a torch for her all these years? She'd had no choice but to get over him. He'd made the decision for both of them.

Enough. It was her turn to start making decisions—or to at least nudge him in a new direction.

"When, Matteo?" Emma asked. "When are you going to stop making it your job to take care of everyone else and finally let someone take care of you?"

He let out a shaky breath. "I *never* said you weren't strong."

"You *thought* it," she amended.

He shook his head. "Not even once."

"Prove it, then," she challenged.

His brows furrowed. "I'm not following."

"Prove you never said or thought I was too weak to handle what those eighteen months were like for you by telling me something new every now and then." She cleared her throat. "When we *see* each other, I mean. *If* we see each other. I'm not suggesting we make regular plans to hang out or anything. You have your job. I have mine. There's this mystery artist to investigate." Emma groaned. "You know what I *mean*."

A muscle in his jaw pulsed. "You *really* want to know?"

Emma nodded. She did. She wanted to prove to herself that she *could* have been there for him, had he let her. She wanted to prove to Matteo that he didn't have to bear it alone.

"I really do," she told him. Emma let go of his hand and held hers out to shake. "You can't change your mind once it's official."

He set the gel pack on the nightstand and gave his shoulder a couple good rolls.

"Good as new," he said.

"You're welcome," Emma responded with an unexpected smile of her own.

Then they both extended a hand and shook on it.

Haddie burst through the open doorway, seemingly from nowhere, holding out her phone and bouncing on her toes. "There's another one!" she called to them excitedly. "Another sculpture!"

"What? Where?" Emma asked, her pulse quickening.

"Lining the steps of the town hall!"

Chapter 14

Haddie full-on belly laughed the second the three of them came to a halt in front of the Summertown town hall where early risers were gathered, pointing and taking photos with their phones.

"Okay, I am certainly no flower expert," she began, "but I think I know enough to *know* that *those* are from, like, Whoville or something, right?"

"*Thneedville,*" Matteo and Emma said in unison, then stared at each other with eyes wide.

"Gesundheit?" Haddie replied to both.

Matteo let out an incredulous laugh. "Our science teacher showed the movie in class in seventh or eighth grade. Mrs. Snyder, right?" He looked to Emma for confirmation.

Emma nodded, her eyes suddenly glassy. Did she feel it too, the overwhelm of something as simple as saying the same thing at the same time?

Or was it possible she was still reeling from what happened—from what they'd both said in the room at the inn—like he was?

I loved you.

He'd hurt her to spare her, and in doing so, he'd lost her. He knew that would be the consequence, but hearing her say it held a heavier weight, one that had thinned the air and made it hard to breathe.

"Yes!" Emma exclaimed, jolting him back to the moment. "We were these squirrely middle schoolers who just wanted to watch the movie, but she kept pausing it to talk about the importance of flowers and trees and how they help the environment, how the Garden Fest that we thought was just about hayrides and roasted corn..."

"And watermelon," Matteo added. "Wilton's farm does a hell of a lot more than take in stray squirrels. Or at least it did before the storm."

Emma nodded. "How did the artist even *do* that?" she asked, glancing up the length of the Town Hall's four white columns that were painted with black and yellow stripes from bottom to top.

Matteo shrugged. "A ladder? Someone has to climb up there to clean the gutters, don't they? I'm sure they make ladders tall enough to—"

"And *more* hubcaps!" Emma interrupted. "This person definitely has a specific style. Hubcaps and other painted metal." She tapped her index finger against her lips as she studied the artificial trees.

He'd *kissed* those lips, not that long ago. Despite the fact they'd both been covered in mud and the humid air had surrounded them with the scent of damp earth, she'd tasted sweeter than any confection.

"Maybe they *want* to be found out," Emma continued, still pondering the town hall's newest decor.

Matteo shook his head as he stared at the overlapping metal circles painted bright pink, yellow, and orange to look like fluffy, swirled cotton. *Multiple* hubcaps arranged in spirals. "If they *wanted* credit, wouldn't they just *say* something?"

Emma shook *her* head right back. "Not if they know the sheriff's office is considering it vandalism." She turned to Haddie. "They're like Dr. Seuss's truffula trees," she explained.

"And that makes you sad because…?" Haddie asked.

So Haddie had seen Emma's eyes well up too.

Emma let out a wistful laugh. "I'm not *sad*. I just… It's nostalgia, you know? Of the blissful ignorance of being a kid, when my biggest worry was whether or not Mrs. Snyder would pause the video *again* or if Mr. Wilton would grow the largest watermelon in the county that summer." She shrugged. "Whoever is doing this hasn't forgotten that feeling—and also must have had Mrs. Snyder for middle school science."

Matteo laughed. "So that would be *anyone* who grew up in Summertown in the past two decades." He held his arms out wide and spun slowly as more onlookers gathered at the foot of the town hall's steps. "Take your pick."

But she was right about the vandalism and the probability of the artist being a local. There were too many similarities to call it coincidence. What he couldn't figure out, though, was if she'd figured out the motive as well. *Wanting* to be caught.

Haddie raised her hand but didn't wait for anyone to actually call on her. "Is anyone else starting to feel like they're walking around in a Tim Burton movie, or is it just me?"

"Like something out of *Edward Scissorhands*," a voice chimed in from behind them.

They all spun to find Harmony Sapperstein, a long white braid hanging over her right shoulder and Pikachu the parakeet perched on her left in a tiny harness connected to a leash clasped around Harmony's left wrist.

"*You're* the one who found it, aren't you?" Emma asked excitedly.

The older woman winked at them. "Not a whole lot happens in this town that I don't know about."

Matteo's mouth went dry as Harmony's eyes met his. Were the rumors of his childhood true? Was the woman who made the candles some sort of sorceress who could read minds?

Of course not, he told himself. *That was some high-level bullshit.* Matteo knew better than anyone that rumors were often the furthest thing from the truth. But the way her eyes stared *through* him, unwavering… He'd be lying if he said it wasn't unnerving.

Haddie laughed. "Looks like she has some dirt on *you*, Paperboy."

"No, no. Of course not." Harmony waved the comment off. "Though if I *did*, I'd never be so bold as to give myself away like that."

"Right," Matteo added. "Not much for me to hide when my history with this town is pretty much public record." Still, he wiped his damp palms on his shorts, wondering what the woman with the bird on her shoulder might have in her depthless well of gossip.

Emma grabbed her friend by the wrist, stepping away from the building. Then she offered her phone to Matteo.

"Would you do the honors?" she asked him.

But before he could accept the offering, Harmony Sapperstein swiped the phone from Emma's hand and shooed them all back toward the building.

"This is for your social media posting, isn't it?" Harmony asked.

Emma nodded.

"Well then, you have to have *people* in your photos to show whoever's watching that the tornado didn't turn this place into a ghost town." Emma opened her mouth to respond, but Harmony didn't give her a chance. "Go on! Two of Summertown's very own standing in front of our town's capitol, showing all those tourists that it'll take more than a tornado to knock *us* down. *Figuratively* speaking, of course. We don't need Mother Nature to test my theory." Harmony nodded toward Haddie. "You too, Haddie. Didn't intend on leaving you out."

But Haddie was already backing away. "I don't do social media, remember?" she said, her eyes on Emma. Then she held up her hands. "Besides, this is a Summertown thing. I think it's best to leave it to the locals." She grinned at Harmony, then crossed her arms and gave Emma a knowing look.

Emma let out a nervous laugh. "If I didn't know any better, I'd say those two are in cahoots."

Matteo barked out a laugh of his own, *his* nerves dissolving to nothing. "If *I* didn't know any better, I'd say you're *nervous* about a photo, Woods. Also… *cahoots*?"

"It's a *word*, Rourke," Emma responded coolly. "And I'm *not* nervous. I just…don't know how we're supposed to pose, okay?"

"Get a little closer, you two!" Harmony called. Pikachu marched back and forth on her shoulder like he was listening to music the rest of them couldn't hear.

Matteo drew in a breath and decided not to overthink it. He draped his arm over her shoulders and pulled her to his side.

"It's just a picture, right?"

Emma looked up at him and nodded. He watched her throat bob as she swallowed.

"Hang on," he told her, then pressed his thumb gently to her cheek. "Eyelash." He pulled his thumb away and showed her the lash now stuck to his skin.

"My phone's camera isn't *that* good," she said softly.

Matteo shrugged, then opened his mouth to blow it off his skin.

"Wait!" Emma cried. "*Not* without making a wish."

His brows furrowed. "It's *your* lash. Doesn't that mean it's *your* wish?" He slowly moved his thumb from his own lips to right in front of hers.

Only now did it register how close she was and that every time he came within inches of this woman—or in this case actually had his arm around her—he wanted… He just *wanted*.

Emma shook her head. "You found it. It's *your* wish. Better make it a good one." She gently nudged his hand back to where it started.

He stared at it for a long moment.

Matteo Rourke didn't believe in wishes. But just in case he was wrong…

He closed his eyes and silently invoked one simple word.

You.

He blew the lash off his thumb, then spun to face their photographer.

"Ready whenever you are!" he called to Harmony Sapperstein.

She strode toward them and held Emma's phone out for her to take back.

"I already got everything you need for everyone to tap that little heart on your post."

Matteo's lips parted into an incredulous smile. He grabbed the phone before Emma did, suddenly desperate to see what Harmony captured when neither of them knew she was already snapping photos. But his smile fell as a figure approached from the square. Deputy Sheriff Dawson Hayes in full uniform, campaign hat and all.

"Good morning, Lemmy," the deputy said with an easy grin.

Matteo's jaw clenched.

"Looks like our vandal struck again," the deputy offered with a wry grin.

Haddie dipped her head toward Emma's ear and stage-whispered. "*Lemmy*? And who is this dashing man in uniform who has a little nickname for my girl?" She didn't wait for Emma to answer.

"I'm Haddie, Emma's closest and dearest friend from Chicago. And you are?" She held out her right hand.

The deputy took his hat off and held it to his chest before shaking Haddie's hand.

"Deputy Dawson Hayes, ma'am. Any friend of Lemmy's is a friend of Summertown."

"You know, I'd usually take issue with the whole 'ma'am' thing, but the small-town charm of a man in uniform is *not* lost on me."

The deputy nodded once. "Appreciate that, ma'am, but I'm afraid that also makes you a suspect. And seeing as how you two made it to the scene of the crime before the authorities..." He unceremoniously dropped Haddie's hand and placed his hat back on his head. "Looks like I'm going to have to bring you two in for questioning."

"Dawson *Hayes*," Harmony admonished. "If you're going to question them, you might as well question *me* too. And Pikachu, for that matter. We arrived mere seconds after they all did." She motioned to the small group.

"What about me, Hayes?" Matteo asked, prying his teeth apart to speak. "We all came here together. Don't you want to bring me in, too?"

He could feel Emma's eyes boring into him, but Matteo kept his gaze locked on the deputy as they continued what felt like a very important standoff. He *was* right, after all. Matteo *knew* he was right. If Dawson thought any of them were suspects, he should suspect *all* of them. But since Matteo knew Emma and Haddie had been at the inn since the crack of dawn—and likely all night—the whole thing felt pretty ridiculous.

"My office is pretty tight, Rourke. Probably best if I get a statement from the ladies first. Then, if I feel like I'm missing anything, I'll follow up with you."

Matteo felt a vein pulse in his neck.

"You don't have to go with him, Emma," Matteo insisted. "You didn't do anything wrong, and it's not like he's arresting you. Isn't that right, Deputy?"

Dawson chuckled.

"Of course. Of course. Your cooperation is appreciated but completely voluntary. You and… I'm sorry, ma'am, what was your name again?"

"*Haddie*," Emma's friend grumbled. "And I changed my mind." She pointed at him. "The 'ma'am' thing isn't charming anymore."

Emma elbowed her friend in the ribs.

"Come on, *Hads*," she murmured out of the corner of her mouth. "It'll be an adventure."

She smiled at Dawson, which only made the vise on Matteo's chest tighten. "Of course we'll answer a few questions, Dawson. Anything to help."

When she spun back toward Matteo, he hadn't moved. He was so still, it was possible he hadn't even blinked.

"We'll be fine," she assured him. "Meet us over there when you're done?"

For several seconds, Matteo didn't move. He stood there against the backdrop of these huge, vibrant, *fake* trees. Haddie was right. The whole thing was like a scene out of an eerie, fantastical movie or dream. Despite Matteo having been back in Summertown for over a year already, it suddenly felt like a fun-house version of the place he once knew—everything down to the woman who'd let him wish on her eyelash.

"Fifteen minutes," Matteo finally replied. But he looked *past* Emma rather than at her. "They're done in fifteen minutes, Hayes."

"Sure, Rourke," Dawson nodded at him with a grin. "Lemmy and her friend are free to go whenever they feel like it."

"*Haddie,*" her friend butted in. "It's *Haddie.*"

Emma gave Haddie's elbow a gentle tug.

"*Haddie* and I will answer the deputy's questions, and *Haddie* and I will decide when we're done."

Matteo knew the comment was directed at him and his slight overstepping of boundaries, but his steely gaze held fast to the deputy's.

"And can we *stop* calling the artist a vandal?" Emma added. "It's obvious that whatever their reason for doing what they're doing, on some level they love this town."

A tall, slender, white-haired man dressed in a short-sleeved blue button-down, khaki pants, and pristine golf shoes strode toward them from the square.

"Now what in the fresh hell is *this*?" Mayor Green asked, sidling up next to the deputy. "Fake flowers in the square is one thing, but this is a place of community business. *My* place of community business."

"Oh. My. God," Haddie said under her breath. "Clint Eastwood lives in Summertown?"

Emma cleared her throat and squared her shoulders, unlinking her elbow from her friend's.

"Mayor Green!" She greeted the public official with more enthusiasm and familiarity than she should have. "I think the columns look…vibrant. Don't you?"

Matteo watched as the older man narrowed his eyes at what to *him* looked like a defaced building—the building that, thanks to no term limits and a town that was resistant to change, he had worked inside of for two-and-a-half decades.

Haddie gasped. "Clint Eastwood is the *mayor* of Summertown?"

Emma elbowed her friend again.

"Ow!" Haddie pressed a palm to her ribs. "What was that for?"

"Vibrant?" the older man inquired. "*Vibrant*? It was one thing for my wife to transform shrubbery into the likenesses of our pets, but I will not have the building *itself* vandalized in such a way. Especially when she's over *there* in Middlebrook with Mayor Munson." A soft growl escaped his lips.

Mayor Green produced a phone from his pocket and, after a few swipes, brandished the screen toward the rest of them.

Matteo squinted to make out the green-on-green shapes in the Instagram photo, but when his eyes adjusted, he realized the shapes were two lush, green shrubs carved into the shape of two small dogs.

"Okay, this is *cold,*" Emma said. "It's one thing for her to up and leave…the *town*…for a new life. But she must *know* Summertown is floundering after the storm, and now she's doing for Middlebrook what we always relied on her to do for us?"

Haddie put her hands on her hips. "With all due respect, Mr. Mayor, why are you calling it vandalism if you're just going to leave the sculptures standing? I saw the lotus flowers on the Welcome to Summertown sign when I got into town, and I can clearly see the sunflowers on the tree stump in the square. The word 'vandalism' has quite the negative connotation, and if I was teaching my first graders about word choice, I would advise them to be careful of word choice that makes anything sound *bad*. If Emma is here to help get the word out about Summertown still being a hot spot for summer tourism, we should be putting a positive spin on this for the community, shouldn't we? For the festival thingy?"

Matteo, Emma, and Dawson's mouths fell open. Harmony chuckled.

"A positive spin on my humiliation?" the mayor asked, scratching at his jaw. He narrowed his eyes. Then he let out a bitter laugh. "I'm not going to waste our time and resources meant for rebuilding this town to clean up this vandal's mess. When we find whoever it is, *they* will be the one to make reparations. As for the contest, the bylaws for the festival clearly state that the entered garden sculptures must be cultivated from their basest origin. That means *seeds*! The beginning! You all might as well know before I make the announcement since it seems our *artist* clearly hasn't planted a thing, and we don't stand a chance against my ex-wife." He sighed. "I'm going to forfeit the festival competition."

Chapter 15

"*Forfeit!*" Emma cried. "Forfeit? You can't be serious. Why? You're just going to *let* her win?"

The mayor crossed his arms over his chest and narrowed his eyes at her. "Ms. Woods, I don't think I need to remind you that I'm the mayor of this town and have been for most of *your* life. There's a reason I've run unopposed for every term since my first, and that's because the people of Summertown trust me to do right by them and this town. That should be all the justification you need."

Haddie grabbed Emma's hand and gave her a reassuring squeeze.

Harmony was feeding Pikachu something from her palm.

Matteo mirrored the mayor's stance as if they were in a showdown.

And when Emma's eyes met Dawson's, he shook his head softly as if her not to proceed.

But she was so damned tired of holding back out of fear.

Emma knew Mayor Green was trying to shut down the argument, but she didn't care. She'd stayed to help get this town back on its feet and because she'd forgotten how much Summertown meant to her until she finally came back. She'd let a broken heart and painful memories keep her away for nearly a decade, and where had it gotten her? Seeing Matteo Rourke again after all this time only brought those painful memories and a whole lot of confusing feelings back to the surface.

"Mr. Mayor," she began, feeling everyone's eyes on her. "Summertown *needs* that prize money. Rebuilding and reclaiming our status as the…the… the garden capital of central Illinois is exactly what it means to do right by this town. I know all too well about loss, humiliation, and how much that hurts." Her hand, still in Haddie's, grew clammy. Emma pulled it free and did her damnedest to keep her eyes focused on the mayor and not steal a glance at Matteo. "But I also know that I let that hurt keep me away from the town that I love, and I regret the years I lost here. If you pull Summertown from the competition before we've even had a chance, you might regret that too."

The older man stared at Emma and her small entourage.

"Look," Emma continued, refusing to let a staring contest intimidate her. She pointed toward the square where a group of volunteers tilled the upturned earth. The debris had been removed, but so had the flowers and much of the grass, thanks to the storm. All that was left was the dirt ground and the few sparsely branched trees.

Mayor Green pivoted slowly so he saw what she saw.

"I'm *looking*, Ms. Woods. But it's nothing I haven't seen before."

Emma bit back the urge to groan. *Loudly.* "Wrong," she told him. "The three sunflowers are new. And while you refuse to see them as art, they are now the only source of color and light in what would be a pretty sad-looking town center if they'd never appeared."

The mayor sighed. "What are you asking me for, Emma?"

"And the town hall!" she added, not ready to answer his question. Instead she spun back toward the mayor's headquarters. "The Dr. Seuss trees make it stand out even more than it did before."

"As a vandal's target," he countered. "I'm not sure I see the pride in that."

Emma's hands fisted at her sides as she tried to maintain composure. "Haven't you ever read *The Lorax*? Or at least watched a film version of it? There's the cartoon from the seventies they used to show us in school. Or the newer one with Danny DeVito...oh, and Taylor Swift and Zach Efron!"

"I'm sorry," Haddie interjected. "But did you just

say that Troy Bolton is in this movie with the weird trees?"

Emma waved her off. "Yes! But that's not my point. My point is that the *story* of the Lorax is all about the importance of these trees and what they support in the surrounding environment. What if these artificial flowers and trees are able to do the same for Summertown?" She held out her arms and spun in a small circle. "Just give me *time*. I'll find a loophole in the bylaws. I'll contact the board of judges. But please don't pull the plug on the fest before we've even had a chance to show what we can do."

Mayor Green scratched the white stubble under his chin, his gaze volleying between the town hall and the square.

"I'll tell you what," he started. "If you and your friend answer all of Deputy Hayes's questions to his satisfaction and *mine*, I'll consider your request."

Emma let out a nervous yet relieved laugh. Then she held out her hand, and the mayor obliged her with a firm shake.

"Thank you, Mayor Green. I promise you won't regret this," Emma assured him.

The mayor raised his brows. "Don't count your chickens so soon, Ms. Woods. I haven't agreed to anything yet."

He dropped her hand and nodded once before shoving his hands in his pockets and strolling toward the town hall.

"Okay!" Emma clapped her hands together, adrenaline coursing through her. "Hads and I will tell you whatever you need to know about our morning, Deputy Hayes."

Dawson tipped his campaign hat and grinned. "Appreciate your enthusiastic cooperation."

"I'll ask around about the bylaws for you," Harmony chimed in. "See if I can't get us a copy to scour and find that loophole!"

"Thank you!" Emma cried, surprising herself as she threw her hands around the older woman's neck, careful not to knock Pikachu from his perch.

Matteo cleared his throat. "And I'm going to—" But he pulled his phone from the armband where he must have had it tucked away for his run. "Um… sorry. I have to take this. I'll catch up with you at the station." And without a second glance he brought the phone to his ear, turned, and strode away.

"We don't know who did it, Dawson," Emma insisted as she paced the deputy's not-exactly-cramped office. She paused to study his various framed certificates, including his associate's degree and his certificate of achievement from the local police academy.

"Hey," she added, pausing in front of a photo of a stone-faced Dawson in what must have been one of his first pictures in uniform and a weathered-looking older man resting a hand on Dawson's shoulder. "Is this your dad?"

Dawson swung his feet off his desk and slammed them onto the already creaky wooden floor.

Emma flinched, and Haddie sprung from her chair.

"Sorry," he told them, standing and smoothing his unwrinkled shirt. "Didn't mean to startle you. I just thought we should stay on task." He motioned toward Emma's empty chair. "If you don't mind, Lemmy."

Emma regained her composure and stepped up *behind* the chair but didn't sit.

"There's room for more in here," she informed him.

Haddie's eyes slowly moved from Emma to the deputy, ready for his response.

"I only have two chairs," Dawson countered. "Plus I wanted to talk to you about how much time it seems you've been spending with a convicted felon."

"Whoa," Haddie said under her breath. "Someone's not pulling any punches."

"That's not what I meant," he added. "I'm just trying to make sure you're safe. *Both* of you. It's bad enough we're dealing with the storm fallout, but now we've got this mystery vandal roaming around *and* Matteo Rourke popping up every time I see you. I know we weren't super close back in high school, Emma, but I obviously know what happened between you and Rourke, and I just think you should be careful when it comes to trusting him again."

Haddie pushed herself up from her chair and moved to stand next to Emma. "So we're *not* being questioned about the giant Tim Burton-esque trees?" she asked. "Because I thought Emma's deal with the mayor depended on what kind of information you got from us."

Dawson nodded once. "Do either of you know anything about the latest installation?"

Emma shook her head. "Only that the kitchen was buzzing about it before the breakfast rush this morning, which was when the three of us headed out to see it."

Another slow nod as Dawson removed his campaign hat and ran his fingers through his dark, rumpled hair.

Wow, Haddie mouthed to Emma when he wasn't looking.

She certainly wasn't wrong. Dawson Hayes was painfully good-looking if you were into the tall, dark, and uniformed type. But his assumptions about Matteo were rubbing her the wrong way.

"The *three* of you? So Rourke was with you already this morning?"

Emma gripped the back of the chair, the tips of her fingers turning white.

"You don't actually think Matteo has anything to do with this, do you?" she asked him.

He shook his head without hesitation. "Not in the slightest. But I am wondering how much you know about the out-of-towner I've seen him talking to a couple of times in the past month."

Emma barked out a laugh. "What, now he's not allowed to talk to people?" But something in her bravado faltered. Matteo and another woman… Of *course* he spoke to other women. It wasn't like she and he made any sort of agreement in the short weeks since their reconnection. But she'd sort of assumed, based on the recent things he'd said to her… Well, what *had* she assumed?

"He's allowed to speak to whomever he wants," Dawson continued. "And I wouldn't have thought twice about this woman showing up again if you hadn't come back to Summertown and if Rourke didn't turn up every time I saw you."

Emma scratched the back of her neck and swallowed. "When was the last time you saw this mystery woman?"

He shrugged. "You mean aside from last night when she was nosing around the Baker Street Pub looking for a place to stay?"

"Wait, this town has a pub?" Haddie asked. "Why haven't we been to the pub?"

Emma huffed out a laugh. "The *actual* pub is the Broken Stool, but it's closed due to a burst pipe."

"From the storm?" Haddie added.

Emma shook her head. "You'd think. The place is just old and needs work. Every time something breaks, they close for weeks on end until they can afford to have it fixed. The Baker Street Pub is the BYOB tent my father throws up on the side lot of the inn whenever the town gets restless for a watering hole. Didn't realize he put it up last night." Or that a woman Matteo had been seeing came looking for a room.

"The inn's booked solid now that *you're* here," she said to Haddie. "So who's the stranger, and where is she staying?"

Dawson's attention strayed from the two women to something outside his window.

"What is it?" Emma asked.

"That's her." The deputy pointed in the direction of where he was looking.

Emma's feet suddenly refused to move, but somehow Haddie propelled her around Dawson's desk and to the window opposite his chair.

There, on the outskirts of the square, stood Matteo and a dark-haired woman in a pencil skirt, a fitted short-sleeved blouse in vibrant red, and matching peep-toe pumps.

Emma pressed her palm to the black cotton tank she'd thrown on with a pair of pull-on green shorts, her *upgrade* from the oversize sleep shirt and yoga pants she'd had on when she pummeled Matteo with the swinging door.

"She looks pretty," Emma mumbled absently.

Haddie nudged her with her hip. "So does my great-uncle Leon from fifty feet away. Maybe they're having a business meeting. She looks like she just stepped out of some fancy office."

"A business meeting where she has to stay in town overnight?" Emma asked.

A business meeting Matteo certainly hadn't mentioned.

A business meeting that had him smiling and holding the woman's hand between his own.

Emma cleared her throat and stepped back from the window. She looked at Dawson.

"She was at the inn last night?"

He nodded. "Briefly. I was having a drink with your father and Old Man Wilton. When your father apologized for the place being fully booked, she left. But I'm positive she's the same woman I saw with Rourke and his father in the square a week or two before the storm. Only reason it raised my haunches last night was because I remembered that first visit. Look, if I'm overstepping, say the word, and I'll let it go. I just thought it was important you knew he was keeping something from you."

Emma nodded. Matteo had a life without her before she came back to Summertown. It's not like he was going to stop living it or like she had any right to ask him to do so. The same went for her. She'd made no promise to him, no commitment to pick back up where they'd left off other than that one mind-blowing kiss.

"Do you know what I think we should do, Hads?" She plastered a smile to her face and pivoted to face her friend.

"Anything you want, Ems. Name it." Haddie's grin was genuine. Not pitying. Not an *I bet you feel pretty humiliated right now* grin.

"Let's visit Middlebrook and see what we're really up against."

Haddie's eyes widened.

"I'll drive you," Dawson said. "If that works for you. I mean, the vandal—or *artist*—might be a local, but it could also be someone who knows the town but doesn't live here anymore."

Emma's brows furrowed. "Lottie Green? Why would she—"

"Guilt!" Haddie blurted out. "What if she feels guilty for leaving the town high and dry especially after a tornado? Maybe she's trying to help in her own way! Oooh, the plot thickens." She laughed. "I think I'm starting to get your dad's love of Sir Arthur Conan Doyle."

Okay, then. Emma had a goal, something to take her mind off of Matteo and his out-of-town friend.

She shrugged. "I guess that settles it. We'll run back to the inn and make sure they can do without us for the day, and then, Deputy, I guess we're going on a field trip to Middlebrook!"

Chapter 16

MATTEO PACED IN THE SMALL SPACE OUTSIDE Deputy Hayes's office. Every time he attempted to place his ear surreptitiously against the door, he got the stink eye from Marilyn Montez, the petite pixie-haired woman who he swore had been the sheriff department's office manager since he was old enough to remember *and* who'd had the same haircut for just as long.

"Last time I remember you in here was after you and your brother, Levi, were lighting bottle rockets and burned down Old Man Wilton's barn. Good thing all the animals *and* Mr. Wilton made it *out* of the barn or you boys could have had a juvenile record."

The memory made his pulse quicken, but it didn't get Matteo to stop walking back and forth. Scared as he and his brother were to get hauled into the sheriff's office, it was nothing compared to getting the *look* from Mrs. Montez.

"What do you think your mother's going to say

when I call her up and tell you what you two boys did?" she'd asked when Matteo was ten and Levi thirteen.

"Please, Mrs. Montez. Let Matteo go. It was my idea. I didn't even want him to come. He followed me to the field outside the farm. We were just trying to have some Fourth of July fun."

"*We?*" Marilyn Montez had asked, arms folded over her chest as she sat behind her desk while Levi and Matteo sat across from her, waiting for the sheriff to return from the scene of the fire. "I thought you said you didn't want your little brother to come. And the Fourth of July was *yesterday*. You know, that day when Summertown has a professional fire-department-sanctioned fireworks display?"

"*Please,*" Levi had begged, somehow flipping a switch and turning on the waterworks. "He's just a stupid kid who doesn't know any better. I'll take the blame. I'll help rebuild the barn. Just don't let my parents find out Matteo was there."

Marilyn Montez had rubbed her swollen, pregnant belly and sighed. "Either I'm falling for your performance, or this little parasite growing inside me is making me soft because—I can't believe I'm going to say this—I'm going to let you off the hook, Little Rourke. But if you ever end up in my office again, just remember that I don't give second chances."

Matteo had hesitated. It was one thing for Levi to cover for *him*, but…

"*Levi*," he'd pleaded. "What about—?"

"Go!" Levi yelled, not letting him finish his question, which would have given up the third party who hadn't been caught—the one who'd procured the bottle rockets in the first place. "Before she changes her mind!"

Matteo had never run so fast in his life, and he wondered if that was where it came from—his connection to the solitary sport of distance running. If he could run farther and faster than his opponents, maybe he could outrun any obstacles life threw in his way.

Marilyn Montez stared at him now over the cat's-eye frames of her glasses, eyes narrowed and lips pursed.

That was the look.

"You'll wear a hole in the floor if you keep doing that," she commented, and Matteo came to a halt. "Plus the door is soundproof. So the most you'll get from trying to eavesdrop is a short lesson from Charlie Brown's schoolteacher."

She glanced back down at her keyboard, not waiting for Matteo to respond.

Normally, he wouldn't give a shit what went on behind closed doors in the deputy's office. But he didn't like the direction this whole artist-slash-vandal thing was going, not if it meant Emma was somehow implicated in what looked to him like a harmless act. No matter what the motivation, the whole situation was getting blown out of proportion.

He crossed his arms and cleared his throat.

Marilyn sighed and slowly looked back up at him from her desk.

"It's been a half an hour. How many questions can the deputy have for someone who knows no more about the sculptures than anyone else in this town? We weren't even the first to find this one."

Marilyn opened a drawer and pulled out a piece of paper. She affixed it to a clipboard and then brandished it toward Matteo. "If you'd like to file a formal complaint about the investigation, please fill out this form. Usually, your form would be reviewed by the official complaint department, and you'd receive a response in forty-eight to seventy-two hours, depending on where your complaint was in the queue. Since the sheriff herself is on maternity leave, the acting sheriff—Deputy Hayes, of course—will have to give his stamp of approval to the form before I can administer a response. Since he's a little caught up in the investigation you'd like to complain about, it could be up to a week or more before you hear back from us. We thank you for your concern and look forward to getting back to you soon."

Despite wanting nothing to do with any sort of

red tape or paperwork—especially if all it would do was land on Dawson's desk—it felt rude to leave the woman sitting there with her arm outstretched and disdain in her eyes, so Matteo reluctantly accepted the offering.

"Do I want to ask who the head of the complaint department is?" he inquired.

Marilyn Montez pursed her lips again.

"*You're* the head of the complaint department."

She stood, brushed nonexistent lint from her skirt, and pulled her glasses off her nose, letting them hang from their bedazzled chain. "I'm the complaint department, the welcome wagon, *and* human resources. So please, make my day and give me more paperwork because you don't like how the deputy does his job."

Matteo gingerly set the clipboard back on Marilyn's desk and held up his hands in surrender. "I was just concerned about Emma and her friend. Didn't mean anything by it."

She relaxed into a smile and rounded the corner of her desk so she was standing in front of him. If she was five foot two even in her heels, he'd be surprised. But what she lacked in stature she made up for in personality. A very intimidating personality.

She reached a hand up and squeezed his cheeks between her thumb and fingers.

Matteo's eyes widened. *Not* what he was expecting.

"You grew up into such a good-looking boy,

didn't you? If I was twenty years younger and there was no Mr. Montez… Though I seem to recall warning you about showing up in my office again."

She released her impressive grip on his cheeks, and he had to give his jaw a stretch before speaking.

"I'm here voluntarily," he reminded her. "As far as I know, there haven't been any barn burnings. Only art sculptures that are somehow being construed as vandalism."

She held him still with nothing more than a stare, sizing him up as if she could tell better than the best detective whether or not he was guilty, though guilty of what he wasn't sure.

"I guess you're right," she finally concluded, then relaxed into an unassuming grin. "Can I get you some coffee?"

Matteo's mouth fell open and so did the deputy sheriff's door. He hadn't realized he was leaning against the door until he stumbled—and righted himself—before any disaster ensued.

He pivoted to face his onlookers and found Deputy Dawson Hayes smiling from ear to ear in full enjoyment of the whole situation. Emma and Haddie, however, were oddly stone-faced.

"You're just in time, Rourke. Now, you weren't trying to listen in and figure out what I was going to ask you so you could plan your answers ahead of time, were you?"

"I'm not worried about *me*," Matteo started,

but for some reason, Marilyn Montez came to his rescue.

"Oh, Deputy, please." She waved him off. "We were just chatting about how unfair it is that I have to do *so* much paperwork every time you start a new investigation. Weren't we, Matteo?"

Matteo's brows furrowed, and Marilyn narrowed her eyes. "Right!" he replied. "Paperwork is the worst. You should probably give her an extra break today with all the hard work she's put in this morning already."

Marilyn winked at him and then sashayed off to get her coffee. She waved at all of them over her shoulder. "I was graduating college when you were praying you'd hit puberty someday, Deputy! I'm going to take my coffee *off* campus."

Dawson beat them all to the punch with an exaggerated guffaw.

"She is *hilarious,* isn't she? There's been an… um…adjustment period since Sheriff Lambert had her baby and went on leave, but I think we're finding our groove."

"Sure, Deputy," Matteo said with a grin. "Whatever you say."

Emma groaned. "Will the two of you let it go already with the pissing contests? Let's all just admit that we're just as scared of Mrs. Montez as we were when we were kids."

The deputy had the decency to look chagrined,

and Matteo wanted to enjoy the moment a little longer. But when Emma's sharp gaze darted in his direction, he swore he saw smoke coming out of her ears.

He sighed. "Okay, fine. She's still scary, but I think she's starting to like me. Maybe I can put in a good word for you, Deputy." Matteo shrugged.

Emma's expression settled back into something impassive and unreadable again.

"Is everything okay?" he asked.

Emma nodded. "Of course." She smiled, but something felt off. "Did you want to tell me anything?"

His brows furrowed. This felt like a test, one he hadn't studied for. "I don't think so…" She wasn't hoping to continue the conversation they'd been having at the inn here in front of everyone else, was she?

"Then I guess we'll catch up later when we get back," she told him coolly.

"From…?" Matteo felt like he was ten steps behind whatever was happening here.

"I'm taking Lemmy and Haddie to Middlebrook," Dawson interjected. "They're going to scope out the competition, and I'm going to take the vandalism investigation over the town line. But don't worry, Rourke. I still have time for you."

Dawson winked, and Matteo wanted to wipe the shit-eating grin off his face. But he also wanted to respect Emma's wishes for the two of them to end the pissing contest, at least while others were around.

So he nodded at Emma and forced a smile. "I hope you find what you're looking for," he told her, then strode past Emma and Haddie and into the deputy's office. "Ready whenever you are, Hayes," he called over his shoulder.

Dawson laughed, then followed him inside.

"She saw you," the deputy said, collapsing into his chair across from Matteo. "Outside with that woman. Told her how she came to see you about a month back too."

Matteo barked out a bitter laugh. "Is that what this is about, Hayes?" he asked, pushing himself to the edge of his chair so his elbows rested on the deputy's desk. "Never saw you as one to perpetuate the rumor mill, but then again, you don't like me. Do you?"

The deputy shrugged. "I don't exactly have a soft spot for convicted felons."

A vein pulsed in Matteo's neck. "And I don't have much of a soft spot for academy recruits who botch investigations and get innocent men thrown behind bars."

"Careful, Rourke. If I didn't know better, I'd say you were accusing me of wrongdoing. And from what I remember, the opioid level in your system that night was well above that of a sober man. Remind me again why you were prescribed those painkillers. Oh, that's right. It wasn't your prescription."

Matteo's hands turned to fists, but he kept them still atop the desk. "I'll deal with the whispers behind my back. But do me a favor, Hayes, and don't pretend like you know my story." He leaned back and crossed his arms.

Dawson sighed and shook his head. "Look, we obviously got off to a bad start here. I just wanted you to know that Emma knows you're seeing someone and that she knows to be careful when it comes to trusting a guy like you."

Matteo laughed. "A guy…like…*me*. Were you this self-righteous when you set off bottle rockets with my brother and let him take the blame for Wilton's farm? My parents grounded him from football for the season. The *entire* season because he took full responsibility for the fire. Do you know what that was like for him?"

A muscle ticked in the deputy's jaw. "I was a *kid,* Rourke. A scared kid who didn't have the kind of home life you and your brother did. It doesn't excuse me for letting Levi take the fall, and I will always live with that guilt, but you don't have the first clue what my old man would have done if he knew I started that fire." He paused for a beat, and Matteo could hear the tremor in the deputy's breath. "You were a twenty-two-year-old adult who drove high and had a glove box full of evidence of your intent to sell. Let's not pretend the two situations are the same."

Matteo's fight-or-flight response went into overdrive, but he needed to stand his ground.

"Fine," he replied. "I'll leave that night at Wilton's farm alone. It doesn't help anyone now to reveal the truth. But the night I was arrested? We're not done there. Not by a long shot."

Dawson stretched his arms and then clasped his hands behind his head. "Suit yourself, Rourke. Your case is closed, as is the statute of limitations to do anything else about it."

"Are you going to question me about this morning's discovery, or am I only here for you to tell me what Emma thinks she saw?"

"Emma and Haddie vouched for you," the deputy admitted. "But as far as you being someone with a record, I'd maybe think twice about getting involved with this whole mystery-artist-vandal thing."

"*Gardener,*" Matteo corrected.

"What?"

"The *Gardener*. That's what Emma's calling your supposed vandal. And all I'm doing is taking pictures. Last time I checked, that wasn't an issue for anyone, regardless of prior convictions."

Every second Matteo was in this room talking about his past with the *last* person he ever wanted to discuss it with, it became harder and harder to breathe.

"No," the deputy said. "The photos aren't an issue. But if you for any reason get caught on the wrong side of this, you could be facing some serious consequences. Emma and Haddie too. Maybe I'm trying to pay your brother back by looking out for you."

Matteo eyed the other man warily. "I'm not a scared-shitless ten-year-old kid anymore, Hayes. I can look out for myself. Same goes for Emma and Haddie."

The deputy nodded. "Of course you can. I was just giving you a friendly warning. I'm not a scared-shitless kid anymore either. I just wanted to be clear that if things go south and we end up on opposite sides of this, I won't be able to help you."

Matteo shook his head. "All this for a few stupid sculptures. Are we done here?"

Deputy Hayes nodded once. "Yeah. We're done."

That was Matteo's cue to finally get the hell out of this room before it caved in. He stood and headed toward the door but suddenly stopped and pivoted back toward the desk where Dawson was now standing too.

"Are you planning on asking her out?" Matteo asked.

"Are you planning on trying to stop me if I do?"

Matteo shook his head. "No," he admitted. "It's not my style."

But this unexpected meeting had planted the seeds of *something*.

Maybe he would never win Emma back after the way he'd hurt her, but what the hell did he have to lose by trying? He'd already *lost,* in so many more ways than one. Either he maintained the status quo or he stopped keeping her at arm's length and finally did something to change that.

His phone buzzed in his pocket, and he pulled it out to see who it was. Only it wasn't *his* phone. He still had Emma's. *And* his.

He glanced back at Dawson with a grin. "See you, Hayes. Thanks for the pep talk, by the way."

Then he stepped outside the office and the entire building as well. He grabbed his own phone from his other back pocket and readied the item he wanted to air-drop to Emma's phone but realized hers was locked.

"Oh good!" Emma called as she jogged toward him. "You're still here. And you have my phone! I thought I lost it."

Matteo decided to shoot his shot and sent the file. Then he quickly brandished her phone toward her face, unlocking the home screen with facial recognition.

She reached for her device, but Matteo snatched it back.

"Wait!" he exclaimed, then subtly swiped his thumb over the button to accept the air drop.

"Nope. I was wrong. Thought I was handing you *my* phone," he lied.

Emma's brows furrowed. "How? Your case is black, and mine is hot pink. Like my Paramore shirt that you stole."

Matteo laughed. "So we're back on the T-shirt thing, huh? Let it go, Woods. *You* lost *your* shirt."

She scrutinized her phone screen, and Matteo held his breath. But when she didn't seem to find anything amiss, she sighed. "Aren't you going to ask where Haddie is?"

He finally realized their chaperone was missing and that Emma didn't seem upset with him anymore. "Okay. I'll bite. *Where's* Haddie?"

"Having *lunch* with the *mayor* at the inn. I know it's harmless flirting on both of their parts, but we might be able to use this to our advantage as far as getting Mayor Green to keep us in the Garden Fest at all costs."

Haddie's absence clicked like it hadn't before. "So…you're going to Middlebrook with Deputy Hayes. *Alone.*"

Emma nodded slowly. "Does that bother you?" Her question could have been a taunt, but came off as sincere.

He shook his head. "I want you to do whatever it is that makes you happy, Emma." And he meant it. But for the first time he let himself wonder if there was a chance that whatever made her happy might actually be *him*.

She pressed her lips into a tentative smile. "I guess I should let Dawson know I'm here."

Matteo nodded. "You know, you can ask me anything, Emma. About whatever…or whoever you want."

He didn't want to assume her seeing him with Lauren was what had shifted her mood. But if she wanted to know, all she had to do was ask, and he'd tell her. Everything.

She opened her mouth, an expectant look in her eye, but then she let it fall closed.

"I'm good. Thanks," she replied instead.

"Good. Good. I'm glad we're good." Before he said *good* one more time, he offered her a parting smile. "Have fun spying on the enemy." He winked and took the steps down to the sidewalk two at a time.

Her time with Dawson was nothing to worry about if Matteo was the one she wanted. He just had to figure out what it would take to win her trust—and her heart—back.

Chapter 17

Emma dipped her finger into the small jar of tinted lip balm and patted it across her bottom lip. Then she rubbed both lips together, finishing off with a loud smack.

"Lip gloss, huh?" Haddie asked, appearing behind her in the opened bathroom door.

Pancake scurried off the bed to greet her.

"And a sundress?" Haddie continued, squatting down to give the fur ball a quick scratch behind the ears. "For a town meeting? I don't suppose this has anything to do with a stranger from out of town and her smart pencil skirt. Oooh, or is it for the deputy? Also, did I mention how over the moon I am that Summertown actually *has* town meetings?"

"I'm starting to rethink giving you a key to my room," Emma replied dryly.

Haddie spun and narrowed her eyes at Emma's bed. "Do you make your bed every morning?"

"What?" Emma asked. She let her dark, wavy hair loose from its bun and then followed Haddie out into the small main room. “I’m living in an inn. You make your bed in the inn. Old habits and all. And is there something wrong with looking nice for an important event?” She tapped open the photo app on her phone and brandished it at her friend. “When Mayor Green sees these, there’s no way he’ll back out of the fest.”

She’d thought about texting Matteo the photos when she and Dawson returned last night, but it still felt like something strange was hanging between them. So she’d played the game of texting chicken—waiting to see if he reached out first—and lost.

Haddie raised her brows. “You may be right about that. I still need confirmation on the outfit, though. Am *I* right about option A or option B. Either way, there’s nary a kitschy T-shirt in sight, so I’m not even sure I know who you are anymore.”

Emma groaned. “Is it too much? Is everyone going to think it’s so out of character for me? It’s not like I live my life in my pajamas. I mean…fine. For work I do if I don’t have any meetings, and even then it’s business on the top and yoga pants on the bottom. And maybe it’s hard to get out of that routine sometimes, but Hads, I *want* to get out of the routine.”

Haddie nodded. “You are *different* here. Good different. I’ll give you that. But you, my dear, need to give me an answer.”

Emma waved her off. "Dawson's just a friend."

Haddie raised her brows. "Are you sure *he* knows that?"

Emma sighed. "He's a good guy."

"A ridiculously good-looking good guy," Haddie added.

"I know." Emma nodded. "He's a great catch."

Haddie crossed her arms. "But not a great catch for *you*."

"You must think I'm such a mess," Emma said. "I don't know what it is, Hads. Like, is it the me from eight years ago feeling the things I feel, or is the me from *now* feeling new things? Or maybe the me from now is the one feeling the old feelings." She plopped onto the foot of her bed. "Am I having an identity crisis? Or an early before-thirty midlife crisis?"

Haddie sat down beside her.

"The only thing I think, Ems, is *I really want you to be happy*." She swung her arm over Emma's shoulders. "I would never judge you for acknowledging your feelings or for wearing that smokeshow of a dress."

Emma stood and smoothed the yellow A-line sundress over her torso. "I feel good."

"About the dress?" Haddie asked.

Emma nodded. "And just about *me*, I guess. I think I know what you mean about me being different here. I feel like for the first time in a long time,

I'm in my element." Was it Summertown? Matteo? A combination of the two? All she knew was that her little "test kiss" in the mud made one thing abundantly clear. Emma Woods was *not* done with Matteo Rourke.

Heat crept up her neck and filled her cheeks. The worry—*Will he hurt me again?*—was, however, just as clear. "Do you think he's seeing that woman?" Emma squeezed her eyes shut as soon as the words came out of her mouth.

"*Ems.*"

Emma opened her eyes and grimaced.

Haddie laughed. "You know, all you have to do is *ask* him."

"Oooh," Emma replied. "So the *direct* approach. Not the seventh-grade approach where I have my best friend figure out how my crush feels about me while I wait in the safety of the girls' bathroom."

Haddie wrinkled her nose. "Since when is a middle school bathroom a safe place?"

Anything was safer than a broken heart.

"Ask him, Ems. Don't put yourself on the side-lines before you even know if you're in the game. That's a lonely place to be."

The way she said that last part made Emma wonder which one of them Haddie was referring to.

"Hads, are you—"

"Food!" Haddie exclaimed, perking up and

changing the subject. "Will there be food at the meeting?" Her stomach growled audibly.

"Didn't you just down a protein shake an hour ago?"

Haddie shrugged. "I'm training for a marathon. I eat to run, and when I run…I need to eat!"

Emma laughed, grateful for the levity. She looked at her friend. "Would it be weird if one person from a town texted another person from that same town to see if that other person was going to be at the town meeting where everyone in town is supposed to be tonight? Hypothetically speaking, of course. I should also probably mention I'm asking for a friend who is definitely not me."

"Come on." Haddie hopped off the foot of the bed and grabbed Emma's hand. "If everyone's going to be there, then there's nothing to text about. This way you can make an entrance. You didn't get all dolled up for nothing, am I right? And I'm not looking too shabby myself."

Emma laughed and nodded at her friend's gray and white strapless floral romper. "You can take the girl out of the city…"

Haddie popped her hip. "But she'll still bring her fabulous clothes."

Emma glanced from her friend's espadrilles to her own flip-flops. "Maybe I should have splurged and gone for the shoes too?"

"Nah." Haddie waved her off. "If you had janky

toes, sure. But you're rocking a nice pedicure. It's not like you're *all* country mouse. Time for us to go reveal our photos to the mayor…and whatever else is on a town meeting agenda."

Emma shrugged. "Probably just storm cleanup status and next steps for replanting or whatever." And making sure Mayor Green saw the Gardener as an asset who could *help* them beat Middlebrook and not as a vandal who was ruining the town. After sneaking some photos of the gardens—or lack thereof—today with Dawson, they were no closer to figuring out *who* the Gardener was, and Emma was okay with that. She felt protective of the artist—despite their mysterious identity—because whoever it was seemed to be the key to winning that prize money and getting Summertown back on its feet.

As Emma and Haddie, arm in arm, followed the throng of guests out of the inn, Emma's thoughts still drifted toward a man who himself was almost as mysterious as the artist. Which puzzle would she solve first? The Gardener…or Matteo Rourke?

"Okay, now that we've cleared up the issue of whether what was salvaged of the Duboses' dragon topiary was the head or the tail, I'm going to ask that all who are in favor of an attempt to replant the tail without the rest of the dragon, please say 'aye,'" Mayor Green instructed with a groan.

A throng of *ayes* sounded throughout the small meeting hall as paddles with "Aye!" written in green were held up.

"Any *nays*?" the mayor added, his voice dripping with disdain.

"I think this is the most fun I've ever had!" Haddie whispered, lowering her paddle even though the mayor said her vote wouldn't count since she wasn't actually a Summertown resident. "My cheeks actually *hurt* from smiling so much. I don't even care that it's hot as Hades in here because I think I just watched an entire town vote unanimously to replant a dragon-butt topiary."

Emma bit back a laugh. "You definitely did." She brandished her own paddle. "Myself included."

Lillian and Freddy Dubose, owners of the dragon butt, erupted into cheers as the mayor reluctantly struck his gavel against the block on his podium, and the rest of the crowd joined them.

Until he shouted a terse "Next!" through his bullhorn.

Silence blanketed the room so quickly that Emma swore she could hear the sweat actively beading on her temples.

"It's time for my final agenda item," the mayor continued. "The issue of the vandal or so-called artist."

Emma straightened in her seat and—for the eleventh time—scanned the crowd for Matteo.

"Maybe these things aren't for him," Haddie whispered, catching Emma in the act.

Emma sighed. Maybe she *should* have texted. But what would have changed? Even if he flat out told her he wasn't going to be at the meeting, he still wouldn't have been at the meeting.

"On the issue of the reward I'd like to offer for identifying our town vandal—"

"What?" Emma sprang up from her seat like a cork shooting from a champagne bottle. A sea of faces spun to look at her, but she didn't care. Maybe she was about to overdo it, but she couldn't just sit there silent while the mayor went back on what he promised her.

Mayor Green looked at her with a curious grin, but nodded for her to continue.

"You..." she started. "You're offering a reward? With what money? Shouldn't all town funds go to the *town*?"

The mayor chuckled, and everyone's gaze volleyed to him.

"I'm sorry for the disruption, folks. Ms. Woods hasn't been to a town meeting since..." He paused and looked her straight in the eye. "When was it, Ms. Woods?"

Emma's parents sat a few rows up. They stared at her pityingly, as if they knew she was fighting a losing battle.

"Okay, fine," she said, tossing up her hands. "So I've been gone for a few years, but that's…that's for personal reasons that I'm not going to discuss with the entire town at this particular moment. But…but that doesn't mean I don't care about Summertown or the people in it, and I'm telling you *all* that the Gardener is *not* a vandal." She picked up her phone from her chair and opened the Summertown Instagram account, holding the phone up for the mayor to see even though he probably couldn't read it from high up at his podium of lies. "Two weeks ago, when the tornado hit, Summertown didn't even have a social media presence. Now it has five hundred followers, which I know doesn't sound like much, but a couple of friends in the business are going to share the account on their channels for this campaign I'm running later this week, and I promise you that number will increase exponentially when it does.

"Plus, Deputy Hayes and I *went* to Middlebrook. I have pictures to prove that despite them—I don't know—*acquiring* Lottie Green, she's only one woman. The topiary photos that were sent to the mayor are the *only* sculptures they have so far. Don't you all get it? We don't need to *expose* the Gardener. We need to let them—I don't know—strike again! Because once the word gets out on travel channels, the tourists will come. And…and when I get finished reading the really, *really* long bylaws for the

Garden Fest, I'm going to find a loophole or something that'll get us back in. I mean, the Gardener has been planting new flowers all over town, right? What if those flowers can get us reentered?"

People began to stir. And mumble. And question. She was reaching them!

"But," she continued. "If we scare the Gardener away, then what? No shtick or quirk in a town that has always relied on shtick and quirk." She laughed unexpectedly. "I forgot how much I loved all that until recently. So if you'll just trust me to do what I know I can do without exposing our artist as a vandal, I promise you won't regret it."

Mayor Green sighed, and for a second she thought she'd reached *him* too, but then he raised his gavel. "All those in favor of a humble reward, something in the realm of say $1,000—that I plan to pay out of my *personal* pocket—please say 'aye.'"

A smattering of paddles raised above the sea of heads, including that of Harmony Sapperstein, who wouldn't look her in the eye, but Emma swore Pikachu looked apologetic when he did.

Haddie jumped up beside her friend and grabbed her hand, giving it a gentle squeeze.

"I'm sorry, Ems," she said against the murmur. "We had a nice little lunch. He's a little lonely and bitter, but I wasn't expecting him to be such a jerk."

Emma's eyes burned, and her cheeks flamed. She couldn't look at her friend because doing so would mean admitting defeat. So she stayed standing, staring the mayor down as he counted the initial votes, hoping the man would have some sort of miraculous change of heart, but it was a Hail Mary sort of hope.

"And those in favor of a more substantial reward to bring our *artist* to the public eye…something more in the realm of $10,000…" He cleared his throat. "Lottie left me half her landscape design earnings in our…um…settlement. I feel it only fitting that the money go back into the town in some way. Do I have any more 'ayes' for that?"

Almost *every* hand went up—Emma's parents included. Could she blame them? They were still paying their small staff, keeping the kitchen stocked and the rooms clean, all for voluntary donations.

Mayor Green's eyes met hers, and his lips curled into a grin as he shrugged.

Then the lights in the meeting hall went out, and a collective gasp rose from the crowd.

Chapter 18

"Is it another storm?" Haddie asked, squeezing Emma's hand. "I don't know how to tornado. Do we duck and cover? Stop, drop, and roll? Why am I forgetting *every* severe weather drill we had in elementary school?"

For a second Emma thought the same thing, but they had walked to town under clear skies as late afternoon turned to dusk.

"Look!" someone shouted. "Outside!"

Through the opened barn door Emma saw spots of colored light dappled across the grass.

Gasps morphed to oohs and aahs.

"*Who* cut the lights?" the mayor snapped through his bullhorn. "Tampering with public property is an offense!"

But no one seemed to be listening or responding as the meeting hall attendees moved like a wave from their seats and funneled through the door.

It was pandemonium by the time Emma and

Haddie made it outside, and as soon as they saw the facade of the meeting hall, they knew why.

"Whoa," Haddie said with a laugh. "Your gardener has some balls. *Big* ones. And seems to be on your team."

Emma stared at the two large tarps, one dropped on either side of the wide-open door from the hall's roof. Hubcaps adorned with LED flower petals and stems were fastened to the one on the left. For several seconds she stood, mesmerized by the patterns of colored light.

"Am I right?" Haddie asked, elbowing Emma in the ribs.

"What?" Emma asked. "Also, *ow*."

"The *note*!" Haddie exclaimed. "Did I mention how much I love this town, by the way? It's like the whole place is one, big live dinner theater. Can we have my birthday party here? Do you think I could talk Mayor Green into turning Summertown into one big escape room?"

Emma's gaze finally volleyed to the tarp on the right side of the door. Painted in bright green were the following words:

Mr. Mayor, how about a wager?

That was it. Nothing else.

"What the hell is this nonsense?" Even without the bullhorn, Mayor Green's voice still carried.

Emma's phone buzzed in her hand. Then it buzzed again. And *again*.

She glanced down to see notification after notification from the Summertown Instagram account.

"What's wrong?" Haddie asked.

"I don't know," Emma mumbled, unlocking her phone and opening the social media app. "Holy shit!"

"Ooh, language, Woods. There are children within listening range."

Emma's head shot up to find Matteo standing over her other shoulder. She knew she was supposed to feel awkward or nervous around him, but right now none of that mattered.

"We have nine hundred followers," she said, holding her phone up for both him and Haddie to see.

"Nope," Haddie responded.

"Not anymore," Matteo added.

Emma dropped her hand back to her own eye level.

"Fifteen *hundred* followers?" she gasped. "*Eighteen* hundred!" Then she noticed she had several messages waiting in her DMs.

One user had shared a post that had Emma—or *Summertown*—tagged. On a quick glance, she saw the user was a contemporary artist who had a modest following of his own and must have been responsible for the Summertown account gaining its initial traction. He'd shared a picture of the LED display from the meeting hall, which seemed impossible since the meeting hall incident was happening right *now*.

Emma whipped her head back and forth scanning the crowd. The Gardener was here. *Now.* One of the many faces she saw every day.

Focus, Emma.

Mrs. Pinkney smiled at her from the crowd. Was it her?

Emma waved, then noticed the older woman massaging her own hand. Right. Her arthritis. Plus, the woman was in her seventies. Not that she wasn't still spry and whip-smart, but she didn't strike Emma as the type who climbed onto roofs in the wee small hours of the morning or just as the sun began to set.

Tilly Higginson stared up at the installation with her arms crossed, as if admiring the work.

Was she admiring her *own* work?

What about the mayor himself? This could all be some big publicity stunt to put Summertown back on the map and—she didn't know—one-up his ex-wife?

She dipped her head back to her screen, to messages piling in the Summertown DMs.

Another account asked if the Woods Family Inn had any vacancies.

The next one wanted to know if The Gardener was single. They didn't care how the artist identified regarding gender. They just wanted an introduction.

And then there was the one that made the hair on the back of her neck stand on end.

> **@summergardener** A wager for Mayor Green—Call off your search until summer's end. If we make it into the fest with my "vandalism" and win (I'm confident like that), you leave well enough alone, and I'll be on my way. No more disturbing the peace. Oh! And the money you offered for the reward? It gets distributed evenly amongst every local business in town. But if we lose the fest (we won't), I'll turn myself in, and you are welcome to make an example of me and my nefarious ways. Do we have a deal?

Emma tapped on the poster's profile and found it was locked. They had no posts and no followers but were following *one* account. Summertown, she assumed. The profile photo was hard to see in the small thumbnail, but it looked like a bird's-eye view of the odd trees, all the proof she needed that this account was the real deal.

"Holy. Fucking. Shit," Emma said this time.

Matteo clapped his hands over ten-year-old Charlie Brewer's ears as he and his mom passed by.

"*Emma,*" he playfully scolded. "Impressionable youth to your right!"

Natalie Brewer, Charlie's mom, gave Emma a reproachful look.

Emma winced. "Sorry!" But then she motioned for Haddie and Matteo to follow her a few paces away from the crowd.

"The Gardener slid into my DMs!" she whispered. "With the full wager for the mayor!"

The mayor who at that very moment was shouting something through his megaphone about finding the circuit breaker and getting back to the vote.

"Okay, this is kind of hot," Haddie told them.

"Hot?" Emma asked.

"Um...*yes*! The Gardener is, like, this masked superhero who everyone is aware of but no one actually *knows*. And he's reaching out to you! You're Lois Lane or Mary Jane or...or...Felicity Smoak!" Haddie exclaimed. "You're the brains behind the brawn. Or vandalism. Or art. Whatever we're calling it. If you play negotiator with Mayor Green, you're officially the caped crusader's accomplice, and it is all very, very *hot*."

Matteo groaned. "How do you even know it's a *he* and not a *she*?"

"Or a *they*?" Emma added.

Haddie shrugged. "I don't. But *you* could use a little romantic upheaval in your life, and you like *hes*, so let me have my little fantasy for you!"

Emma laughed. "Okay, okay. But what am I supposed to do with this?" She pointed at her phone screen, then waved her hands at all the people milling about in front of the meeting hall. "I can't get the mayor's attention with all this chaos."

Haddie held up a finger, then produced her own phone. She opened an app. "Cover your ears," she warned Emma and Matteo, then tapped the screen and held the phone high in the air as it emitted an earsplitting sound, not unlike the horn at the end of an NBA game.

Emma jumped, despite the warning. But after several gasps and shrieks, the crowd went silent.

"The floor is yours, m'lady," Haddie said with a bow. "Do your thing, and I'll get on damage control with the mayor since you're about to steal his thunder." Haddie started backing away but gave her friend the double thumbs-up before disappearing into the crowd.

"Oh!" Emma said. "Right. Okay." She cleared her throat, strode a few more feet to the sidewalk park bench in front of the meeting-hall lawn and climbed atop it. "Hey, everyone!" she called, projecting as best she could in the wide-open space. "Um, can you hear me?" Bodies turned, and heads nodded. She searched the crowd until she saw the man with the megaphone, who was having a hushed conversation with Deputy Hayes. "Mayor Green!" she continued, and the older man paused, sighed, and finally glanced her way. "I have a message for you from the Gardener about the wager."

The mayor handed his loudspeaker to the deputy and crossed his arms, nodding for her to continue.

"Would have been nice if he lent me the stupid

thing so I don't have to yell," she mumbled under her breath but then proceeded to read the terms of the wager to Mayor Green and basically the rest of the town. "You do realize," she continued after she finished the Gardener's message, "that qualifying for and *winning* the Garden Fest on the twentieth anniversary will be more than just a much-needed monetary boost for the town. It will prove we're resourceful and resilient, and that we can shine creatively without anyone else swooping back into town to do it for us. Think about it. If we support this artist rather than hunt them down and ferret them out—then we *all* get credit when we win this thing."

Mayor Green, lit by the glow of the LED display on the side of the meeting hall, stared at her for several long moments before reaching for his speaker and bringing it to his lips.

"How, Ms. Woods, do you envision the whole town taking credit if we simply rely on your *artist* to do all the work?" he asked.

Emma worried her bottom lip between her teeth. He was right. She was flying by the seat of her pants here. While she was an experienced marketer, she usually ran her campaigns with carefully thought-out plans—wireframes, storyboards, and mockups.

Matteo hopped up on the bench beside her. "We'll keep working!" he called out to the crowd.

"We'll keep planting and replanting. We'll help each other out with repairs wherever we can. We'll pay special attention to cleanup efforts at the art installation sites…"

"So the sculptures are highlighted as a point of pride!" Emma chimed in. "As something being done *for* Summertown rather than *to* it!" She went back to the town's Instagram profile on her phone, her eyes widening as she noticed the follower count had grown to over two thousand. "Thanks to our artist…" Though she wasn't sure yet what he'd done. "Our social media account is growing at an exponential rate, and—"

"We just got a booking at the inn! From an actual paying customer!" a voice called out from the crowd. Emma's mother. "No! Make that two! No, three! And they're asking for a tour of the Gardener's sculptures!"

Emma's heart swelled, and she couldn't wipe the grin from her face if she tried. "I told you all we needed was time, and I think everyone else would agree. What do you say, Mr. Mayor, should we take a vote?"

Even in the dim light, she could make out the slight shake of his head before he brought the megaphone back to his mouth. "All those in favor of working *with* the vandal until the Garden Fest, please say 'aye.'"

Like a practiced choir, the voices rang out in unison with a resounding vote in favor of the Gardener.

"Any *nays*?" Mayor Green asked with a sigh, but no one responded. "Then…I suppose the motion is carried."

Cheers erupted from the crowd, and without thinking, Emma threw her arms around Matteo's neck. As soon as she realized what she'd done, she attempted to let go and step away as best she could while they were still standing on the park bench. But he was already hugging her back, lifting her onto her tiptoes as he stood to his full height.

"You were amazing, Emma," he said against her ear, and goose bumps rose on her arms as his stubbled jaw brushed against hers.

She tilted her head back to look at him, though her hands were now clasped behind his neck, his at her hips.

"I was, wasn't I?" she teased, though she had to admit she was pretty damned proud of herself. "And you're a pretty decent wingman." Then she finally remembered the events that had taken place before the meeting-hall blackout. "You were late, by the way. I was getting my ass handed to me by the mayor, and I could have used a wingman then as well."

Matteo huffed out a laugh. "I was in back with Old Man Wilton the whole time. Was at his farm depositing a furry friend and gave him a ride back to town. Mr. Wilton…not the furry friend. I'm sorry I didn't jump in to help you out sooner. I really thought you had him until he upped the award amount."

She narrowed her eyes at him. "Then why couldn't I find you when...?" She clamped her mouth shut, but it was too late. She'd already given herself away.

He raised his brows. "You were *looking* for me."

The corner of his mouth turned up into the crooked grin that still did things to her she didn't want to admit.

"Yeah, well...so what? Maybe I was." She jutted out her chin, but it tapped against his, which kind of blew the whole defiantly breezy vibe she was going for.

"Should we go find Mr. Wilton so he can vouch for me? I should probably see if he needs a ride back or if Mrs. Pinkney is taking him home. *Again.*"

Emma gasped, and she finally loosened her grip on the man in front of her, her hands sliding down to rest on his chest.

"Old Man Wilton and Mrs. *Pinkney*? Everyone in this town seems to be hooking up except for..." Again she smacked her lips shut. Again she was too late.

"If, um, hooking up is something you're interested in, I think the deputy might be interested... *Lemmy.*"

Matteo's tone was teasing, but she noticed a vein pulse in his neck as he said the words.

"Dawson is a friend, and if I didn't know better, I'd say you sound a little jealous."

Matteo raised his brows. "Maybe I am," he admitted without an ounce of hesitation.

Emma closed her eyes and took a steadying breath. *Just ask him.*

"The woman in the square?" She let out a nervous laugh. "Is she…someone you're seeing?"

The corner of his mouth twitched. "Lauren is an investigative reporter from Chicago. The current story she's investigating involves me and my time *away*."

Emma's chest tightened. She wanted to know about his time…away. But it also scared her as much as her feelings for Matteo did.

She nodded. "Just a reminder that I can handle anything you want to tell me." She wanted to believe her own words.

He nodded. "But maybe somewhere quieter. And *not* standing on a park bench."

She grinned.

"You were jealous too?" he asked.

Emma nodded.

"And you're not interested in Deputy Hayes?"

She shook her head this time. "I'm standing here on a park bench for all to see, admitting I have *feelings* about seeing you with another woman and looking like I'm about to kiss you. Isn't that answer enough?"

His thumbs pressed firm against her hips. "I'm out of practice, Em. I needed to be sure. And in case you haven't noticed, *no* one is looking at us. They're too busy figuring out next steps now that you got the ball rolling in the direction of winning this festival thing."

She glanced down at the sea of people who up until recently had been giving her their undivided attention. He was right. *No* one paid them any mind. Plus, they were pretty much shrouded in darkness now that dusk had turned completely to night.

"See?" he said when her gaze returned to his. "Invisible right out in the open. But there's still the question of your vigilante. Is *he* the one you're hoping sweeps you off your feet for this hooking up you speak of?"

Emma laughed. "That's *Haddie*'s fantasy. Not mine. Though if he *is* a *he,* and he works out on a salmon ladder, I may have to amend my answer."

But as her thumb absently tracing the white embroidery of Matteo's name above the pocket of his work shirt, Hollywood actors were the furthest thing from her mind.

He dipped his head, his lips dangerously close to her ear. "What's your fantasy, Emma Woods?"

She swallowed, then tilted her head toward his, the answer already on her lips.

"*You.*"

Chapter 19

How had they gotten to her room? Matteo couldn't remember the walk—or *run*—from the meeting hall to the Woods Family Inn.

"What if Haddie comes looking for us?" he asked breathlessly as Emma fumbled with the buttons of his shirt.

"Haddie's a big girl," Emma said, her own breathing erratic. "She'll be fine without me for a bit. Plus, this is the only room up here other than the storage closet, which leads to the attic. No one's going to bump into us up here. Though I have to admit that this situation doesn't bode well for Haddie's chaperoning skills."

Matteo grinned. "Are you insinuating that you need a chaperone around me?"

For a second she stopped what she was doing and narrowed her eyes at him.

"I'm trying—and *failing*—to get you naked, Matteo Rourke. But I think it's safe to say that without proper supervision, I might get myself into a wee bit of trouble." She waggled her brows, then went back to work on his buttons, her hands slightly trembling.

"Hey," he said softly. "Emma. We don't have to do this if—"

With a firm grip and a surprisingly strong tug, she *ripped* the top three buttons from their holes, sending them scattering across the wooden floor.

Matteo's mouth fell open.

"Oh, we're *doing* this, Rourke. Because I haven't *done* this in… You know what? Let's not talk numbers, okay? Let's just stick to the task at hand."

She tore his shirt the rest of the way open and stopped to stare at his now bare torso.

"It'll be fun explaining *this* look on the walk back through town later tonight." He laughed.

Emma was still staring. She licked her lips and then pressed her palms to his chest, slowly letting her hands slide down over his abdomen.

"You didn't look like this when…" Her voice trailed off. "I mean, it was so many years ago the last time that we…" She squeezed her eyes shut and shook her head. "Nope. We are staying in the here and now." She opened her eyes again and blew out a shaky breath. "Here and now, Matteo Rourke, I am so ridiculously attracted to you that I don't even know what to do with myself." Her chest rose and fell with each breath.

"Emma Woods…" Just saying her name like this, *to* her, breathed new life into Matteo's long-neglected heart. "You *are* and have always been the most beautiful girl—no, *woman*—I've ever known."

He hooked a finger under the strap of her dress and let it fall off of her shoulder. He did the same with the other, then gently tugged the thin cotton down over her breasts. Her *bare* breasts.

"Jesus, Emma," he hissed. Then he dipped his head to kiss the soft flesh above the tightened peak of her nipple.

She gasped, so he moved lower, taking her into his mouth.

She whimpered, her nails digging into his flesh as her knees buckled.

Matteo caught her around the waist. He nipped at her with his teeth, and this time she cried out.

"Did I hurt you?" he asked, tilting his head up.

Her eyes were closed, her lip between her teeth. "No!" she whispered. "God, *no*."

He grinned even as his erection strained against the zipper of his jeans. Then he lifted her in his arms, hooking her legs over his hips as he piloted her to the bed. She kicked off her flip-flops, and he dropped her down on her back.

She smiled up at him, and for a second he swore his mind was playing tricks on him, the way it had so many times when he wasn't sure what time it was or even what day, week, or month. So he closed his eyes and tried to steady himself. When he opened them, she was still there, still smiling.

"This is real?" he asked, surprised to hear his voice crack.

Emma nodded and grabbed his hand, placing it over her breast.

"It's *real*," she whispered, and because it was Emma's voice and not the one in his head, he believed it.

Matteo slid the dress over her hips and took her panties with it.

Yes, this *was* the girl he'd loved since he was barely a teen…and the one he'd lost before becoming a full-fledged adult. Her breasts were fuller. She had curves he didn't recognize…and a trio of small scars on her right side that hadn't been there before. He brushed his fingers over the raised flesh.

"Appendix?" he asked.

Emma nodded. "Three years ago. Went to the ER for stomach cramps and came home one organ lighter."

He laughed even as his throat tightened. He'd missed so much, yet somehow the universe was granting him this second chance. But he knew not to look a gift horse in the mouth. This one night could very well be all he got, so he was going to savor it, appreciate it, and make sure Emma would always remember it.

He knelt next to the bed and kissed all three of her healed wounds.

"Thank you," he told her. "For taking care of Emma *then* so I could be with her now."

With his finger he drew a soft circle around each spot where his lips had touched and then extended down her center until his hand fell between her legs.

She sucked in a sharp breath.

"Is this okay?" he asked. "Do you need your inhaler?"

Emma let out a breathless laugh. "No! I mean *yes*," she whispered. "What you're doing is very, *very* okay. And no, I don't need my inhaler. This is a very different kind of being out of breath."

He smiled, relieved, then traced a line down one of her folds and then up the other.

She squirmed.

"And this?" he asked again.

Another whisper. "Yes."

He dipped a finger into her warm, wet center, and she bucked against his palm.

"What about this?" he asked, his voice rough with need. "Is this okay too?"

"Matteo," she whimpered. "I can't… I'm not gonna… It's been so long since…"

He pulsed his finger inside her and she cried out, her hands fisting the duvet.

"*Please*," she said, grabbing his arm. "I don't want to do it alone."

He was prepared to make her come apart without ever unbuttoning his jeans. Maybe it was some penance he thought he owed or maybe it was simply because watching her—*feeling* her—react to him was beyond any sort of pleasure he'd ever imagined possible.

"*Please,* Matteo," she asked again, squeezing his wrist and tilting her head up to look at him. "I want *you* too."

He nodded slowly, then reluctantly pulled his hand from between her thighs.

He shook off his ruined shirt, then stood, unbuttoned and unzipped his jeans, and slid them off along with his briefs, socks, and work boots.

Emma wrapped a hand around his hardened length, and Matteo swore he saw stars.

"Matteo Rourke," she whispered as she stroked him from root to tip. "You are and have always been the most beautiful man *I've* ever seen."

He barked out a nervous laugh. "Hey," he growled. "That's plagiarism." But realization suddenly set in. "I don't have a... I mean, I wasn't planning on..."

She let out a nervous laugh of her own. "I'm on the pill, have been for years. And I haven't... I mean, it's been a long time since anyone..." She groaned, and Matteo crawled onto the bed, bracing himself on all fours above her.

"Let me see if I've got this straight," he started. "You've got birth control covered; we're both nervous as hell and way too close to climax; and neither of us has had another partner in longer than we'd like to admit?" Even though he had one hundred percent just admitted as much about himself.

"That about sums it up," she confessed as well.

"Okay, then." He dipped his head and kissed her, long and slow and lingering because he knew there'd be no going back or slowing down once they took the next step. "And you promise you're sure about this?" he asked one more time.

"I promise," she replied with zero hesitation.

"Then I guess..." He kissed her one more time. "There's only one thing left to do."

He nudged her opening and found her more than ready for him, so he buried himself as deep inside her as he could go.

Something primal tore from Matteo's chest as Emma hooked her heels behind his legs and attempted to pull him even deeper.

Together they found a rhythm.

Together they touched, tasted, and explored.

And together they branded a memory in his head to which he vowed to always return when he once again forgot what it felt like to be happy.

"*This,*" he whispered with his final shuddering breath before collapsing next to her, his limbs shaking and his muscles a pile of Jell-O.

That was the last thing he remembered until the inn room door swung open however many minutes or hours later, and he was awakened by a scream.

Chapter 20

Emma burst out from the bathroom, toothbrush in hand and mouth full of paste wearing nothing but Matteo's no-longer-able-to-be-buttoned shirt.

Matteo sat bolt upright in the bed with his palms crossed over his groin while Haddie stood at the door clutching a pile of linens to her chest as she stared at his naked form and yelled, "Ahhhhhh!"

"Hads!" Emma cried, but then she had to run back into the bathroom to throw her toothbrush in the sink and spit out what was in her mouth. When she stepped into the bedroom once more, Haddie was still yelling, but she'd now turned her gaze to the *nearly* naked Emma.

Emma stormed over to her friend and clamped a palm over her mouth. "Do you want to be responsible for showing my *parents* what you're witnessing right now?" she whispered-shouted.

Matteo clutched at the duvet with one hand while trying to maintain his cover with the other, but he couldn't gain purchase.

"Who makes a bed this tight?" he exclaimed. "And how long have I been out?"

Emma—hand still over her friend's mouth—pivoted to face her recent bedmate. "Good morning, sunshine. It's 6:00 a.m. I tried waking you after I showered last night, but it was like trying to wake the dead. Truly. If I didn't see your chest move when you took a breath, I was ready to hold a mirror over your mouth and nose to make sure you *were,* in fact, still alive."

"Six?" he asked, incredulous. "In the *morning*? That's not possible."

Emma turned back to Haddie, who'd stopped making noise. "If I drop my hand, do you promise not to yell again?"

Haddie rolled her eyes, and Emma took that as a yes.

"Em*ma*!" Haddie scolded as soon as she was set free. "As much as I'd love to stare at your boobs and bush all day long, can you cover up so we can have a serious conversation?" Then Haddie narrowed her eyes at Matteo. "And it looks like Miss Hospital Corners not only short-sheets but also makes sure the duvet fits the bed like leather pants fit Ross Gellar."

Matteo—now wearing a pillow as a loincloth—furrowed his brows.

"*Friends*? Good lord, does Summertown not get streaming services? Are we in some sort of suspended-in-time situation here? I'm not living the same day over and over again, am I?" Haddie strode into the room and dropped the linens on the foot of the bed so she could check her watch. "Nope. Time is still passing. And I think I would remember walking in on this over and over and *over* again."

Emma padded to the other side of the bed and yanked at the duvet, but it didn't budge. She growled as she tried once more but to no avail.

"Okay, *fine*. I make the beds too tight. My own included." She hopped up next to Matteo, pulled his shirt over her breasts and placed the other pillow over her lap so they were wearing matching loincloths. "Please," she said to Haddie. "Continue with your scolding."

Haddie stood at the foot of the bed with her arms crossed.

"I'm not *scolding* you." She sighed. "You are two consenting adults who disappeared last night, and I covered for you because I figured you two just had some big-time talking to do considering—oh, I don't know—a tumultuous past?" She pointed at Emma. "I trusted you to make good choices, young lady. I trusted you to…" She sighed. "Okay, I'm scolding you. But that's only because you wanted me here to *keep* you from doing exactly what you did last night, but if this is what you really want, then I'm happy for you. For *both* of you."

Matteo turned to face Emma. "You *didn't* want last night to happen." It wasn't a question. "It was just a product of poor judgment? When you mentioned Haddie being your chaperone last night, I didn't think you meant it *literally*."

Emma opened her mouth to protest but couldn't stop thinking about the fact that they were both sitting in bed with pillows over their nether regions while Haddie stood at the foot of the bed staring back at them.

"Hads?" she glanced at her friend. "Do you think you can give us a minute?"

Haddie nodded. "But I'll be right outside the door if you need me." She pivoted toward the still-open door and strode through it, keeping her back to Emma and Matteo.

"*Close* it, Hads," Emma called after her.

Haddie reached behind her without turning around and pulled the door shut.

Matteo immediately hopped off the bed and around to Emma's side where his jeans still sat in a pile on the floor. He had them pulled up, buttoned, and zipped before she could even get a word in. When she opened her mouth to say something, he handed her her wrinkled yellow dress and nodded at the shirt she was wearing. *His* shirt.

"*Matteo,*" she said softly. "Can we talk about this?"

"Sure," he answered coolly. "Just let me reclaim what's left of my dignity."

She bit back a smile as she wriggled out of his shirt and into her dress before sliding off the bed to stand before him.

His shirt, of course, hung open, and his hair was an adorable rumpled mess, so much so that she couldn't help reaching up and tousling it some more.

"*Emma...*" He gently swatted her hand away. "That's not exactly helping me in the dignity department."

She smiled.

"What?" he asked, crossing his arms.

She shrugged. "You're cute when you're pouty in the morning."

"Pouty?" His eyes widened. "I'm not...*pouty*."

"Okay, Pouty Pouterson," she teased. Then she tugged at his wrist, urging him to uncross his arms so she could wrap hers around his waist.

"What are you...? Emma, you don't have to do this."

She kissed his chest, and Matteo groaned.

"Okay, now you're not even playing fair," he told her. "I'm having a crisis of conscience, and you're activating my libido, which is making it *very* hard for me to think."

She rose onto her toes and kissed his neck and then his chin. For a few seconds he let her continue, but then she felt his hands on her shoulders and him pushing her an arm's length away.

"Emma, *wait*."

She pressed her lips together and did as he asked.

"Last night was... It was unexpected," he began. "But I wanted it. I wanted it more than I'd like to admit, and I don't regret a second of it...unless the only reason it happened is because *you* weren't thinking clearly."

Emma raised her brows. "Can I talk now?"

Matteo cleared his throat. "Um...yes. If by talking you mean using your words and *not* your powers of seduction."

She stifled a laugh. "Was I drunk last night?"

His brows furrowed. "No. Shit...I don't think you were. Were you?"

Emma fisted her hands at her sides and let loose an exasperated groan. "*No,* Matteo. I wasn't drunk. And I was of sound mind and whatever other legal mumbo jumbo means I was capable of making my own decisions. Look... Those first few days when we kept running into each other and our *lips* ran into each other that one time, I was confused. I don't know how to process these feelings that are either resurfacing or new or a combination of both.

"And then there's the fact that whatever happens between us is finite because you live in Summertown, and I don't anymore. I think I understand why you pushed me away all those years ago, but does it still scare the hell out of me that it might happen again? Of course it does. So yes, I might have asked Haddie to help me keep my head on straight while I was sorting it all out. I don't think I should have to apologize for that. And I—"

"Emma," he interrupted. "I wasn't asking for an apology. Don't you get it? I know you already have regrets when it comes to me. Do you think I want to add to that?"

She chanced it and took a step closer to him again, and this time he didn't object.

She grabbed his hand and gave it a reassuring squeeze.

"Whatever feelings I have about what happened eight years ago, I *never* regretted falling in love with you." She blew out a shaky breath as he stared at her wide-eyed and speechless. "Just because I've been running from our past ever since I graduated doesn't mean I wish it never happened. And just because Haddie wasn't there last night to talk some sense into me doesn't mean I wish last night hadn't happened either." The corner of her mouth turned up, but he still wasn't smiling. "That was a *joke*. As much as I hate to admit it, I'm an adult, which means I need to be able to make my own decisions and *trust* my own decisions. And last night I decided that I wanted to be with *you*." She yanked gently on his hand and placed it on her hip. Then she grabbed his other hand and did the same.

He didn't let go.

"I don't sleep," he finally said.

She looked up at him, her hands over his. "What do you mean?"

"I have insomnia. It's been like that for...for a lot of years. But last night... I don't get it. I *slept*."

She closed the distance between them and wrapped her arms around his torso once more. But this time, instead of using her *powers of seduction*, she pulled him into a hug.

What must have happened to make him unable to sleep? Did he not feel safe? Did he have bad dreams? She hoped he'd tell her when he was ready.

"Thank you for sharing that," she said softly, then pressed a soft kiss to his freckled chest. "And in return I owe you one thing about me, right?" As much as she wanted to look away, she glanced up at him and held his gaze. "I–I always hoped that once you were released, you'd look for me."

He swallowed. "I wanted to, Em. More than fucking anything. But I didn't think I deserved you in my life again after what I did to you. I still don't think I do, but somehow I'm here with you, and I truly don't know why."

Emma bit back the threat of tears.

"You were barely more than a kid, Matteo. You're a different person now, and I'm not going to hold over you a decision you made eight years ago. It took finding you again for me to realize I could let go of that hurt and see you for who you are."

He shook his head as if he still didn't believe her. "Who am I?"

She stood on her toes and softly kissed his lips.

"You're a good man who takes care of his father, who is always ready to lend a hand to someone in need, whether it's trapping a squirrel or being someone's wingman when they're standing up to the mayor."

His lip twitched into an almost-grin.

This time she spoke while peppering kisses up his neck. "And for someone who claims (like *me*) to be out of practice, you are quite skilled in bed."

"*Emma*." He hummed a soft moan after whispering her name.

She tilted her head back to look at him and finally, *finally*, he smiled.

"You think I'm that easy?" he teased, but his voice was hoarse. "That you can just have your way with me whenever you want?"

She nodded, and he laughed.

"Yeah, well, you're one hundred percent right. You can have your way with me whenever you want."

She bit her bottom lip. "How about right now?"

"*Except* right now." He buried his face in her hair and kissed the top of her head. "I have the walk of shame back to my truck to attend to right *now*."

"Are you *really* ashamed?" she asked with a knowing grin.

He shook his head. "Not even a little bit. Unless your parents see me."

She laughed. "I'm sure they're going over the top with prep for arriving *paying* guests and won't even notice whether you're coming or going. But they *might* notice that shirt. At least let me grab you one of my dad's T-shirts to wear underneath. You can't go out there looking like the cover of a romance novel."

Matteo took a step back and casually motioned to his well-defined torso.

"Emma Woods, are you trying to tell me that this is the stuff of romance novels?"

She swallowed as his fingers brushed over the line of fine ginger hair that started below his belly button and disappeared beneath his jeans.

Her core tightened. "Are you *sure* there's no chance of *right now*?"

"*No!*" Haddie yelled from outside the door. "The inn will be fully booked once the new guests arrive as early as noon! The two of you need to check your thirst at the door and get to woooorrrk! Also *stop* making me be the bad guy when I'm supposed to be the *fun* one!" Haddie whined.

Emma snorted, then covered her mouth.

Matteo tucked his shirt into his jeans and somehow got it to overlap enough that it almost looked *not* ruined.

"I'll take a rain check on that T-shirt," he whispered

in her ear and then had the audacity to nip at her lobe.

Emma whimpered.

"Just remember," Matteo continued. "There's a thirst trap underneath waiting for your poor, parched lips."

Emma's mouth fell open as Matteo strode to the door.

"I'll make sure our attic friends are contained before I leave so I can say I was here on official business," he added, then opened the door. Haddie stumbled inside as he exited and headed straight for the storage-closet entrance to the attic.

"I wasn't eavesdropping!" Haddie protested as she gained her footing, but Emma was still staring out the door at the ghost of Matteo's recent presence. "Are *you* okay, Ems?" she asked.

"I've been so worried about getting hurt again that I forgot about this part," Emma told her, finally shifting her eyes from the empty hallway to her friend.

"Which part?" Haddie asked.

"The blissed-out feeling of new love…er, *lust*. It's definitely lust right now. I mean, the guy just called himself a thirst trap, and I didn't even laugh because the thirst is *real*, Hads, after a drought that was even *more* real, if you know what I mean."

Haddie crossed her arms and looked her friend up and down. "Exactly *how* real, darlin'? Because this moony, puppy-love thing you've got going on is a look I have never seen on you before."

"How real would you rate eight years?" Emma winced.

Haddie kicked the door shut behind her and pointed over her shoulder.

"He's the only *one*? And you haven't—"

"No!" Emma interrupted, rounding the bed to face her friend. "I mean, *yes*. Sort of. There was David, the guy who came *after* Matteo. He was..." Emma groaned. "An assignment from my therapist."

Haddie huffed out a laugh. "Sounds like a lucky guy."

Emma scratched the back of her neck and plopped down on the foot of the bed.

"We didn't *sleep* together but we did...you know...other things. Anyway, he was a good guy. A *great* guy. But he wasn't—"

"The right guy," Haddie continued, finishing Emma's sentence with a sigh. "But is there really such a thing as the *one* right person for you?"

Emma shrugged, then laced her fingers through Haddie's and squeezed. "I don't know. I mean, Matteo's dad lost his mom, and now he might be finding love again. Apparently Old Man Wilton and Mrs. Pinkney—both widowed—are a thing as well. I think maybe we can have multiple loves in our lives. I'm just not sure I'm finished loving my first love." Whoa. There was the admission of the century.

Haddie squeezed Emma's hand back. "Even though your first love broke your heart and ruined you for therapy-assignment David?"

Emma laughed. "I heard he's married now with two kids, so I'm guessing he did all right."

"But are you sure you know what *you're* doing getting involved with Matteo again?"

Emma rested her head on Haddie's shoulder. "I don't. All I know is that last night was wonderful and unexpected, and when I woke up next to him this morning, I didn't panic, you know? The past couple weeks, whenever something happened between me and him, my fight-or-flight kept kicking in. Which was really a problem when I didn't have my inhaler with me. But last night was different." She straightened and pivoted to face her friend. "I think it might have something to do with the Gardener."

Haddie's brows furrowed. "So you have the hots for the mysterious vigilante too? Is this like some sort of sexual surrogacy where you pretend Matteo is the superhero, and… Ooh! Is it a role-playing thing? That could be a fun way to shake things up!"

"*No!*" Emma rolled her eyes. "I just mean with things falling into place with the Gardener. The mayor is backing off. Tourists are coming, and I'm going to find a loophole to enter us in the fest. All just seems right with the world, and last night with Matteo was kind of like the cherry on top. Does that make sense?"

"Kind of?" Haddie replied. "That blackout stunt last night was pretty badass."

Emma nodded. "You know the Chicago Botanic Garden?"

Haddie nodded.

"Think of a whole town interspersed with all of that…plus some really over-the-top topiaries." She laughed. "*That* was Summertown. But the sculptures or pieces the Gardener is creating? There's meaning to them. The sunflowers in the square? The lotus flowers at the town entrance? The LED flowers like constellations? All of it points toward a new beginning. A fresh start. A *do*-over."

Haddie lifted their clasped hands and pressed them to her chest. "I hope you're right and that you're not just looking for something to justify getting involved with Matteo again. You know I support you no matter what, but it's also my job as your best and smartest friend to look out for you."

Emma smiled. "Fair enough."

"Hey…" Haddie continued. "You're pretty badass too, you know. Standing up to the mayor and calling him out on that bullshit reward? I'm impressed."

Emma's chest filled with pride. "He's backing down for now, which is great. But the fact he has to walk into work each morning under what looks like cotton candy trees is giving me more joy than it should."

Both of them laughed.

And for the rest of the day—despite the frenzy of preparing and greeting the few new guests—Emma held on to a feeling she thought she'd never grasp this way again.

Happiness.

Pure, unbridled, fills-every-bucket *joy*.

Chapter 21

MATTEO CLIMBED UP INTO THE ATTIC, FLASHlight held before him. When he made it through the trapdoor and straightened to his full height, he startled to find a figure standing in the darkness, waiting for him.

"Shit, Emma!" he hissed, almost dropping the flashlight, stumbling back, and almost falling through the hole in the floor from which he'd just emerged. "Are you trying to kill me?"

She stared at him for a long moment, hands on the hips of her khaki shorts, a white Woods Family Inn T-shirt stretched over her sexy curves.

Instead of answering, she grabbed him by the wrist and led him to a corner of the attic where she'd laid out a checkered picnic blanket and a couple of pillows.

"You're not serious, are you?" he asked. "Here? I have another house call in thirty minutes. Mrs. Pinkney thinks there's a skunk under her porch. If she's right, you're gonna want to steer clear of me for at least another few days."

Emma groaned. "*Another* few days is why I put together our little make-out corner. I've barely seen you all week. I'm not expecting you to let me have my *way* with you in a dusty attic—unless you *want* to, of course—but I *am* going to ask that you lie down on that blanket and make out with me for at least five to seven minutes."

He pointed his flashlight down at the blanket and then back at her. "How long were you standing there waiting for me? I'm thirty minutes later than I was yesterday."

She let out a nervous laugh. "Let's just say that if you don't make immediate use of the make-out blanket, someone is going to come looking for me and the replenishment bars of soap for the guest rooms I said I was coming up here to fetch."

A scratching sound came from his left and he spun, flashlight pointed at the part of the chimney that held the trapped squirrels.

"They're fine," Emma insisted. "I checked on them before you got here. Mama still has outside access and the babies look well fed and not so much like mole rats anymore."

He hesitated, knowing he was here to do his job, but also knowing he could trust Emma's word.

He spun back to face her.

She gestured aggressively toward the blanket. "Clock's ticking, thirst trap."

Matteo laughed, but then his expression grew

serious. He ran the beam of the Maglite up and down the buttons of his work shirt. "Before you go getting all handsy, just remember I have to wear this to my next job."

She dropped down onto the blanket and collapsed onto her back with an exasperated sigh.

"Notice that I'm giving you *zero* directives about whether or not *you* can get handsy with *me,* mister."

His brand-new erection strained against his jeans and reminded him that he was wasting precious time.

He turned off the flashlight and tossed it on the blanket, then dropped down over her, sliding his knee between her thighs and covering her mouth with his own. She immediately parted her lips, inviting him inside, and he growled his need for her as he tasted the bittersweet remnants of coffee on her tongue.

"We cannot let another day go by—not to mention *days*—without doing this again, okay?" she asked when they quickly parted to breathe.

"Deal," he said, then kissed her again as she arched beneath him.

He rolled onto his side to get a good look at her, his eyes now adjusted to the dark.

"Even dressed like a camp counselor, you're still the sexiest woman I've ever seen."

Emma scoffed. "*Camp* counselor! How dare you, Matteo Rourke. And to think I was going to let you touch my *breast*!"

Matteo chuckled, then cupped her breast in his palm, which made her go from haughty to Jell-O in mere seconds. "Did you miss the part where I called you *sexy*?" he asked.

"Did *you* miss the part about playing fair?" she squeaked as he brushed a thumb over her hardened peak. "Do you *really* have to keep that appointment with Mrs. Pinkney?"

He gave equal attention to her other breast as she sucked in short, sharp breaths.

"I do if I want to get paid," he told her. "But I am just now remembering something you said about having my way with you. I think I might be able to do that without ruining any of my buttons."

Matteo slid his hand down her torso and to her shorts, flicking open the button and tugging the zipper down.

He crawled over her again and quickly yanked her shorts and panties to her ankles, then lowered his head between her knees.

"Matteo, what are you—"

But her words were cut short with the first swipe of his tongue… Until five to seven minutes later when she might have cried out his name and an expletive or two.

He stood up, leaving her lying there limp as a noodle, and did his quick check on the squirrels, freshening their food and water from the supplies he now kept in the attic.

"You okay down there?" he asked with a grin, producing his flashlight and shining it where she lay.

She pulled her shorts back up but hadn't fastened them or tucked her shirt back in. The soft, creamy skin of her abdomen begged to be kissed, but Matteo knew if he crawled back down beside her, he'd never leave.

She smiled, eyes softly shut and hands clasped behind her head.

"I ammm…" she hummed. "The most okayest person to ever be okay, thank you very much."

"God, I love you, Em." The words leaped from his lips before his brain had any freaking clue what was going on. But it caught up pretty damned quickly…and so did Emma.

She shot up from where she lay boneless just a millisecond before.

"What did you just say?" she asked.

He turned the flashlight off and pivoted back toward the trapdoor, hoping to hell he saw it before he fell through.

"Nothing!" he called over his shoulder. "I'm late for the Pinkney call! We can catch up later! Don't forget the soap!"

He didn't think the trapdoor had a firehouse pole, but he was down the ladder about as quickly as if it did.

That was it, he thought, as he kept putting one foot in front of the other on his way to the high school track. His last words to Emma Woods: *I love you,* and *Don't forget the soap.*

This was *her* fault, actually. She was the one who set up that damned make-out blanket, and *she* was the one who said he could have his way with her. And it was *Emma* who lay there all glowing and beautiful because of him. Because of *them.* Because even now, after all that happened, they still somehow made sense. She still wanted him just as much as he wanted her.

Earlier that evening, Matteo had slipped quietly out of his apartment and through the mudroom door. He'd dropped to a squat on the driveway and laced his running shoes. Then he paired his earbuds to his phone and picked this evening's playlist.

"Teo!" his father called from the front door.

Almost, Matteo thought with a sigh.

"Yeah, Dad?" he asked, backing down the driveway to the street.

"Tilly made *qui-no-a*? I'm not sure how you say it, but it's supposed to be good for you. Won't you stay for dinner?"

Matteo pointed to one of his earbuds and shrugged. "Music's starting! I can't really hear you! But I'm pretty sure it's *keen-waa*...the healthy stuff!"

He was slowly jogging backward now, waiting for his father to retreat.

"You'll like her once you get past this, Teo. And we still need to talk about scheduling my surgery!"

Matteo waved, childishly pretending like he was definitely out of hearing range now rather than avoiding both the subject of his father having a girlfriend *and* the man's impending spinal surgery.

Denny Rourke finally threw his hands in the air, admitting defeat, and headed back inside.

Matteo spun so his body was finally facing the same way he was moving and let his feet hit the pavement with purpose.

He knew better than to let his subconscious lead him to the inn tonight. While he was thrilled the place was booming with *actual* business and that Summertown's Instagram channel was still growing, he hadn't had the balls to face Emma again after saying what he had said.

Despite the truth of his words, he never wanted to put pressure on her to make this more than it was. He wasn't an idiot. She had a life in Chicago and he had… Well, he had his father to worry about and a business to keep running.

Running. He was good at that, sometimes to a fault.

He pushed himself harder, ran faster as he passed through the gates and onto the school grounds. Except someone was already there. Running on *his* track.

She saw him approach and picked up speed, so he followed her lead and turned his jog into a sprint.

Haddie was fast. He had to hand it to her. But Matteo was fueled by adrenaline and urgency. What had Emma told her? Had he completely blown it?

So he pushed on, catching up and eventually overtaking her before finally running out of steam.

Thankfully, so had she.

She slowed to a stop a few paces ahead of him, her hand on her side and her chest heaving.

"Well done, Rourke," she said through gasps for breath. "I only have myself to blame for the screaming stitch in my side."

"Here," he said, striding toward her as he hit Stop on his playlist. "Do this. It'll help." He reached his hands high overhead, stretching his fingertips toward the stars.

Haddie groaned but followed his lead.

"Now stretch over the same side as the stitch and hold it there for about thirty seconds," he added.

Haddie leaned to her side, and Matteo mirrored her with his own stretch, which they both held for the requisite amount of time.

She exhaled as she straightened. "Thanks for the tip. I don't usually overdo it like that. I just saw you coming, and my first instinct was to make you eat my dust."

Matteo laughed. "Fair enough. Mind if I ask why? Something I said or did? The list is pretty long."

She tapped her lip with her index finger, then crossed her arms. "See, that's the thing. I know you and Ems have this complicated past, but I only know what she's told me. I know she's been acting really weird all day, like spacey-head-in-the-clouds, keeps-forgetting-why-she-walked-into-a-room weird, but she won't tell me why. I know that she's all into you again even though she's only here for the summer and you're not doing anything to stop the momentum of her falling for you again, which means this can only end with her getting her heart broken. *Again.* And despite all of that, the only thing I've seen from you since I've gotten to town is this really great guy who has nothing but heart eyes for my friend, and I don't know what to make of it all because I've never seen her this happy." She threw her hands in the air. "So I thought maybe I'd run the answer out of you, but you made me eat my own dust instead. Lesson learned." She shrugged.

Matteo took a moment to let it all sink in. Emma was…*happy*? Even after what he'd said in the attic—after how he'd hurt her all those years ago. "So she said *nothing* to you about what happened this morning?"

"This *morning*? All I remember is her taking a really long time to get the soap replenishments from the top floor, and then when she finally came back downstairs, she'd forgotten the soap. See what I mean? *Weird.*"

Matteo held out his hand to shake hers.

"Hi there," he said. "Forgotten Soap. Nice to meet you."

Haddie's mouth fell open. "Of *course* you are. Okay, so be honest, Forgotten Soap. Should I be worried? Because I have loved that girl for, like, more than six years now. And I am fiercely protective of the people I love. Lucky for Ems, she's the *only* person I love, so she gets all of my fierce protection."

He scrubbed a hand across his jaw. "Aside from family, of which I have very little, she's the only person *I* love, and I kinda blurted it out this morning."

Haddie gasped. "I can't believe she didn't *tell* me! What did she say? What happens next? Are you, like, star-crossed lovers reunited? Are you moving to Chicago?"

Matteo stared at her blankly. He couldn't answer a single one of those questions.

"I bailed on her," he finally admitted. "I took off from the attic so fast, I'm not even sure I used the ladder."

"What? Why?" Haddie laughed and pushed him playfully on the shoulder, the one that hadn't properly healed in eight years.

He hid the wince of pain the best he could, but the memory it jogged had nothing to do with that night in the prison dining hall. Instead he saw

Emma through the glass partition, her eyes glassy with tears she wouldn't let fall after he told her not to come see him again.

His throat tightened.

"Because as much as I want it—as much as I'm actively fighting for it—I can't get past the idea that I don't deserve her love in return. Not after what I did."

Haddie lifted a leg and wrapped her arms around her knee, stretching like she was ready to take off around the track again. She stared at him, her jaw tight. Then she dropped her foot to the ground and lifted the opposite knee.

"You're either in or you're out, Paperboy. Because regardless of what you think *you* deserve, Emma deserves the world."

"You're right. She does." Matteo sighed. "I never *wanted* to hurt her, you know."

She crossed her arms. "Prove it by doing better this time."

He let out a nervous laugh. "Tall order."

"You're damn right, it is."

"But *you're* willing to give me a chance." He crossed his arms as well so they were now in some sort of a runners' standoff. "That's got to say something."

She reached her hands behind her head and undid and redid her ponytail before squatting down and taking her mark.

"Talk to me in 400 meters, and we'll see," she said with a wink.

Matteo let out a long breath, his shoulders finally relaxing as he took his mark in the lane beside hers.

"I'm faster," he taunted.

"I'm younger," she replied.

"*Ouch!*" But he laughed. "Guess that makes me more experienced."

"I guess," she conceded. "But there's one thing I haven't told you about my competitive streak."

"What's that?" he asked.

She launched forward like she was shot from a cannon. "Sometimes I cheat!" she called over her shoulder.

One surprised laugh loosed itself from his throat before he took off after her.

Sometimes you had to bend the rules to win, and if he had even the slightest chance in hell at making things right with Emma, he'd twist the rules into a tangled mess of knots if it meant never losing her again.

Chapter 22

Emma had never climbed a trellis before, but how hard could it really be? The white wooden squares were certainly big enough for her feet, and if it was fastened securely to the side of the Rourke family house, it would hold her weight—*securely* being the optimum word.

"Here goes nothing!" she told no one in particular, hoping to psych herself up for the task.

It's romantic.

It's charming.

It's something you'd never *do in Chicago.*

It's just a ladder, and it's not like you're afraid of heights.

That you know of.

Okay, tonight would be a really shitty time to learn that she actually did harbor a deep-seated case of undiagnosed acrophobia.

Finally, she exhaled, stuck her toes into the first square, and gave the not-quite-a-ladder a tug before attempting her ascent.

She held her breath the entire way to the roof of the garage, silently cursing Matteo and his father for not building a balcony or an outside set of stairs.

When she made it to the top, she found little relief climbing onto the slanted roof. She dropped to all fours, then slowly rolled to her back, bracing her heels on the gutter for purchase before shimmying up high enough to grab Matteo's windowsill.

A mosquito buzzed in her ear, and Emma yelped, then clapped a hand over her mouth.

She saw him then, sitting on his bed with his back propped against the headboard, folders, papers, and books strewn to his right and left in front of his raised knees.

She pulled herself to sitting and leaned her elbows on the concrete sill, resting her chin on her arms. She could see the white earbuds, which saved her from revealing herself too soon. He tapped a pencil against his lips and pushed a pair of glasses up the bridge of his nose.

Glasses?

The Matteo she knew never wore glasses. Or sat on a bed surrounded by books. He looked so immersed in what he was doing that Emma almost second-guessed about knocking until she reminded herself that going down might not be as easy as climbing up, and she really wasn't ready to find out yet.

She squinted through the screen and gasped.

He was wearing the *black* Paramore concert tee. *His* concert tee. The one he'd said was *hers* when she accused him of stealing the pink one!

Without another moment of hesitation, she rapped her knuckles against the glass.

Matteo didn't even blink.

The *earbuds*. Shit.

She knocked again, but still no reaction.

Emma groaned.

She took a chance on the fact that no one in Summertown ever locked their doors and pushed up on the screen.

Without any hesitation, it rose, as did the window behind it.

She peeked over the ledge and saw no desk, dresser, or any other piece of furniture in the way, just a small two-foot descent, so she clumsily crawled through the opening and just as gracefully dropped onto the floor of his room.

In a blink, strong hands gripped her biceps, pulling her off the floor and bracing her against the window frame.

Emma shrieked, and Matteo swore.

"Shit, Emma!" He jumped back and held his hands in the air.

"What the hell was that?" she asked, rubbing her arms. "That was like Batman in some dark alley with a...a...a hooligan type shit."

"I'm sorry! I overreacted. But jesus, Emma. You

just broke into my room when you could have just as easily come to the front door." He moved toward her again, reaching hesitantly toward one of her arms. "Did I hurt you?"

For a second she was held captive by the tinge of pain in his voice.

"No," she told him. "You...surprised me. That's all."

"You mean I *scared* you." He pulled his glasses off and tossed them on the bed, then pinched the bridge of his nose.

What *else* happened to him when he was in prison? Was it more than the incident in the dining hall? Was he always on alert like this? Or had she simply been naive enough to think that Summertown existed in a vacuum where no one worried about anything more threatening than an artist who "vandalized" public property?

"I was trying to be romantic," she said with a nervous laugh. "I haven't heard from you since this morning, and I wanted to make sure everything was okay after...I mean, before you left..." She groaned. "I didn't take what you said seriously, okay? I know it was in the moment and that there's no way that you feel like *that* when it's been so long and—"

"Right," he interrupted. "It was in the moment. Because that would be moving way too fast, especially when you're leaving at the end of the summer." He paused. "Aren't you?"

Of course Emma was leaving the end of the summer. She lived in Chicago. *Pancake* lived in Chicago. And Haddie. That was Emma's life, which meant Emma's life was in Chicago. So why wasn't she answering him as quickly as he'd asked the question?

"Chicago!" she finally exclaimed. "I live in Chicago." She spoke the words as if she were an amnesia patient repeating her biographical information as the doctor read it to her. "*Not* in Summertown." So what was she doing here, trying to be romantic after Matteo accidentally told her he loved her this morning?

"Emma?"

Right. She was still standing there not saying anything.

"Yeah?"

He laughed softly. "Can we maybe back up and try this again? You can break into my room, and I can *not* think you're an intruder, and you can be… What was it again? Romantic?"

Her cheeks warmed, and she bit back a smile.

"Did you really climb the trellis?" he added.

Emma nodded. Then she stood on her toes and peeked over her shoulder.

"If I didn't know any better, I'd say you were studying for a final exam." She shuddered. "I'm almost thirty, and I still have those nightmares of waking up and having missed all my finals. When does that end?"

His brows furrowed. "So final exams is your idea of romantic?"

Her mouth fell open. "*No,* I had some *very* romantic things in mind, but you were sitting there, looking all studious, and you had *glasses* on. When did you get glasses? I don't remember you… *Wait.* Hold the phone. We interrupt this regularly scheduled program to bring you the fact that Matteo Rourke is wearing the *black* Paramore concert tee!"

He glanced down at his attire and then back at her.

Busted.

"You *lied* to me." She gasped dramatically.

He nodded. "And you *knew* I was lying. You saw how small the pink one was on me, but you didn't push it."

He had her there. But that was right when she'd gotten to town. Pushing him would have meant engaging, and her fight-or-flight had been way too volatile. Now she felt like she had some semblance of control, no matter how fleeting it might be. "Maybe it's because I knew it would be more fun to simply catch you in the act," she continued, which was not entirely *un*true. "Ever think about that? Now that I have caught you, I'd like to know why."

He studied her for a second and then simply said, "Maybe because I *wanted* you to catch me."

She squinted at him and pursed her lips. "Touché, Matteo Rourke. Touché." She flicked her index finger up and down in the direction of his bed. "And the final exam scenario?"

Matteo sighed. "It's exactly what it looks like. I wasn't exactly avoiding you today. I mean…I was a *little*. It's not every day you accidentally tell someone something that's way too early and out of line to say. I needed to regroup. And cram for this final tomorrow."

She still couldn't puzzle the whole thing out.

"But it's summer. And you're *thirty*." She stepped around him and toward the bed, suddenly aware that while she was in Matteo Rourke's childhood home, this little studio apartment situation was brand-new to her. It was *adulthood* Matteo's home. With adulthood Matteo's bed. And adulthood *Matteo*. "Art history?" she added. "Isn't that, like, a gen-ed one?"

She heard him chuckle behind her.

"It is. At the 300 level, though, I might add. I… uh…was actually a few credits shy of graduating my senior year. Left myself some room for a couple blowoff classes, and wouldn't you know it? I didn't get the chance to blow them off."

Emma swallowed and turned to face him.

"Because your mom passed away."

Matteo nodded, but then he let out a bitter laugh. "Why do people do that?" he asked.

"Do…what?" She hesitated, her stomach pooling with dread.

"The euphemisms. They don't soften the blow." He shrugged. "Whether you say 'passed away' or 'pushing daisies,' she's still dead. Still gone. Not actually saying the *thing* doesn't make the thing untrue."

"I'm sorry," she started. "I didn't mean to upset you. I've never been good with this kind of stuff. It made me wonder… I mean, the weekend of her funeral… Did I not…?" She swallowed, her throat dry. She couldn't come out and ask the one thing that had been in the back of her mind since the day she visited him and he told her never to come back.

He stepped forward, cupped her cheeks in his palms. The nearness of him…the scent of him… Even in her spiral of doubt, something as simple as his skin on hers could turn that doubt to dust.

"Emma…" He buried his face in her hair and inhaled before pressing his lips to her forehead. "Nothing that happened between us had anything to do with you or how you supported me through one of the two hardest times in my life. It was *all* me. No matter what I said to you back then, you at least need to *listen* and hear and believe that it was *All. Me.*"

Emma nodded. "What about the second time?" She cleared her throat. "What was the second-hardest time in your life?"

"The second I knew I had lost you."

His jaw ticked, and Emma's breath hitched. She pressed her palms to his chest, over *his* concert tee.

"I should have fought you on it. I should never have left you there alone. But I was hurt and confused and—"

"It was *me*, Em. *Me*."

She shook her head. "It was *us*. I'm so sorry, Matty Matt. For what both of us lost."

Fine. So the pain would always be there. But Emma didn't have room for anger or regret or blame. Not when they'd both made mistakes. So she decided right there in the home of the man who was the boy she once knew to finally let it go.

She brushed her lips softly against his, and he let out a trembling breath.

"I forgive us, Matty," she whispered. "Can you do the same?"

"*Em*," he whispered, the nickname she told him not to utter again.

But instead of protesting, she answered him with, "Yeah?"

"I...can't have sex with you right now."

She huffed out a laugh. "Geez, Rourke. Can't a girl kiss a guy without an ulterior motive? I didn't come here to seduce you." Yes she did.

He raised his brows. "So you climbed the trellis and broke into my ridiculously impressive apartment above my dad's garage just to kiss me and be on your way?"

She scoffed. "*No.* I climbed the trellis, *shimmied* up the roof, and broke into your ridiculously impressive apartment to kiss you *and* help you study for your exam."

She grabbed his wrist and tugged him toward the bed full of books.

"Emma, seriously, you don't have to—"

"Um, excuse me, but I am only doing this because of the sheer joy I get out of making flash cards. And thanks to *not* having to sit for any sort of exam in quite a few years, I've been deprived of such joy. Are you going to take that away from me?"

"What about the inn?" he countered. "Aren't you guys fully booked?"

She nodded. "Yep, thanks to our gardener friend. And thanks to *my* friend, Haddie, I have the night off." She gave him another tug, but he hesitated.

"Haddie knows where you are?"

Emma nodded triumphantly. "I am fully trusted to make good decisions fully unchaperoned. But maybe don't tell her about the trellis and roof shimmy. Not sure that falls under the good decisions column now that I think of it." She yanked on his hand a *third* time. "Come *on*, Matteo. Grab me a pack of index cards and let me party like it's the early 2010s!"

Matteo shook his head and laughed but did as she said, producing the already-started stack of flash cards he had on his bed.

"Hmmm..." Emma said with a grin. "Looks like some of my better habits stuck with you all these years."

Unable to contain herself, she beamed at him as she climbed onto the bed, crossed her legs, and got to work. She only lost her focus for a millisecond when Matteo sat down across from her and put his tortoise-shell-framed glasses back on.

"You okay?" he asked when he caught her staring.

"Mm-hmm," she lied. Because she wasn't okay. No matter how flippantly she'd blown off his accidental use of that four-letter word this morning, Emma Woods was clearly still in love with the glasses-wearing, final-exam-studying, wild-life-controlling stranger she'd also known most of her life.

So instead of dwelling on what she couldn't control, she focused on what she could.

Flash cards. Studying. Having definitive answers for important questions.

"*American Gothic* is one of the most recognizable paintings in the world. Who painted it?" she asked, a good hour into the quiz portion of the study session.

"Grant Wood," Matteo replied, looking up at her from where his head rested in her lap.

"Where did Van Gogh paint *The Starry Night*?" Emma continued, raising her brows at the answer.

"The Saint Paul Asylum," he responded with a yawn.

Emma looked at her watch. "It's almost eleven," she said. "And you have not gotten an answer wrong yet. Maybe I should head back and let you get some sleep before your exam."

"Not yet," he said, his eyes blinking closed. "Give me a few more."

But when she asked him to name three Chagall paintings produced before 1920, he answered her with a soft snore.

Emma covered her mouth to keep from laughing and tipped her head back against his headboard. Only when she'd regained her composure did she glance back down at the man conked out in her lap.

She pulled his glasses from his face and folded them onto his nightstand. Then she ran her fingers through his hair, listening to him sigh as he seemed to fall deeper into sleep.

He'd sort of already told her something new tonight about his life back then—that he never graduated. So she owed him one in return.

"Okay," Emma started. "Since it's my turn, I'm going to give you a two for one. Something about me back then that's still true now." His chest rose and fell. Rose and fell. So she pushed on. "I loved you, even when you pushed me away. And I'm pretty sure, despite everything, I've loved you ever since. Even now." She let out a shaky breath, but Matteo remained fast asleep.

She *should* go back to the inn. But he had a test tomorrow, and she remembered what he'd said about his insomnia, yet he was sleeping again. With *her*.

She somehow managed to pull her phone from her pocket without jostling him too much and fired off a text to Haddie.

Emma: Back in the morning. Cover for me. We're JUST sleeping.

The three dots denoting Haddie's response appeared immediately.

Haddie: You do you, Ems. JUST sleep. JUST sleep and then some. If you're happy, I'm happy. And yes, I'll cover.

She ended the text with a kissy face emoji, which Emma reciprocated.

Then, thanks to some deft maneuvering, she transferred Matteo's head to a pillow and her body to the barely vacant spot among the books and study materials surrounding them.

She turned to her side and placed her head on the pillow beside his. When she kissed his temple, he rolled to face her, his bleary eyes fluttering half-open.

"You don't have to stay," he whispered groggily, then tucked a lock of her hair behind her ear.

She froze.

"Did you hear…?"

His forehead crinkled between his brows. "Hear what?"

Emma shook her head. "Nothing. Don't worry about it. And I know I don't have to stay," she told him. "But I want to. Is your phone charging and an alarm set?"

He nodded sleepily, and she smiled.

"Hey," she whispered. "Forgot to tell you something pretty cool. The traffic on the Summertown social was thanks to this pretty well-known contemporary artist guy who somehow got ahold of the LED display and shared it in his stories. Said the Gardener is a former student of his! That's super cool, right? We've got a connection to a famous artist right here in Summertown, and we don't even know who it is."

Matteo hummed a soft sigh before his eyes fell closed again.

"Super cool," he mumbled. "Find where he taught, and you might find your vandal."

He laughed, but the laugh morphed into a small snore, and he was out like a light again.

Emma, however, was now wide awake. Why hadn't she thought of that?

Phone in hand, Emma brought up the artist's Instagram account, sighing with relief she hadn't been caught in her admission but wondering if the Gardener had different plans for him or herself.

Wyatt Kim. Where did you teach…? But more important, who *was your student, and why does it feel like they want to be caught?*

Chapter 23

SNEAKING BACK *DOWN* THE TRELLIS AT THE crack of dawn seemed like the only thing for Emma to do rather than wake Matteo or his father *or* run the risk of surprising his father and an overnight guest, if that was the case. She hoped Matteo would sleep until his alarm went off and that he felt refreshed and ready for his exam. She also hoped she could make it back to the inn before the sun was fully up and she had to explain why she was out so early. *Not* that she had anything to be ashamed of. But it took some getting used to, being back in a place where everyone knew everyone and wanted to know every*thing* about you.

Emma strolled past the Dubose house and laughed when she was greeted with the newly replanted topiary dragon's behind at the edge of the property. She came from strange stock. That was for sure. But there was a certain pride to the strangeness of Summertown, a pride the storm could have destroyed. Yet the Gardener, whoever they were, seemed to be infusing that strangeness and pride back into the town.

Her first instinct was to avoid the square and take the long way around when she saw the streetlights go dark and the sun illuminate a figure standing in front of the first sculpture, the sunflowers. At first she thought it was a local simply admiring the art, but then she watched the figure back up and drop down to one knee as they pointed a camera at the once lush tree.

Something raised her hackles and propelled her straight toward Summertown's epicenter.

"Hey!" she called out. "Did Mayor Green put you up to this? Or are you one of the deputy's spies, trying to gather 'evidence'?" She finger quoted the word. "Because if they're not holding up their end of the bargain to…to…cease and desist…" That was intelligent-sounding legal mumbo jumbo, wasn't it? "We had an agreement!"

She was still shouting even though she was a stone's throw from the intruder because whoever this guy was, she'd never seen him in her life. Despite almost a decade away, Emma certainly knew a stranger to Summertown when she saw one.

The guy—probably a few years older than she was—stood and let his camera go slack in its strap around his neck. He brushed his palms on his jeans and then held out a hand as he flashed her a toothy grin.

"Sorry," he said as she reluctantly clasped his offered palm and shook. "We usually like to do our initial photos for the newsletter without disturbing the locals. Which reminds me…the festival committee is still awaiting Summertown's registration. I tried reaching out to the mayor but haven't heard back. Would that have anything to do with the spies you were shouting about?"

Emma's brows furrowed as he dropped her hand and went back to fiddling with his camera. "I'll be out of your hair in a bit," he told her. "Just need to get a couple shots of the meeting hall. Already grabbed the lotus flowers on the entrance sign. Really remarkable. *Not* that I'm passing any official judgment. But the committee *is* looking forward to Summertown shaking things up this year."

Emma stared at him for several long moments. Maybe she was sleep-deprived from going down the rabbit hole of the countless places Wyatt Kim had taught because something wasn't clicking.

"I'm sorry, who did you say you were?" Emma asked.

"Oh! Right!" The stranger laughed. "I didn't actually introduce myself, did I? Sorry. This is only my second year on the committee. Ted McFarland. Commercial horticulturist and newest member of the Twin Town Garden Fest. Born and raised in Middlebrook, but don't hold that against me." He laughed again. "I'm just the surveyor. I don't get to vote."

Emma warily eyed the man who was technically the enemy. "Well, Ted McFarland who doesn't get to vote, do you know who *is* on the voting side of the committee this year?" Every fest boasted a new panel of voters that included varying professors from nearby colleges or universities who specialized in horticulture, floriculture, botany, and the like.

He nodded. "Of course. But so does Mayor Green. He's already received the panel members' names. I've actually reached out to him personally to confirm registration so Middlebrook doesn't win by forfeit. There's no fun in it that way."

She shook her head. "Okay, none of what you're saying is adding up. Everyone in Summertown has been up in arms about will we or won't we be admitted to the fest without actual living sculptures, and you're telling me that it's all a matter of Mayor Green, like, signing some form?"

Ted grinned as if she'd just spelled the final and most difficult word in a spelling bee.

"More or less," he told her. "There is the matter of the entry fee, which goes toward the making of the trophy and also the small stipend we give to the judges, but with the damages Summertown suffered, we've been giving the mayor a bit of extra time to get things in order as we're sure finances are tight."

Emma scoffed. "Right, but he has ten grand to offer up for information on the Gardener."

Ted McFarland's brows furrowed this time. "I'm not following."

"So what *you're* saying is..." She pointed at him. "Summertown qualifies for the competition even though most of our greenery was tossed like a salad?"

"Of course," he told her, as if this was not brand-new information to her and likely anyone else in town who *wasn't* Mayor Green. "The bylaws of the festival clearly state that the entered garden sculptures must be cultivated from their—"

"Basest origin," Emma interrupted, remembering the exact words dripping off the mayor's lips. "And these count?" She gestured to the sunflowers. "And the LEDs and even the lotus flowers? Even though they weren't grown from seeds?"

Ted Shrugged. "The rules are vague for a reason, so we can evolve and adapt. Especially when Mother Nature is against us. The sculptures started as *not* flowers, and through what was evidently a lot of work—especially for that light display—*became* flowers. So, yeah. Summertown is in, but we need confirmation from the mayor by the end of the week."

Emma grabbed the man's hand and shook it vigorously this time.

"Thank you!" she exclaimed. "You might be from...*over there*." She whisper-shouted the last two words out of the side of her mouth. "But you actually don't suck."

He barked out a laugh. "You *are* competitive, aren't you?"

Competitive and ready to give Mayor Green a piece of her mind…or a very sternly worded email. *No.*

She shook her head. She needed to march into his office and *watch* him sign the registration, pay the fee, and whatever else he could have done days ago when the committee initially reached out.

"Are you okay, Ms…"

"Emma!" she blurted out. "Emma Woods. It was lovely meeting you, Ted McFarland. Truly, the best." Since their hands were still clasped, she gave him one more good shake before letting go. "But I have to head home to get reinforcements, and then I need to storm the town hall."

She took off in a slow jog, adrenaline overtaking her lack of sleep, and soon she was running the rest of the way toward the inn. Her lungs were screaming by the time she'd made it to the front door, but thanks to her earlier attempt at trying to fake her running prowess, she had her rescue inhaler in her pocket waiting for an occasion such as this.

It took two good puffs to get her breathing back to normal just so she could break into a sprint up the stairs to Haddie's room once she got back inside.

"What *time* is it?" Haddie groaned the second Emma slammed her door shut. "And *why* are you here at what I know is an ungodly hour even for me?"

Emma looked at her watch and winced. "A little after six, but the sun is up, so that means the day has begun, and there is *so* much to tell you. Also, how do you even know it's *me*?"

Haddie pushed herself up onto her elbows, her sleep mask still fastened securely over her eyes.

"I can sense your presence. Also, you're wheezing."

As if on cue, Pancake poked his head up from beneath Haddie's duvet.

"There's my little fur ball!" Emma exclaimed. "I guess my lungs sensed *his* presence. Also, I just ran home from the square."

She strode toward the bed as Pancake crawled onto Haddie's chest, spun three times, and then settled himself back into a purry little ball.

"By the way, when did you steal my cat?"

"You slept out, remember? I wasn't going to leave the little guy all alone," Haddie retorted. "Also, shhh! It's two to one for staying asleep. So either crawl in next to us, or come back in no less than two hours!"

Emma groaned, but it wasn't as if the town hall offices were open yet, so she did as she was told and kicked off her shoes, then padded to the other side of the bed. She hopped in next to her friend and her cat, propping herself up on her elbow as she scratched Pancake under the chin.

He cracked one eye open, gave her a half-assed meow, and then settled back into kitty dreamland.

"I'm sorry I've been neglecting you, mister," she said softly, switching to a belly rub as he rolled onto his back, stretching all four paws in the air.

"Do you think you could neglect *me* a little more?" Haddie mumbled. "We were up so late with the game-night folks who kept insisting their host—yours truly—join them in another glass of wine. I swear if I never hear 'Colonel Mustard in the library with the candlestick' again or never drink another glass of sparkling rosé, it'll be too soon."

Emma snorted. "Sounds like my dad didn't waste any time getting drunk Clue going again. Did he wear his deerstalker cap?"

"Yes!" Haddie exclaimed. "I know you said he likes his Holmes, but I was not prepared for his level of fandom… *Or* the endless bottles of rosé." She finally slid her eye mask up to her forehead. "So I'm awake now?"

Pancake stretched, stood up, and resituated himself—after spinning three times—in the space between Emma and Haddie.

Emma beamed. "You *do* still love me, Mr. Pancake."

Haddie sighed. "Your fur ball is going to have to take a back seat if you're going to be shtupping your ex."

Emma let loose a combination laugh-sneeze, then rubbed both her eyes that were suddenly itching like crazy.

"Shit. I forgot my nighttime meds because I stayed at Matteo's." She sniffled. "Okay, I'll be brief and then let you go back to sleep for a *little* bit more."

"*Stayed* at Matteo's? Is that what we're calling it now?" Haddie gave her an exaggerated wink.

Emma lovingly kicked her friend's foot. "That's *actually* all I did. I stayed there while he studied for his exam… Did you know he hadn't finished his degree? It makes sense, but I guess I didn't realize everything affected by his arrest. So he's apparently taking a few classes to round out his last semester, and he had an art history final this morning. So I helped him study, he fell asleep, and then I went down a Wyatt Kim rabbit hole."

"A Wyatt *who* what?"

Emma waved her off. "That's not the *point*."

"Oh my god, woman, are you ever going to *make* a point so I don't regret letting you stay?"

"Right!" Emma said, hopping back onto her train of thought. "So I bumped into this guy in the square, Ted from the festival committee—and also Ted from Middlebrook, but apparently he can't vote—who told me that Mayor Green has already been given the green light to enter Summertown into the Twin Town Garden Fest competition based on the Gardener's sculptures, but he's been dragging his feet on signing the paperwork and paying the registration fee! Hads, I think your friend Walter *wants* Summertown to lose."

Haddie bolted upright, her mouth wide open. Then she clamped it shut and rolled her eyes.

"Ems, that has been obvious from almost the get-go. He clearly *hates* the Dr. Seuss trees on his building, the sunflowers, the LEDs. Don't you get it? He *wants* Summertown to lose, and by forfeiting he does it while not having to face You-Know-Who. The man has been living in his ex-wife's shadow for years. The storm was out of his control, but using it to his advantage is not." She leaned back against the headboard and closed her eyes, pausing for a long moment before perking up again. "I have a theory, and if I'm even close to being right, we might truly be fighting a losing battle here."

Emma sneezed again and sighed, then sat up so she was eye level with her friend.

"What do you mean?" she asked.

"I *mean* that it was Colonel Mustard in the library with the candlestick." Haddie laughed. "Mayor Green doesn't just want out because of the storm. He wants *out*. Permanently."

Emma's eyes itched and watered, and she felt another sneeze coming on. She wiggled her nose to try to keep it at bay.

"He wants to wipe the slate clean, which means no more festival." Her smile faltered. "*Ever*."

Haddie sighed. "Exactly. And right when he thought he had the bull by the tail with this whole vandal-slash-artist situation, you went and rained on his parade."

"What?" Emma scoffed. "I mean, *maybe*. But why should Summertown have to pay for his dignity?" Emma was one to talk. Hadn't she made Summertown—and the people she loved, like her parents—pay for *her* broken heart by staying away so long? "Also," she added. "That doesn't give him the right to turn the Gardener into a criminal when they actually saved Summertown from financial ruin during our biggest tourist season."

Haddie patted her friend on the head. "I know, I know."

"Um, I'm not a first grader who needs to be patronized, thank you very much." Emma crossed her arms with a pout and a sneeze.

Haddie laughed. "No, but it's really hard to take you seriously when *Achoo!* has basically solidified itself as part of your vocabulary. *Which,* I might add, is *very* first-grader of you."

Emma swiped at the allergy-induced tears leaking from her eyes, then groaned as she only made them itch more thanks to Pancake's dander.

"I am going to go load up on the meds, shower, and throw back a cup of coffee or seven. Then we are heading down to the town hall as soon as the doors open to make sure Walter Green dots all his *i*'s and crosses all his *t*'s to enter Summertown into the twentieth-anniversary Twin Town Garden Fest."

Emma gave Pancake one last belly rub, climbed out of the bed, and sneezed three times in a row.

"And what about this Wyatt Kim person you mentioned before?" Haddie asked.

"One mystery at a time," Emma replied, then sneezed again. "We deal with the mayor first, and then I find my gardener."

Haddie's brows rose. "*My* gardener, huh? Are we forming an attachment to our vandal, Ms. Felicity Smoak?"

She was forming an attachment to Matteo *Rourke*.

"Let's just say I need a mission to focus on to keep my mind off things I'm not ready to focus on yet."

Haddie nodded, still smiling, but Emma swore she saw a hint of sadness in her eyes.

"You know I'm here if there's anything you need to talk about or process, right?" Haddie asked. "And that I support whatever makes you happy?"

"Of course," Emma said. "I know that." She punctuated the moment with yet another sneeze.

"Oh my god, *go*," Haddie ordered. "Or I'm going to drop Pancake at the nearest rescue shelter."

Emma gasped. "Don't you *dare*! My immune system and I have an arrangement. As long as I hold up my end of the bargain with medication, I get to continue living with my furry soul mate." She stared down at Pancake who was blissfully unaware. "Don't you let Auntie Haddie take you for any rides in the country," she warned him. "You dig your claws into that duvet if you have to and hold on for dear life until Mama gets back, okay?"

Haddie threw a pillow at her, which Emma caught against her chest.

"You truly need to get out more," Haddie teased.

"I know," Emma admitted. "Next stop, the office of the illustrious—and still brokenhearted—Mayor Green."

And then, once again, she sneezed.

Chapter 24

It was early afternoon when Matteo returned home after his exam. He'd expected to feel drained, exhausted, or the need to face-plant straight into the pillows on his bed, but instead he found a surprising pep in his step as he strode up the driveway and headed for the door.

Again he'd slept through the night with Emma Woods beside him.

How had he not scared her away yet, especially when he'd responded to her romantic gesture by almost slamming her against the wall.

He closed his eyes and shook his head as he gripped the front door handle.

It had only taken the first of his six months in county to teach him to hit first, apologize later… or not at all. That sort of survival mode remained burned into his psyche, no matter how long it had been.

He blinked his eyes open and blew out a long breath. He hadn't hurt her, physically at least.

"Dad?" he called, finally stepping into the house. "We get any appointments this morning?"

But instead of his father's booming voice in response, Matteo was greeted with nothing but silence.

"Hellooo?" Matteo called again.

Still nothing.

He made his way into the kitchen and set his phone and keys on the counter, realizing his phone was still powered off from his exam.

He turned it on, his pulse quickening as he saw he'd missed several texts and calls.

He ignored the texts and went right to his voicemail.

"Teo, it's me," his father began in the first message. "Something's not right. I can't get out of bed. If you can come home as soon as you're done with your test, I think I might need to go to urgent care."

"Shit," Matteo hissed. "Where are you, Dad?"

He hit Play on the second one. "Teo..." He could hear the panic in his father's voice. "I–I can't feel my right leg. I don't want you to worry, but I think I might have to call 911."

His throat felt like it was closing, and it was getting harder to breathe. He wasn't sure he wanted to press Play on the third and final voicemail because whatever message was on the other end, it couldn't be good.

He held his breath, already light-headed from

the oxygen seemingly disappearing from the room, and tapped the blue triangle.

"Hi, Matteo," a woman's voice began, and Matteo's knees buckled. He slammed his palms onto the counter for purchase and forced himself to keep listening. "It's Tilly Higginson," she continued. "I was able to get your dad into my car and drive him to the hospital. They've got him on medication and in traction, but it looks like this herniated disc situation is causing so much pressure on the nerve that he's losing feeling in his right side below the waist. His GP is coordinating with the spinal surgeon to get him in the OR as soon as possible, but he may be stuck like this for a day or two before they can operate. I know he'd like to talk to you before anything happens, but I just want to warn you that he's pretty doped up right now, so he's not making a ton of sense when he's awake. Anyway, he's in room number..."

Matteo was already back out the door and heading to his truck.

He didn't remember pulling out of his driveway or exiting the town limits. All he knew was that his father needed him, and he hadn't been there. So as soon as he was on the interstate, he put the pedal to the floor and just drove.

Until blue and red lights flashed behind him less than a mile before the hospital exit.

"Dammit," he growled and for a few seconds kept

his foot on the gas, but the patrol vehicle was picking up speed, gaining on him, and he knew if he did anything that looked like an evasive maneuver that he'd be in deep shit, so he pulled onto the shoulder and came to a stop. He slammed his palms against the steering wheel and banged his head against the back of his seat before lowering his window and waiting for the officer to approach.

"Going a little fast, weren't you," a low, male voice chided as the officer placed his hands on the window frame and dipped his head into view.

"Fucking hell," Matteo growled. "You've got to be kidding me."

"Good afternoon to you too, Rourke," Deputy Dawson Hayes replied with a grin. "I clocked you at twenty-five miles over the speed limit. Ten more miles, and that's a Class A misdemeanor. Could cost you another year, maybe more if you already have a record."

"Fine, Hayes. You win." Matteo thrust his hands out the window, wrists up. "You want to cuff me? Then cuff me already. Just do me a favor and call over to Grand Valley and let my father know I won't be showing up for his goddamned spinal surgery because of your hell-bent agenda to get me back behind bars."

The deputy stood and backed away from the car.

"Step outside the vehicle, Mr. Rourke," Deputy Hayes commanded.

Matteo shook his head and huffed out a bitter laugh. Because why would the universe work in any way other than this? He didn't deserve Emma's help last night or the confidence of having aced his exam today. Of course he had to be taken down a peg, and who better to do it than Deputy Dawson Hayes?

"Faster, Rourke," the deputy added. "We don't have all day."

Matteo clenched his jaw, turned off the truck, and pulled the key from the ignition. He threw open the door and, despite his sunglasses, squinted at the glare of the sun. When his eyes adjusted, he saw the deputy nod his head toward the Sheriff's Department SUV.

"Get in," Dawson said.

Piss off, Matteo thought, but strode toward the driver's side of the vehicle, stopping at the door to the back seat.

"The *passenger* side, Rourke," the deputy added with a groan. "The *front* seat."

Matteo spun back to face his rival, his brows furrowed behind his aviators.

"I'm not arresting you...*yet,*" Hayes told him. "Now, can you just get in the damned car and stop wasting our time?"

Matteo walked around the vehicle in a confused haze and climbed into the empty passenger seat.

The deputy hopped behind the wheel and

powered up the vehicle. Then he stared at Matteo from behind his own mirrored lenses.

"I can't let you drive in the state you're in because you obviously aren't making good decisions. But I can do this..." Deputy Hayes threw on both the lights and his siren and launched the SUV back onto the road.

Matteo was too stunned and confused to respond until the deputy sped onto the exit for Grand Valley Hospital and Medical Center.

"You're taking me to the hospital?" Matteo asked, still not sure he was reading the situation correctly.

"Perceptive," was all the deputy said as he plowed through the red light and onto the street that led to their destination.

"And you're *not* arresting me," Matteo added, this time a statement rather than a question.

Dawson's jaw pulsed before he answered. "I really want a reason to," he admitted. "But there's no fun in winning by default. Plus..." He sighed as they pulled into the drop-off lane at the hospital's main entrance. "Your dad's a good guy. My beef isn't with *him*."

The vehicle jerked into park, and Matteo pivoted to face his driver.

"You don't deserve her," Deputy Hayes said, still staring out the windshield.

"Maybe not," Matteo admitted. "But maybe I do. Either way, forcing me out of the picture isn't going to change how she feels if she does for some inexplicable reason still care about me."

The deputy nodded. "Doesn't mean it wouldn't be enjoyable for *me*," he said with a bitter laugh, then finally turned his head toward Matteo. "Now get the hell out before I change my mind about taking the high road." He nodded toward the door.

"Thank you, Hayes. You're not a *total* asshole."

Dawson huffed out a laugh and shook his head. "Can I ask you something?"

Matteo checked the time on his phone. "I'm kind of in a hurry."

The deputy nodded. "I just want to make sure that you know the statute of limitations for litigation due to wrongful arrest ran out six years ago."

"Your point is?" Matteo had his hand on the door, ready to pop it open.

Dawson shrugged. "I know that woman is poking around the case. You did your time, Rourke. Why not let it be?"

Matteo's jaw tightened. "Because I'm not the guy everyone thinks I am. And I'm going to prove it." He didn't wait for the other man to respond before exiting the vehicle and sprinting inside.

Matteo startled awake and for several seconds had no idea where he was. Then his father's hospital bed came into focus, the older man still sleeping while somehow strapped into the traction apparatus that kept his legs elevated and the pressure off of his spine.

He pressed the heels of his hands to his eyes and heard a quiet whooshing sound as the hospital-room door brushed over the tile. He glanced up to find Emma pushing her way through with her shoulder on the door and a to-go coffee cup in each hand.

He rose to greet her and lighten her load. Then he nodded for them to head back the way she came so they wouldn't wake his dad.

She somehow understood and pivoted back toward the hallway, leading him toward the waiting area before he had a chance to give her a free hand.

"Here," she finally said when they made it to the small nook that boasted three chairs, a love seat, and a television tuned to a game show network that was playing *The Price Is Right*. "An Americano with an extra shot."

He scratched at the stubble on his jaw as he accepted the offering. "You remember?"

She smiled nervously and nodded. "Of course I do."

It was a small gesture, one most people would take for granted. Not him. Not anymore. Not when it meant she still cared.

A reassuring warmth bloomed inside him, and he felt an invisible tether pulling him closer to her, like a sunflower grew toward the sun.

She lowered herself onto the love seat, and he backed toward the chair that was kitty-corner to it.

"Sit next to me?" She patted the spot beside her, and Matteo caught himself mid-sit, straightening back to his full height.

"Um...yeah. Sure." He sat down beside her and knocked his knee against hers.

Emma smiled, and despite the turn of events that afternoon, everything inside him felt like it was glowing.

"I feel really underdressed," he admitted, noting his T-shirt and jeans. "You look beautiful, by the way."

"Oh, this old thing?" she asked, her cheeks turning pink as she glanced down at the red sundress that lay softly against her curves. "It's Haddie's. I had to pin the straps to make it fit my significantly shorter torso."

He took a sip of his coffee and sighed. "How did you know this was exactly what I needed? And how did you know I was even here?"

She tapped her knee against his again. "Dawson told me. I came as soon as he did."

"You know, that guy is making it really hard for me to keep thinking he's a dick."

Emma laughed, and Matteo let his head fall against the wall behind the love seat. "I thought I dreamed you were in the room with me, but it was real, wasn't it?"

She nodded and looked up at him, skimming her fingers along his temple. "Even after sleeping through the night, you must be so drained after your exam and then coming home to find out about your dad. You dozed off pretty soon after I got here."

He pressed his cheek into her palm, then tilted his head to press a kiss into it.

"Thank you," he told her, then dipped his head to brush his lips against hers. "Thank you," he whispered against her.

He straightened and cleared his throat.

Emma slid her free hand onto his and threaded their fingers together. She gave him a soft squeeze.

"Seems to me like you have a lot of lost sleep to catch up on," she told him. "I'm just happy I can help."

Tilly Higginson materialized from around the corner and smiled at Emma and Matteo.

"Your father's awake," she said. "And the surgeon is in the room to discuss next steps."

Matteo shot to his feet, inadvertently pulling Emma up with him, their hands still entwined.

"You'll come too, right?" he asked.

Emma nodded. "Whatever you need."

Whatever you need?

Matteo needed to understand why, after already experiencing the devastating loss of one parent, he might have to go through it again just shy of his thirtieth birthday.

He needed to understand why Deputy Hayes had helped him when he could have so easily used the law against him, especially knowing his record. And why he cared whether or not a reporter found the truth to Matteo's story.

And he needed to understand why Emma Woods was standing beside him, her hand in his, after all he'd put her through. Had he finally forgiven himself? Did she really bear the responsibility of it all with him?

He didn't know. All he could do was put one foot in front of the other, the same thing he'd been doing for the past eight years, and hope he came out the other side.

Tilly opened the door for Matteo and let him and Emma inside before following behind them.

"Teo!" his father exclaimed. "How was your exam?" He turned his attention to the doctor. "Dr. Geiger, this is my son, Matteo. Smartest kid I know who's about to become a college graduate."

Matteo let Emma's hand go so he could shake the doctor's.

"Matteo Rourke," he said with a nervous laugh. "I think you might need to dial his medication back a notch because it sounds like he forgot about his other son who already *is* a college grad."

"I can be proud of both my boys, can't I, Doc?" his father added.

"Nice to meet you, Mr. Rourke," the doctor

said to Matteo, then turned back to her patient. "Absolutely, Denny. But let's talk about how we can get you out of that bed and back home *with* your boys as soon as we can."

Matteo crossed his arms and stared down at his dad. "Is Levi coming home?"

His father waved him off. "He's hosting two different camps this summer for his players. I don't want to worry him."

Matteo sighed. This was not the time to play the comparison game between himself and his older brother. "Fine. So what's the story with you and what looks like is now unavoidable surgery?"

He glanced from his father to the doctor.

"Using traction, we've been able to relieve the pressure enough from the slipped disc that was causing the numbness, but the other disc is dangerously close to the nerve, and permanent traction really isn't an option. I'm recommending spinal fusion to eliminate movement between the vertebrae where the discs are bulging. With time and physical therapy, your father should be able to return to full mobility."

Matteo nodded slowly. "I hope you don't take this the wrong way, but...you *have* performed this procedure before, right?"

Emma backhanded him on the ribs. "*Matteo!*"

Dr. Geiger laughed. "It's okay. I get that a lot. I'll chalk it up to good genes. But I performed fusions dozens of times during my residency and probably twice as much since then. Counting my residency, I've been doing this for almost a decade, and I promise your father is in good hands. But I can provide patient references for you if that makes you feel better. You're also entitled to a second opinion, should you choose to go that route."

"No," Denny Rourke replied. Tilly Higginson stood beside his bed, his palm sandwiched between both of hers. "I'm fifty-five years old and otherwise healthy as an ox. I want to get back to work. I want to live my life so you can get back to living yours, Son. The sooner I'm out of this bed, the better."

"Well," Dr. Geiger began before Matteo could reply. "It's not an outpatient procedure. You'll be here for several days following and then might have to spend a few more in a rehabilitation facility before we give you the all clear to head home. After that it will be months of physical therapy to slowly get you back to full mobility. So no matter what you decide, it's a long road ahead." She nodded toward Matteo's dad and then at him. "I'll give you some time alone to discuss. Just have one of the nurses page me when you're ready to discuss next steps, whether they involve me or not."

She shook Denny Rourke's hand and then Matteo's. "It was nice to meet you, Mr. Rourke. I'm looking forward to seeing your father up and about again soon."

"Thank you, Dr. Geiger," Matteo replied, and then she left the four of them alone to make their decision.

Emma pressed her palm to the small of Matteo's back, and he blew out a shaky breath.

"Nothing to discuss, Teo," his father began. "I want out of this damned bed, and I don't want to waste a single second hemming and hawing over who's going to cut me open because my mind is already set on Dr. Geiger."

"But, Dad—"

"No 'But, Dad!'" his father exclaimed. "Look at me, Son. I'm a damned prisoner in this bed. Right when I decide to start living again instead of cocooning myself in my safe, *lonely* little world, I'm stuck."

Emma cleared her throat. "Um, excuse me for a minute. I just have to..."

She didn't finish the thought but instead pivoted on her heel and barreled through the door as the three of them watched her go.

"I'm going to give you boys a few minutes," Tilly told them. She kissed his father on the forehead and then rounded the foot of the bed. She squeezed Matteo's forearm. "And I'll check and make sure she's okay." Then she followed Emma through the door.

Matteo slowly paced at the foot of his father's hospital bed.

"Matteo," his father said softly, but Matteo kept at it. "*Teo,*" he called again.

After a few more paces back and forth, Matteo finally stopped and faced his dad. He braced his hands on the foot of the bed, hung his head, and sighed. Finally, he met his father's eyes.

"You want me to say it, Dad? Fine. I'll say it. I'm scared, okay?"

"I know, Teo. I am too."

Matteo strode around to the chair on the side of the bed where he'd been dozing earlier. He sat.

"I'm not just talking about the surgery," he admitted.

His father used the button on the mechanical bed to raise himself to almost sitting. "What do you mean?" he asked his son.

Matteo scrubbed a hand across his jaw. "I want you to be happy, Dad. I do. But I already feel like I'm forgetting, you know? Mom's smile. The sound of her voice. The smell of her perfume…"

"Or the smell in the kitchen when she somehow managed to burn eggs," his father added.

Both men laughed.

"See?" Denny Rourke said. "She's still with us. And she always will be. Just like I will always love her. But that doesn't mean I should put that part of my life on the back burner. I did for a lot of years, and it only made me lonelier. Made me miss her more. With Tilly I don't have to pretend she didn't exist because she knew your mom. They were friends. We can talk about her and remember her... keep her spirit alive."

Matteo nodded. "I know. Logically, I *know* that all of this makes sense. But..." He sighed.

"But maybe *we* should have talked about her more over the years," his father admitted. "If I hadn't tiptoed around you when you first came home... God, Teo. What it must have been like for you to have to grieve by yourself!" His father's voice cracked. "I'm going to do better with you once I get through this. You'll see."

Matteo leaned forward and rested his elbows on the side of the bed.

"Just get through this, Dad. That's all I need."

Denny Rourke nodded and grabbed his son's hand. "Deal," he said.

"I'll hold you to it."

Chapter 25

Matteo found Emma in the lobby a few minutes after Tilly headed back up to Denny's room. He sat down in the chair next to her, which wasn't as intimate as the love seat upstairs, but she still appreciated the nearness of him. Even if they weren't touching.

"You could have come back up with Tilly if you wanted to visit longer. I know my dad and Mrs. Higginson are kind of a thing right now, but deep down I know he's always had a crush on you."

Emma's cheeks warmed and she laughed, her eyes dropping to her coffee cup.

"You…um…you didn't leave because of what my dad said, did you?" he asked.

Emma's head shot up. "What? *No.* I mean… What?"

Matteo shrugged. "I don't know. He just said that thing about cocooning himself into his safe little world, and it seemed like it triggered something for you."

Emma's stomach tied itself into a hundred knots.

"Is it too late for me to make up some elaborate lie about leaving because I had to pee really badly or had contracted coffee-induced food poisoning?"

He laughed. "I'll buy whatever story you're selling as long as you're okay."

She waved him off. "I'm fine. You have enough to worry about with your dad."

He pulled the coffee cup from her hand and shook it, seemingly having guessed it was empty. So he set it on the table on the far end of her chair.

"I can still worry about you too," he told her. "It's called multitasking."

Emma let out a weak scoff and nudged his shoulder with her own.

"Don't be funny and charming when I'm at an emotional crossroads," she said.

He held his hands in the air. "Any humor or charm I may give off is purely by accident, I promise."

She narrowed her eyes at him. "*That!*" she exclaimed. "That, what you just said, is humorous and charming. *Stop. It.*"

He pantomimed zipping his lips, then leaned back against the side of his chair and crossed his arms over his chest.

She shook her head and laughed again, then blew out a long breath.

"I'm scared, okay? Of how I feel about you after all these years," Emma admitted. "I'm scared that you don't feel the same way, and I'm also scared that you *do*. Because there is no winning here. If we fall for each other again, it's going to hurt like hell to leave and go back to Chicago. And if *I* fall all by myself? Well, then I guess that's just the universe telling me to get back in my damned cocoon and play it safe for the rest of time."

Okay, then. Talk about ripping off the Band-Aid. She'd all but confessed that he was it for her. Getting her heart broken once by him was devastating, but she'd survived. Only after seeing Matteo again, though, did she realize that surviving was all she'd truly been doing for the past eight years, and she wanted to start *living* again. But that meant commitment to whatever was happening between them now. It meant figuring out what came next at the end of the summer. And it meant letting them both tell their stories of the past eight years—reopening and reliving their painful past to understand it better.

He pantomimed *un*zipping his lips. "May I speak if I actively try to be neither funny nor charming?"

Emma laughed, realizing that even after all this time apart, Matteo not only knew when she needed to smile but could say just the right words to get her to do it. "Good luck with that one, multitasker," she told him.

"So, I just talked to my dad like I've never talked to him before. It was…weird, I guess? But in a good way."

"How?" Emma asked.

He ran a hand through his already tousled ginger hair, evidence—Emma guessed—of the compounding stress of his day. She felt the need to smooth it, or maybe it was just an excuse to touch him. But instead she simply listened.

"I think we both just realized that we've kind of been living parallel lives since we lost my mom. You and my dad aren't the only ones who know how to barricade themselves behind some super-safe, super-high walls. It's so much easier to play it safe after loss so we don't lose any more."

Safe was *so* much easier. Emma felt like she'd already stepped so far outside her comfort zone with Matteo, and it was terrifying.

"I'm scared too," Matteo continued. "Which is not something I've been able to admit out loud before. Scared for what's going to happen with my dad if he has this surgery that he's already decided he's having. Scared for what it means if his surgery is a success, and he no longer needs me to run the business. Then what? I have to figure out what *I* want when most people my age already have it all figured out. I'd accepted living in limbo a long time ago, Emma. But seeing you again makes me want what I don't feel I deserve."

Emma opened her mouth to say something, but she wasn't sure what. She couldn't assuage any of his fears any better than she could her own.

"Thank you for telling me all that," she told him instead. "Does this mean other people on the cusp of thirty *don't* have it all figured out, or are we the anomalies?"

He laughed. "My dad is fifty-five, and I don't think he has much more of a clue than we do. I think it's just about taking the next leap and hoping we land on our feet...or that someone we trust is at least there to catch us if we fall."

Emma groaned. "Great. So this adulting thing just keeps getting harder? Why the heck were we in such a rush when we were kids to get here?"

Matteo slid his hand behind her neck and wrapped his arm around her.

She sucked in a breath at first, then relaxed, letting her head fall against his shoulder.

"See?" he said. "I was terrified to do that just now, but I took the leap, and it paid off."

She laughed. "When did you get so wise?"

He kissed the top of her head. "Don't worry. I'm still riding high after this great and unexpected study session I had last night with an equally great and unexpected—also kind of sexy—study partner. I'm sure I'll do something really stupid in the not-too-distant future. Speaking of sexy, I didn't get the chance to ask what the special occasion was for the dress. I'd like to think it was for me, but I know neither of us had a trip to the hospital on our agenda toady."

She straightened and turned to face him, her spirit brightening after the events of the morning.

"Right! I forgot to tell you! Haddie and I met with the mayor. We're in! Summertown is officially *in* for the Twin Town Garden Fest. Mayor Green is not thrilled…for reasons I'll let him break to the public himself. But he signed the registration papers and sent in the fee, and we are set!"

Matteo's eyes widened. "And…the Gardener's sculptures count as part of the town's entry?"

Emma nodded, a smile spreading across her face. "Yes! They absolutely count! But…" Her voice trailed off, her smile fading.

Matteo crossed his arms. "Of course there's a *but*. Mayor Green has it in for this gardener person for whatever reason, doesn't he?"

"No." Emma shook her head. "I mean, yes, he does, but the *but* isn't because of him. Turns out there has to be a name attached to the sculptures with our entry. In years past, Lottie Green was always the designer listed for Summertown's entry. Even though many of our residents cultivate their own gardens—like my parents do for the inn—the overall design was always attributed to Lottie. If she's stricken from this year's entry, which according to the mayor she most definitely is, we need a designer's name for Summertown. The committee has accepted our entry, but we need to submit the designer's name by the end of the week. Basically, before close of business on Friday." She cleared her throat. "So, I'm just going to reach out to the Gardener on social media and tell them the good news and hope they don't disappear altogether. Yay!" She forced a smile and added a final flourish of jazz hands, but Matteo didn't share her sentiment.

"So thanks to this development, the mayor gets his way whether we win or lose."

Emma nodded slowly. "But if we win, do you really think he'd prosecute the Gardener after all they've done for the town? I mean, we're still a few weeks away from the contest, and we've already got a booked inn; retail business is up in the square; and Haddie's even taken on giving tours of the sculptures for an extra fee added to the inn's room rate. How anyone can call all the good that's come of this 'vandalism' is ridiculous." She pulled out her phone and opened up Summertown's Instagram profile. "I'm just going to message the Gardener and lay it all out, and if they don't want to come forward then...I don't know...I guess I'll say *I'm* the Gardener if I have to."

"*No!*" Matteo snapped.

Emma flinched.

"I'm sorry," he continued. "I didn't mean to scare you, but Emma... *No*. I'm drawing the line here."

She scoffed and sprung out of her seat. "*I'm* sorry, but what right do you have to draw the line on what I do or don't do? I make my own decisions, Matteo.

You lost the right to weigh in *eight* years ago." She gasped and covered her mouth, but it was too late. Those last words were out, and she couldn't take them back.

"It's okay," Matteo told her, reading her mind. "I deserved that." He pushed himself up from his seat as well. "I'm actually glad to finally see you react directly to what you won't let us talk about. But shit, Emma. I may not have the right, but that doesn't mean I'm going to sit by and watch you put your neck on the line for someone who might not do the same for you."

She squared her shoulders and jutted her chin out. "Hasn't the Gardener already done just that for the entire town?"

"*Emma*...Mayor Green already threatened to loop anyone in who might be the Gardener's accomplice. What do you think he'll do if he finds out the woman who took him down a peg in front of the entire town is the one behind all of the 'vandalism' in the first place? You have a life and a career. Are you going to jeopardize that for some stupid small-town garden show?"

Emma replied without hesitation. "Yes!" she exclaimed. "You're the one who just said we should start taking the next leap and hoping we land on our feet. With every new sculpture, the Gardener risks getting caught. But they're taking the leap. This is *my* chance to take the leap, Matteo, for everyone in this town who needs this win—Mayor Green included. He's *not* going to arrest the Gardener."

"How do you know?"

She threw her hands in the air. "I don't. But I'm coming out of the cocoon. And you know what? It feels good." She groaned. "I honestly don't know why we are fighting about this, and I'd really love to, like, storm out of here and make you think about how unreasonable you're being, but I know you need a ride to your truck, so..."

"Right. My truck." He sighed. "Thanks. I appreciate the ride."

It was a short enough ride, but the trip felt interminable thanks to the silence stretching out between them. Emma had to do a U-turn in the middle of the interstate, which was easy enough thanks to the lack of traffic. Such a huge change from Chicago.

She pulled onto the shoulder and came to a stop behind Matteo's truck.

"Did your dad set a date for the surgery?" she asked, grasping at whatever she could so they didn't end the day with anger.

He nodded, still staring out the windshield. "Friday. Looks like your artist and I both have a deadline to contend with." He turned to face her. "Promise me you won't do anything stupid, Emma."

"I'm an intelligent woman," she told him, brows raised. "That alone should be enough for you to trust that I'll do what's best for me."

He let out a bitter laugh. "Says the same woman who asked her best friend to chaperone her so she didn't wind up in bed with her ex, and look how that worked out."

She banged her head lightly against the steering wheel and groaned. "Why does it feel like one step forward, two steps back?"

He shook his head. "I don't know."

She gripped the wheel even harder, her knuckles turning white.

"Will you at least look at me?" he asked.

She blew out a shaky breath, knowing that as intelligent as she was, she still didn't know if she could trust her judgment when it came to Matteo Rourke.

"*Em...*" he insisted, and she finally let her hands fall to her lap as she pivoted to meet his gaze.

"Maybe..." she started, her throat tight. "Maybe we *should* take a step back for a bit. You have your dad to focus on, and I have a decision to make based on the response I get from our artist." She put a hand on his knee and gave him a gentle squeeze. "I don't want to fight with you, Matteo."

He nodded, then leaned over the center console, cupping her cheeks in his palms.

"I don't want to fight with you either," he whispered, then kissed her softly, his lips lingering on hers for a long moment before he pulled away. "Do you think that maybe before you offer yourself as tribute to the mayor, you might be able to pop by the hospital on Friday? Surgery is supposed to begin at 8:00 a.m. and will last four to six hours. Tilly will be there, of course, but I wouldn't say no to another friendly face."

"Of course," she said. "No matter what happens between us as an *us*..." She motioned between them. "I'll always be there as your friend if you'll let me." She smiled. "That was a really good step, you know...asking for support."

One corner of his mouth turned up as he smiled back at her with the crooked grin she'd never grow tired of. "Look at me taking a tiny little leap of my own! Guess I can't be the wise one if I don't take my own advice, huh?" He grabbed the handle and pushed the passenger door open. "Thanks for the ride, Em. And for showing up last night and again today. The hard parts are a little less hard when you're there."

He climbed out and closed the door before she could muster a response.

Did they just break up after admitting they were falling for each other again? Were they even officially together?

Emma pressed her hand to her chest and realized

neither she nor her heart was crumbling into a thousand tiny, irreparable fragments. So she and Matteo had taken two steps back, but Emma had also taken her first leap by confessing her feelings, and she'd survived it.

Well…one good leap deserved another.

She opened her Instagram app again and went to her message with *@summergardener.* She could see that he was logged on, which meant he'd likely see her message the second she sent it.

Emma took a steadying breath and then began to type.

> Hey...so...new development. The contest committee needs someone's name to put on the sculpture designs. By Friday. Any chance you're willing to come forward regardless of the wager?

The word *Seen* appeared below her message almost immediately. Emma held her breath as *@summergardener* typed.

> Is Mayor Green offering punitive immunity?

Then they added a GIF of Dwight Schrute from *The Office* with the caption, *The worst thing you can do for your immune system is to coddle it.*

She snort-laughed remembering Matteo's

relentless teasing back in high school when she admitted her crush on Dwight.

"He's a sociopath," Matteo had insisted during one of their weekend meetups in college where they'd order in and binge her favorite show. "You have the hots for a sociopath. I'm not sure what that says about me."

She'd shrugged and then kissed him. "Just means I'll still love you even if you conduct a safety drill by trapping me in my dorm room after setting a garbage fire in the hall."

He'd bought her a Dwight T-shirt that Christmas, one she'd packed away since then but hadn't had the heart to get rid of.

She stared at the GIF, and a rush of goose bumps raised the fine hair on her arms. Then she scoffed and shook her head, clearing it of the nonsensical thoughts beginning to form.

> No promises. But if what you're doing really is for the town, don't you want the credit?

Again the word *Seen* popped up on her screen, so she waited once more with bated breath. But after several seconds that turned into one minute, then two and three, Emma realized a response wasn't coming.

So that was it, then? The Gardener was simply going to bail.

It wasn't until Thursday evening when Emma and Haddie were splitting a pint of Salted Caramel Pretzel Crunch ice cream at Sweet that *@summer-gardener* popped onto her radar again.

Chapter 26

Emma and Haddie sat at a table, laptop to laptop, idly dipping their spoons into the shared pint, surrounded by pink and while shelves lined with ready-to-go gift boxes of Mrs. Pinkney's homemade chocolates.

"When I die," Haddie started, "please bury me in a vat of this ice cream because I'm going to spend eternity with it."

"Mm-hmm..." Emma said absently. "Sure. Just put it in your will." She was back in the Wyatt Kim rabbit hole, trying to find the connection between him and the Gardener, but she couldn't find a single thing tying him to Summertown or anyone in the town.

"And then I want you to dance on my ice-cream-filled grave," Haddie continued.

Emma nodded. "Totally. All the dancing," she replied.

Haddie stood and bent down over Emma's side of the table, shoving her head between Emma's and her screen.

Emma jumped back and yelped, her chair screeching against the tiled floor.

"Hellooooo? Anyone there? Or are you perfectly lucid and actually planning to dance on my grave when I die?"

"What?" Emma's eyes widened. "You're dying? When? Why?"

Haddie groaned and sat back down. "I thought our night off was a night *off*. Why don't you just slide into this Wyatt Kim guy's DMs and *ask* him how he knows the Gardener?"

Emma picked up her phone and opened her Instagram DMs before brandishing the screen full of unanswered DMs she'd already sent Wyatt Kim.

"Oh," Haddie said, her shoulders slumping. "So what's the story, then? You're going to unmask the Gardener without their consent so Summertown can enter this contest?"

Emma's eyes widened. "What? No! Of course not. I'd never..." She sighed. "The Gardener is scared of something, right? They have to be or else they'd have come forward already. Maybe they don't trust me enough to tell me the truth, but if I find out the truth on my own and *don't* turn them in, then they'll see I'm someone they can trust. *And* maybe I'll understand their anonymity. It's a win-win. Sort of..."

Emma reached for her spoon sticking out of the pint, but Haddie grabbed the entire thing and held it to her chest.

"Or maybe this is your way of avoiding dealing with your feelings for Matteo and the fact that he's actually respecting your time off."

"You know, withholding ice cream from a friend in need is just cruel."

Haddie shrugged. "Cruelty? Tough love? I say potato, you say po-tah-to."

Emma pouted. "I'm seeing Matteo tomorrow. I told him I'd be there for his dad's surgery, and I'm a woman of my word."

"But...?" Haddie asked, taunting Emma by shoving a giant spoonful of ice cream into her own mouth.

Emma tried shooting lasers at her friend from her eyes, but Haddie just sat back and enjoyed her ice cream. No, *their* ice cream.

"I don't know. He respected my wishes, so it's completely illogical for me to be disappointed that he hasn't tried to text or see me. Unless..."

"Unless...?" Haddie asked.

Emma groaned. "Unless I scared him away by telling him I loved him while he was sleeping?"

Haddie gasped. "After he told *you* in the attic?"

Emma gasped. "How did you know about that?"

"How did you not tell me?" Haddie retorted.

"Because he didn't *mean* it. He just got caught up in the moment. He admitted it!"

Haddie narrowed her eyes and pointed at Emma with a dripping, chocolaty spoon.

"Was it after *you* suggested as much?"

Emma's mouth fell open. Then her stomach clenched, and her heart began beating erratically.

"So he *loves* me?" she asked, incredulous.

"Yeah. Surprise, Ems. You're in love. So whether or not you're taking a step back doesn't matter. He loves you. You love him. It's a whole thing."

Haddie handed her the pint of ice cream, which Emma snatched away willingly.

Mrs. Pinkney appeared behind the candy counter from where she'd been closing up shop in the back room.

"Can I get you girls anything else before I lock the cooler?" she asked, her white hair shining like silver in the bright lights.

Haddie swooped her long arm across the table and stole the pint back. "How many of these are there in existence?" she asked. "And can I start some sort of layaway plan to ensure that all of them go to me?"

The older woman laughed and waved Haddie off. "As long as I'm still kicking, I can always make more. Thank goodness for folks like you who keep coming 'round and gobbling up what I make. Keeps me young. And thank goodness my store fared better than my house." She shook her head. "Though I may be able to leave the inn sooner than I thought now that Matteo's repaired the roof and the broken porch step."

Emma's eyes widened. "He's been doing work on your house?"

Mrs. Pinkney nodded. "Mine, Harmony's. I think he helped replant that dragon behind as well." She laughed. "And of course the work he does at Wilton's Farm. Sad what happened to that boy after his mama passed, but it sure is good to have him back in town."

Emma swallowed. She knew Matteo didn't see himself in the same light Mrs. Pinkney saw him, but whether or not he believed it, he was beloved by Summertown. He *belonged* in Summertown. Emma felt like she was straddling two different lives, both of which were important parts of her identity. So where did *she* belong?

"Um, Mrs. Pinkney?" Emma cleared her throat. "Speaking of staying young. Does Old Man… I mean, does *Mr.* Wilton deserve some credit for that?"

Mrs. Pinkney answered with a flutter of a laugh. "Oh my. I suppose there is no privacy in a town like ours, is there? Yes, yes. I suppose Andrew is courtin' me these days."

Emma's mouth fell open. "Old Man Wilton's name is *Andrew*?" She clapped a hand over her mouth. "Sorry! I didn't mean…" she sputtered, behind the muffling of her palm.

Mrs. Pinkney just laughed. "I suppose the two of us have seemed rather ancient to you, having been around since before your parents were born. But don't you know that seventy is the new fifty? And fifty is the new thirty?"

Emma winced. "So that makes me what? A ten-year-old?"

"Nah," Haddie chimed in. "Only that you have the emotional maturity of one. And shoe size."

Emma stuck her tongue out at her friend and then realized she was only proving Haddie right.

"So…" Emma continued, turning her attention back to the woman behind the counter. "You must see a lot of Matteo at the farm if you're spending time there, huh? I mean Old Man…" She stopped herself and redirected. "*Andrew* takes in a lot of the displaced wildlife he rescues, right?"

Mrs. Pinkney nodded slowly and seemed to size Emma up through a narrowed gaze.

"Sure, sure," the other woman said, busying herself with tidying up behind the sweet counter. "He spends quite a bit of time on the farm."

Emma's brows furrowed, and she looked at Haddie who shrugged and wrapped her mouth around another ice-cream-filled spoon.

"Spends time there?" Emma inquired. "Like, he hangs out with you and Andrew?"

Mrs. Pinkney raised a brow. "I believe Matteo would be better prepared to answer your questions, Ms. Emma. Don't you?" She slipped back into the stockroom without waiting for Emma to answer.

"That was weird, right?" she asked Haddie.

Haddie tapped her empty spoon against her bottom lip. "I don't think so. She's an eccentric woman, sure. But who in this town isn't?"

Emma opened her mouth to protest, but Haddie pointed at her with her spoon.

"Don't even try to deny it, Emma Woods whose wardrobe includes more cats than should be legal."

Haddie's gaze dipped to Emma's current attire, a maroon tee with the print of a fluffy black cat that read, "Fluff you, you fluffing fluff."

"Fine," Emma conceded. "I'm eccentric. This town is eccentric. But that little evasion when she was talking about Matteo was more than eccentric. It was downright cryptic."

"If you say so," Haddie responded with a laugh. "Now can we please close the laptops so I can pretend I actually *don't* work in the summer and you can maybe do something fun before your big admission to the mayor tomorrow?"

Emma sighed. Haddie was right. She'd already wasted a good chunk of their night going down one dead end after another. She closed her laptop and grabbed the pint.

"I left you the last bite," Haddie told her.

"So generous," Emma replied, then scraped what was left onto her spoon, savored it on her tongue for a couple of seconds, and swallowed it in one delicious gulp.

A notification popped up on her phone, and she and Haddie saw it at the exact same time.

A message from *@summergardener*.

They both gasped.

"Okay, *that* is weird," Haddie admitted.

Emma nodded. The hairs on her arms stood on end just like they had in her car the other day. This was it. The deadline was tomorrow, so either Summertown's artist was going to come through for the town, or Emma was going to take a giant leap and come through for Summertown instead.

She unlocked her phone and tapped open the app to find seven short words.

@summergardener Wilton's Hill. The last sculpture. Come alone.

"Tell me *that's* not cryptic," Emma said.

Haddie huffed out a laugh. "That's cryptic AF. We're going, right? I mean, we have to go."

Emma shook her head.

"*Ems,*" Haddie started. "It's almost 8:00 p.m."

Emma glanced out the shop window. "It's not even dark yet."

"It will be by the time you get there. What if this person isn't even the actual gardener? What if it's some poseur? Did you think of that? Like, this could be some baddy who wants to hurt you."

"Who just happened to text at the exact right

time the night of the town meeting? I mean, fine. Sure. It could be anyone, but whoever it is, they're from Summertown. There's no way these sculptures are popping up unnoticed without whoever the Gardener is knowing a thing or two about the town and when to avoid detection." Emma stood up, took one last glance at the message, and then dropped her phone in the back pocket of her jeans. "Take my stuff back to the inn, and if you don't hear from me in an hour, *then* you can worry."

"And call 911?" Haddie asked.

"And call 911," Emma replied.

"I'm also going to track you on my phone," Haddie added.

Emma laughed. "I'd expect nothing less. But I'm pretty sure I'm going to be okay." She motioned to her laptop and tote bag. "You've got all this, right?"

"Yeah, yeah. I've got it. Be careful. Okay?"

Emma kicked up her sneaker-clad foot. "Look, I'm even wearing hill- climbing shoes. I got this."

Haddie clenched her teeth, then leaned over and hugged her friend. Hard.

"Aw, *Hads*."

"Tell anyone about my voluntary show of public affection, and I will deny it," Haddie whispered.

Emma kissed her on the cheek and laughed. "Noted." The two women broke apart, and Emma smoothed out her T-shirt over her jeans. "Okay.

Here I go. I feel like I should wear my dad's deerstalker or something."

Haddie shook her head vigorously. "Hard pass on that. You look ridiculous enough in that T-shirt."

Emma's eyes widened, and her mouth fell open.

"Kidding!" Haddie said with an eye roll. "Now go so you can be home safe telling me *everything* in no more than an *hour*."

"Okay. Here I go!"

She pivoted on her heel and strode toward the door and out into the last shreds of daylight.

Lightning flashed in the distance as Emma ascended the hill outside of Wilton's Farm. No sound of thunder followed, so she took comfort in the fact that even if a storm was coming, it was still far enough away.

Still, the air grew thick with humidity, and her breaths felt shallower with each inhale.

"Not wheezing," she said out loud, listening for the telltale whistle as she sucked in a breath.

Finally, she made it to the top of the hill, lungs intact. At first, all she saw was Wilton's Farm below on the other side. Probably because the only light above was the moon shrouded behind the overcast sky. She pulled out her phone and turned on the flashlight, then swept it across the grass to her left, right, and then a few feet down the hill toward the farm.

There it was, a couple yards away, something blue peeking up from the thick green grass.

She followed the light and knelt down beside a hubcap intricately painted to resemble a Himalayan blue poppy.

Her breath caught in her throat.

A few feet ahead and further down the hill she saw another. And then another one beyond that.

She fought the urge to run, the hill steeper going down than up, and ignored the thinning air as the humidity grew denser.

The distance between them was so perfectly measured that she found a new poppy every few feet, each one more beautiful than the last.

Emma was wiping away tears by the time she reached the bottom of the hill, though she still wasn't entirely sure what this all meant. Maybe she hadn't taken the festival all that seriously before now because it had been all she'd ever known. Flower gardens and topiaries, while eccentric to the outsider, were always the norm for Summertown.

Until Matteo gave her a small bouquet of Himalayan blue poppies for their first Christmas home after leaving for college.

"I wanted to give you something you'd never seen before," he told her.

"Where did you even get these?" she asked.

Matteo laughed. "My roommate is a botany major. Because of course I leave Summertown to end up with a buddy who studies plants. They take *two* freaking years to bloom. Can you believe that? He started this project in the campus greenhouse his first year. You can't grow these in Summertown, so consider yourself lucky to have the one and only bouquet in central Illinois."

He'd spent a fortune on the rare flowers to keep his roommate from selling them to anyone else, and she'd kissed him—and then some—to show him how lucky she felt, not just for the flowers but for having him in her life.

It had been the one and only time she'd seen the flowers in bloom, but Emma was certain the flowers leading her down the hill were the very same variety.

Rain started falling before she made it to the foot of the hill, so she ran the rest of the way to the barn, where the trail of poppies ended.

She threw open the heavy door as the drizzle quickly turned into an all-out downpour and ran inside, struggling to pull the door shut behind her against the howling wind.

Where she thought she might find a host of wild rescue animals taking shelter from the storm, she instead found herself surrounded by hubcaps and scraps of metal strewn across shelves and on the worktable in the center of the space. But one more poppy sat propped on the table among the raw materials, and as she strode closer, she saw a file folder sitting next to it with a sticky note attached that said, *Read me. I'm ready to get caught. Message me when you're done.*

Emma's eyes darted around the dimly lit room, but she found no one else there. So she sucked in a deep breath, cursing the telltale whistle of her narrowing airways, and reached for her tote bag to grab her inhaler.

"Shit," she hissed out loud, remembering she had asked Haddie to take her stuff back to the inn… including her tote.

She breathed in and out slowly, trying to steady herself enough to ward off the impending asthma attack. According to her phone, she'd been gone thirty minutes already. It should only take her a few minutes to read whatever was in the folder, and then she could text Haddie to come get her with her inhaler in tow.

She brushed her hands over the sticky note, clearly recognizing the same handwriting she saw all over Matteo's study notes those few nights ago.

Her fingers trembled as she lifted the flap of the folder to find what was inside. It was time to leap and hope she either landed on her feet or that someone was there to catch her.

On top of a sheaf of papers sat a printout of a web article: *Local Artist Wyatt Kim Heads Up*

Art Rehabilitation Program at Illinois County Correctional Facility.

The article included a photo of the artist and his star pupil, a young man who'd been prone to frequent outbreaks of fighting with the other inmates but who had turned himself around, finding an unexpected outlet through art. It didn't matter that his name wasn't printed in the article because Emma would recognize those eyes and that crooked smile anywhere.

"Matteo," she whispered.

Along with the article were sentencing documents, most of which she didn't understand other than the time between the dates of his incarceration and release.

Next were medical files denoting a ninety-day stay at a drug rehabilitation facility and documentation of driving while under the influence of a controlled substance—which turned out to be his brother's pain medication—and an empty prescription pad plus thousands of dollars of illegally acquired prescription opiates hidden under the back seats.

She knew all this. Why bring it up now? Why—

Muffled shouts came from outside the barn.

Emma coughed. She felt confused. The air in the barn kept getting thinner.

Her hands shook as she reached for her phone and opened up *not* her Instagram but her list of personal contacts instead.

She tapped the green icon to initiate the call, but he didn't answer.

Again she heard the shouts, this time closer to the door, so she moved toward it even as her vision blurred.

"I said to leave it alone!" a male voice yelled.

"You asshole!" someone yelled back. "You took close to two goddamn years from me. And *Emma*. Jesus, *Emma*!"

The barn door flew open, throwing her to the ground as two figures, wet and muddied, barreled through without even noticing her.

Matteo threw Dawson to the ground, but the deputy was quick, knocking Matteo's feet out from under him. She heard a crack as something hit the ground. His head? Oh god. She couldn't tell.

"Matteo!" she managed to yell just as Dawson, pounced, landing a blow.

Both men scrambled to their feet. Emma tried to do the same, but her limbs felt like wet noodles, and she was suddenly so cold.

"Em?" Matteo yelled, running to her. He dropped down to his knees. "Em?"

"What's wrong with her?" she heard Dawson ask.

"Emma, where's your inhaler?" Matteo yelled, sounding frantic. "She's asthmatic, Hayes. Fuck, her lips are blue."

He pulled her into his arms, and she reached a limp hand toward his face. "You're bleeding."

"Where is it, Emma?" he yelled over the rain as it started pouring again. "Where's your inhaler? You promised you wouldn't forget again. You fucking *promised*."

"Haddie," she coughed. "Tote."

He yelled something at someone, maybe it was her? Maybe… Who else was there? Then he laid her down on the damp ground and leaned over her.

Emma closed her eyes and waited for his kiss.

Chapter 27

If Matteo made it through this day, he swore he would *never* step foot in a hospital again.

"Go!" Tilly said softly as she pushed open his father's hospital door.

"Why?" Matteo's eyes widened. "Dad's surgery just started, and Dr. Geiger said she'd send a nurse with an update as soon as she got him opened up and could really see the damage he'd done."

She shooed him with her hands as she strode toward the chair next to his.

"I'll text you the update. But I just ran into Lynette Woods in the restroom. She said Emma's awake and is asking for you."

Matteo sprung out of his chair, his heart in his throat.

Her parents and Haddie had tag teamed all night long, rotating shifts at the hospital and at the inn. But Matteo had been with her the whole time, from the emergency room breathing treatment to a restless Emma slipping in and out of sleep until she finally couldn't fight slumber anymore.

"Okay," Matteo said, hurrying toward the door, but he stopped just before passing Tilly by.

"What's the matter?" she asked.

Matteo shook his head. "Nothing. I just..." He threw his arms awkwardly around the woman who had always been their neighbor but from here on out he knew would be so much more. "Thank you," he whispered, then straightened to his full height. "My dad is really lucky to have you."

Her mouth opened, but no sound came out. For the first time since Matteo had known her, Tilly Higginson was at a loss for words.

"Don't forget to text me an update," he added before spinning back toward the door and practically sprinting to the elevators that would take him to Emma's floor.

Getting to her room was a blur, but once he was there at the door, he wasn't sure he could go in.

He peeked inside the cracked-open door and saw Emma sitting up and laughing, her mom and the doctor standing opposite her bed.

He sucked in a steadying breath and inched the door open just enough to quietly slip through... and barrel straight into the nurse and her cart who were apparently in his blind spot when he was spying only moments ago.

"Sorry!" he exclaimed, catching the nurse by her shoulders. "So sorry."

She laughed and patted him on the arm. “No worries, buddy. I was just on my way out.”

And she left him standing there with Emma, her mother, and the doctor staring at him and his subtle entrance.

“Good morning, Matty,” Lynette Woods said. “The doctor was just finishing up with Emma’s discharge orders.”

The doctor nodded. “Paperwork will be here within the hour, but according to your vitals, Ms. Woods, you are good to go.” He shook Emma’s hand. “I’ll send the prescription with the discharge information.”

“Thank you, Dr. Mitchell,” Emma said.

The doctor smiled at Matteo and headed through the door.

“I’m going to go upstairs and see how Tilly’s doing,” Mrs. Woods said. “Text me if you need me, okay?”

Emma nodded and gave her mom the double thumbs-up, and then the last buffer between Matteo and Emma left the room, leaving just the two of them.

He stopped at the foot of her bed and crossed and uncrossed his arms.

“You look good,” he said.

Emma tugged at her hospital gown. “What? This old thing? I’ve had it for ages. Can’t believe it still fits.” She looked up at him. “Are those stitches above your eye?”

He nodded as he made his way to the chair opposite her bed. He sat but then stood right back up. "I can't, Em. I can't sit and make small talk and pretend like you didn't almost *die* last night because you left your inhaler behind *again*."

"I know," she conceded. "But do you think part of your anger might be connected to the fact that learning you're *him*—the Gardener—and that it all came from the horrible stuff you went through might have gotten me so distraught that it might have *induced* the asthma attack?"

Matteo threw his hands in the air. "Shit, Emma. Of *course* that's why I'm angry. I'm the reason you're here. I'm—"

"*You're* the reason," she interrupted, "thanks to your mad CPR skills, that I am sitting up and talking to you right now." She whacked her head against the pillows that propped her up. "I was *kidding* about it being your fault. *I* should have had my inhaler. I'm sorry. I was just trying to break the ice because I don't even know where to begin."

He ran a hand through his hair. "Are you okay?" he asked. "Like, *really* okay?"

She nodded. "But just in case I find myself in such a situation again, the doctor is prescribing a few more inhalers for me to keep with people I see often or at places I frequent. I was thinking that maybe *you* could hang on to one for me?"

She worried her bottom lip between her teeth.

Matteo's throat grew tight. "Em, you're going to have to explain what you mean by that in short, slow sentences so I don't miss anything because it sounded to me like even after everything that's happened, you still want me in your life."

Emma pressed her lips into a smile, but her eyes grew glassy. Then she scooted to the side of the mattress and patted the empty spot.

"I read the documents last night, and I read the local coverage when it happened. But I want you to tell me, in *your* words, what happened the night you were pulled over—and what happened last night. Even though I was there last night, the events are a little fuzzy. The stuff in between I'll listen to whenever you want to talk about it. Every day if you want to or never again if that's what you need."

He crawled in the bed and wrapped his arms around her, pulling her to him so all he could smell was her apple-scented shampoo. He buried his face in her hair and kissed the top of her head. It was the only air he wanted to breathe for pretty much the rest of time.

"Levi was in the middle of a game when he found out about our mom. He blew out his knee on a tackle."

Emma nodded, burrowing into the nook between his arm and his chest. "I remember. He was on crutches at the funeral."

"He was on some pretty heavy pain meds in the

weeks after, before they could schedule his surgery. He was a mess. My dad was a mess. And I…" He hadn't said any of this aloud to anyone other than his therapist, and that had been years ago.

"You were holding it together for everyone else, like you always do," Emma continued. "I should have stayed home longer." She squeezed her arms around him. "You should have *asked* me to stay."

"No," he told her. "I'd already accepted that I might have to finish the semester in summer school, but I wasn't going to ask you to do the same. So, yeah, I held it together as long as I could. One night I was so goddamn desperate to fall asleep. Levi's meds always made him groggy. So I took one. It was only supposed to be *one*." He pressed his thumb and forefinger to his eyes. "I should never have gotten behind the wheel that night. I own that, and I'll regret it for the rest of my life. But Emma, the shit they found in the car—the shit that put a goddamn *felony*—on my record? It wasn't mine. And I know how that sounds. Every convicted felon says he's innocent, so I don't expect you to believe me, but—"

"I believe you," she interrupted without hesitation.

He paused. "You…you do?"

She nodded, tilting her head up at him. "Of course I do."

He let out a shaky sigh. "I don't think I knew how much I needed to hear you say that until now. It makes the bullshit from last night feel like—bullshit."

She smiled, and despite her lying in a hospital bed because he'd almost lost her the night before, Matteo wasn't sure if he'd ever been happier than he was right then, at that moment.

"So are you going to let Lauren's newspaper run the article about Dawson's father?" she asked.

Matteo's eyes widened. "You know?"

She nodded. "Dawson came by about fifteen minutes ago. Told me your reporter friend traced a tip she'd received back to the academy recruits. Didn't take her long to connect Dawson and his father with Mr. Hayes's prior substance abuse history. But Matteo. He was—"

"A scared kid who made a really bad decision?" He let out a bitter laugh. "Not gonna say I can't relate." He shook his head and tucked her hair behind her ear. "It's too late for me to have any legal recourse, but I thought at least I needed to clear my name. But you know what? Taking someone else down isn't going to give me back what I lost. And I don't want to be stuck in that time anymore, Em. I want to move forward. With *you*."

She slid her leg between his and pulled his head down to hers.

"I love you, Matty Matt." She kissed him. "I don't think I ever stopped, even when I thought the worst about you."

He grinned. "I know. You told me the other night."

Emma gasped. "You *heard*?"

He laughed. "I don't mind hearing it again."

She narrowed her eyes at him but couldn't keep herself from smiling. "I *love* you, Matteo Rourke, my vandal gardener."

He laughed. "Who the town already thinks is a criminal." That part did still sting, but he had to let it go.

She shook her head. "The town that *loves* you, Matteo. It's time to start seeing yourself how they *actually* see you and not how you assume they see you."

She kissed him again, and every time her lips touched his, Matteo felt the door slowly and finally begin to close on the past he'd been trying to outrun for so long.

"I have loved you for more than half of my life, Emma Woods," he told her. "And if it's okay with you, I'd like to love you for the rest of it too."

She snuggled in close, burying her face against his neck and peppering it with featherlight kisses that made it impossible for him not to smile.

"That sounds like an excellent plan, Mr. Rourke. I'm glad I took the leap last night."

He squeezed her tight against him. "And I'm glad you trusted me to catch you."

They stayed like that for several minutes, just

wrapped in each other, knowing there was nothing left between them they couldn't handle or overcome.

"Wait!" Emma propped herself up on her elbow. "Today's the deadline for the Gardener to reveal himself to the mayor."

He nodded. "And the deadline for Lauren's story. It's all taken care of." He pivoted to his back, then pulled out his phone and opened up the Summertown Instagram page. He handed the phone to Emma.

She stared at the latest post—a picture of Old Man Wilton posing just inside his open barn, surrounded by all of Matteo's materials and works in progress.

> Farmer Andrew Wilton reveals himself as **@summergardener**. Turns out the mayor's brother-in-law was the one responsible for Summertown's boom in tourism even after a devastating tornado tore up the town. Looks like the artistic touch runs in the family. **#Summertown #twintowngardenfest #wejustmightwinthisthing**

Emma's jaw dropped. "Old Man Wilton is Lottie Green's *brother*?" She buried her head in her hands. "Oh that poor man. First his wife divorces him, and now this? What's keeping Mayor Green from arresting *him*?"

Matteo raised his brows. "Apparently Lottie is offering quite a nice chunk of change as long as Walter upholds the tradition of Summertown's involvement in the annual festival. It means the Gardener is untouchable."

"That's great!" Emma exclaimed. "But then why Andrew as a front?"

He kissed her. "Because as soon as the Gardener strikes again with Farmer Wilton in plain sight, the mystery begins again."

She laughed. "You *love* being the eccentric mysterious artist!"

He shrugged. "Apparently it's good for local business, and some offers to purchase pieces have started to trickle in."

She slid her arms around his neck. "My brilliant, talented vandal of art."

"My smart, sexy, asthmatic accomplice."

She scoffed, but Matteo made up for the slight—albeit a *true* slight—by pressing his lips to hers.

Chapter 28

Emma, Matteo, and Haddie backed up to admire the twentieth-anniversary Golden Topiary atop the inn's mantel.

"Is it a dragon?" Haddie asked.

"I think it's a bird," Emma replied.

"I'm pretty sure it's a dog," Matteo said.

"*This* is what all the hoopla was about?" Haddie continued. "Because that statue thing is actually going to give me nightmares."

Emma snorted, and Pancake rubbed his head against her ankle.

"It's the title that matters to the town," Lynette Woods called over her shoulder as she strode through the lobby. "And don't forget the cash prize!"

"Right," Matteo said. "And the title of *Winner*. We won the Twin Town Garden Fest on our own, without Lottie Green having to swoop in and save us like she always did. And now we are well on our way to live gardens for next year and getting this town back into shape."

Emma laughed and wrapped her arms around his waist. "Says the guy who swooped in and saved us."

"Shh!" Matteo looked left and right, then over his shoulder with feigned paranoia. "I have no idea what you're talking about."

Emma laughed, then stood on her toes and pressed a kiss to his cheek. "You're adorable when you're a small-town superhero."

Haddie mimed vomiting. "Just kidding. You two are *adorable* with all your love and happiness and public displays of affection."

Emma let go of Matteo and turned her attention to her friend. "Do you really have to go back today?" she asked.

Haddie nodded. "I want to finish my training running the actual course a few times. You promise you'll be back in time for the race?"

Emma grabbed her hand. "Wouldn't miss it. We'll drive up the week before. Matteo wants to see the apartment before I pack it up."

Haddie's lip wobbled, but she breathed in hard through her nose and pasted on a smile.

"Are you *sure* you want to chuck your studio-apartment-slash-home-office…and *me* for a town that's looking more and more like the *Willy Wonka* movie set each day?"

Now Emma's lip was wobbling, and she didn't have it in her to try and sniffle it away.

"I didn't realize how much I missed home until I finally let myself come back."

Matteo slipped his hand into hers, and she laced their fingers together.

"Also, the beauty of the home office is that I can work from anywhere I call home, and Summertown is home…for now at least. But you're coming for Thanksgiving and New Year's, right? And you always have a summer job at the inn. Plus, I can head back to the city for one of your many three-day weekends."

"Like Labor Day?" Haddie asked with a sniff.

Emma nodded. "And Presidents' Day, and whatever other Mondays are deemed non-attendance days. This isn't goodbye, Hads. It's just going to be longer stints between our visits, but we can FaceTime every day."

"*Twice* a day?" Haddie asked, brows raised at Matteo.

"No more competition between you two," Emma told them both with a laugh. "I love you both equally and in very different ways, so there is no reason to compete because you *both* win, okay?"

Both Haddie and Matteo grumbled something under their breath, and Emma took that as agreement to the moratorium on rivalry.

"Take care of her when I'm not around," Haddie told Matteo. "And never go anywhere without her inhaler."

Matteo patted the side pocket of his jeans. "Always with me."

Haddie patted the tote hanging from her shoulder. "Same here."

"Do you mind if I walk her to her car?" she asked Matteo.

He gave the two women a soft bow and then backed away.

Emma hooked her arm through Haddie's, and side by side they strolled out onto the Woods Family Inn's porch.

They both squinted into the early August sun as the early morning temps began to rise toward what promised to be another scorcher of a day.

"I knew," Haddie said when it was just the two of them. "I knew the second I saw you with him that you weren't coming back."

Emma let loose a tearful laugh. "I wish someone had told *me* how in love with him I still was."

Haddie tugged her close. "You had to figure that out for yourself, Ems. That's the only way to believe it."

"And what about you?" Emma asked. "I worry about you all by yourself in the big city."

Haddie waved her off. "I'm never short on company. Plus, we're going to FaceTime three times a day." She winked, and Emma laughed. Then the two of them stepped down the porch steps and onto the sidewalk that led to Haddie's car.

"It's *not* goodbye," Emma reminded her friend as Haddie blew her a kiss from the open car window. "I'll see you in a couple weeks!"

Haddie gave her one last wave before idling out of her parking spot and slowly pulling away.

Matteo was waiting for her on the porch with open arms when Emma trudged back up, tears leaking from the corners of both eyes. He pulled her to his chest and ran his fingers softly through her hair.

"We can move to Chicago," he whispered, the same thing he'd been offering for weeks.

But she shook her head and sniffled, then looked up at him with what she hoped came off as a hopeful smile.

"I stayed away for so long because I was afraid Summertown would remind me of you. Now I want to stay because it reminds me of *us*. The us that we were and the us I know we're going to be."

He kissed the tip of her nose. "In that case, do you want to go pack up half-a-dozen squirrels from the attic and take them to Wilton's Farm?"

Emma laughed through her tears. "Why yes, I would. I thought you'd never ask."

That night, as they lay in bed, a tangled mess of sheets and limbs, Emma scrolled through the photos on her phone.

"You're not *working*, are you, Emma Woods?"

He traced soft circles around her belly button as she began selecting photos for the post.

"We *won* the fest," she told him, sucking in sharp little breaths as he tickled her already sensitive skin. "The Gardener needs a retrospective post of his best work."

She scrolled all the way back to the beginning. The sunflowers, the lotus flowers, and the Dr. Seuss trees. She was scrolling so fast that she almost missed it. *Almost.*

"Matteo?"

He was kissing her shoulder. "Yeah? I'm a little busy, Em. Just because *you're* working doesn't mean *I* have to."

"Matteo," she repeated with a little bit more force, and this time he looked up.

"What is this?" she asked, showing him the aerial photo of the Seuss-like trees. "Whoever took this photo of the trees was on the *roof* of the town hall. How do I have this photo?"

He offered a sheepish grin in response.

"Remember how you left your phone with me when you were being questioned by the deputy?"

She furrowed her brows. "*Yes…*"

He propped himself up on his elbow. "And remember how you thought I was jealous of Deputy Hayes?"

"Uh-huh…"

"Well, when he admitted to me that he was interested in you, I decided I was done sitting on the sidelines. I mean, he's a good person—even if I hate admitting it—and I tried telling myself to just let it happen with him and let you be happy with a guy who doesn't have a messy past and an uncertain future. But I couldn't do it. I couldn't go down without a fight. So I decided right there on the Sheriff's Department steps that I was going to tell you my story, bit by bit, until you were ready to hear the whole thing. So I air-dropped the photo before I gave you back your phone."

Emma rolled onto her side to face him.

"You told me you were the Gardener *that* day."

He nodded.

"And the LED display, the Instagram DMs, those weren't just for Summertown to win the Garden Fest?"

Matteo shook his head. "The festival win was a fortunate by-product, but no. The garden was always my shot in the dark at a second chance…" He brushed his lips over hers. "With *you*."

She pulled him over her, letting her legs fall open, inviting him inside.

"Again?" he asked with a wicked grin.

She felt him nudge her opening and sucked in a breath. Looked like he was ready for round two as well.

"We've got eight years to make up for," she teased. "This is just the beginning."

"Okay, but..." He nipped playfully at her bottom lip. "I'm definitely going to need a protein shake and a nap after this one. Possibly in the reverse order."

She laughed. "I think that can be arranged." Then he sank deep inside her, filling her with love and hope and trust that no matter how far or how high she leaped, he'd always be there to catch her.

And if he ever stumbled again, she'd catch him right back.

Epilogue

"Dad? Tilly?" Matteo called as he and Emma stepped through the front door. "We're here!"

No one answered them back, and Matteo felt the same sinking feeling he'd felt months before when he'd come home to find his father gone and all the missed texts and voicemails he'd sent before winding up in the ER.

"Something's not right," he said. "They knew we were coming." But the kitchen and living room were empty. His phone was text and voicemail free.

"Are you sure they said to meet here?" Emma asked. "Maybe we were supposed to meet *at* the restaurant."

While Matteo had never been big on birthdays, even he had to admit that this one was important. He was *thirty*. His father was back at work, while he and Emma were about to launch the Gardener's gallery and e-commerce site. His life was so full, and for the first time in years, he wanted to celebrate that with the people he loved.

"No," he finally replied. "Also, do you feel a draft?" he asked. The sheer kitchen curtains billowed over the back door. "What the hell? He left the back door open."

Matteo threw back the curtain and grabbed the opened door only to feel someone shove him by the shoulders so that he stumbled out onto the deck.

"Surprise!" a chorus of voices yelled.

Then he heard a click, and hanging lanterns lit up the perimeter of the deck. When his eyes finally adjusted, Matteo saw his father and Tilly, Lynette and Hank Woods, Old Man Wilton and Mrs. Pinkney, and a face he hadn't seen in years.

Wyatt Kim. The art teacher who, eight years ago, unwittingly changed the course of Matteo's life.

For several seconds, Matteo couldn't speak. He wasn't even sure he was still breathing, but took the fact that he was still standing as evidence that he was.

"Happy Birthday, Matty Matt," Emma said, appearing at his side.

He draped his arm over her shoulders.

"Did you plan all this?" he asked, finally able to form coherent words.

"Maybe?" she admitted. "But I had plenty of help."

He spent the night on sensory overload, not used to all attention pointing to him, but for the first time in as long as he could remember, not hating it either.

"Wyatt," Matteo started, finally getting a chance to pull him away from the group. "This is Emma."

"It's nice to finally meet you, Emma."

Wyatt extended his hand for Emma to shake, but instead she stood on her toes, throwing her arms around his neck, which was no small feat considering he was at least an inch or two taller than Matteo.

"Oh," he continued, still facing Matteo. "She's a hugger!"

Wyatt laughed and hugged her back, lifting her off the ground as he straightened and then lowering her back to her feet.

"We chatted via email," Emma confessed. "I mean, I had to hunt him down to get him here, right?"

"And I was more than happy to oblige," Wyatt said. "Especially for my star pupil who dropped off the map for almost a decade before calling in a social media favor."

Matteo winced. "Yeah, about that disappearing act…"

Wyatt held up his hands. "No explanation necessary. We all need our time and space to figure life out. I'm just happy to see things going so well for you, and that you're painting and creating again. You know, County has made the art rehab program a yearly thing. They're always looking for more artists to mentor those who need mentoring."

"Me?" Matteo asked. "Why?"

Emma grabbed his hand. "How about because you're brilliant and talented and a perfect example of how the program made an impact on you not only while you were there but also further down the line?"

Wyatt shrugged. "She's a smart one, Rourke. I'd keep her. Look. You don't have to say yes right now, but if you decide you want to give it a try, I'll recommend you, write a letter of reference, whatever it takes to get you in there."

"I don't know what to say, Wyatt. This is really unexpected."

Wyatt grabbed Matteo's hand and gave it a firm shake. "Say you'll think about it because I think—no, I *know*—that you're the perfect man for the job."

Matteo swallowed the lump in his throat and nodded. "Okay. I'll think about it."

When they made it to the foot of Wilton's hill, Matteo stopped short and turned to Emma.

"Inhaler?" he asked.

She rolled her eyes and tapped the side pocket of her jacket.

"Inhaler?" she parroted.

Matteo patted the chest pocket of his puffer vest. "I never leave home without it, which is more than I can say for you, Ms. Woods."

Emma groaned. "It's been three months. Are you never going to let this go?"

He shrugged. "Probably not. Now are you ready for your birthday surprise?"

Her brows furrowed. "It's *your* birthday, silly. Not mine."

He tugged her beanie down over her ears and kissed her cheek, her nose, and then her other cheek.

"Don't worry," he told her. "I promise the surprise is completely self-serving."

She laughed. "Well, in that case, shall we?" She nodded toward the top of the hill.

Matteo pulled out his Maglite and turned it on to illuminate their path to the top. Once they got to their destination, though, they wouldn't need it anymore.

The air was brisk and thin, and when they paused at the hill's peak, he made her take a puff from her inhaler, even though she claimed she didn't need it. Then he pointed toward the barn, which at the moment was simply a barn.

"My brother and I rebuilt it after the fire," he told her. "That's why Wilton lets me use it now that he doesn't anymore. He says it's mine anyway. So it's kind of been my real home, you know? The place where I can just be."

Emma nodded.

"And now that you're here, the place where my

heart lives..." He pressed his palm over the left side of her chest. "I wanted to ask you something."

He felt her pulse quicken beneath his palm, and he smiled. Then he pulled his phone from his pocket and opened the LED app, igniting his display. The roof and outer wall of Matteo's home away from home lit up with three simple words. *Marry me, Emma.*

She gasped, and when she turned back to face him, he was down on his knee, the sapphire and diamond ring pinched between his thumb and forefinger.

"Oh my god!" Emma covered her mouth and nose with trembling hands. "It's a poppy."

"I know. I decided I needed to make you *one* more." He let out a nervous laugh. "It's a question, by the way. The words on the barn. Not a command. I just didn't have enough lights to add the 'Will you' part."

She dropped to her knees in front of him and held out her hand.

"Only if it fits," she said, trying to tease him, but the tears gave her away.

"Only if it fits?" he asked. "And if it doesn't, do I get to go door to door until I find someone with the right-sized finger and ask *her* to be my wife instead?"

Emma grabbed the ring and shoved it onto *her* finger. Of course it was a perfect fit.

"I'm not an amateur, Ems. I measured your finger while you were sleeping a month ago."

She stared at her finger with wide glassy eyes and the biggest, most beautiful smile he'd ever seen. Still, he had to ask to be sure.

"Is that a yes? Because it would be really reassuring just to hear the word."

She tackled him, and he crashed flat on his back against the grass with a thump.

"Sorry!" she cried. "But I am very happy and very full of adrenaline right now, and that might be giving me superhuman strength."

"Noted," he croaked, still catching his breath. "But you still haven't answered."

"Oh!" Emma exclaimed. "Right. What was the question again?"

He closed his eyes and groaned.

She lowered herself so her lips were a breath away from his.

"Yes, Matty Matt," she whispered. "Forever and always, *yes*."

Acknowledgments

Thank you so much to my editor, Deb, for giving me the chance to do something a little different. Don't get me wrong...I love my cowboys, but it was fun coming up with this quirky little town and their mystery garden art!

To my agent, Emily, I'm so grateful to get to work with you on *all* the things. Here's to many more fun projects in and out of Summertown!

Lea, Megan, Jen, and Chanel...my sisters by choice...I love that we've all been in this together since the beginning. Thank you for the daily support, laughs, and occasional sprinkle of peppermint oil.

S and C, my two favorite humans, I'm so lucky to have you both, but remember that you have to take a cat with you when you go to college. M and W, thank you for the dedicated bookshelf in the new house. D and I, thanks for making the stores go and grab the book from the back if it's not on the shelf yet on release day.

And always, my wonderful, supportive readers, thank *you* for letting me do this thing I love. It means the world that you love it too.

About the Author

A corporate trainer by day and *USA Today* bestselling author by night, A.J. Pine can't seem to escape the world of fiction, and she wouldn't have it any other way. When she finds that twenty-fifth hour in the day, she might indulge in a tiny bit of TV to nourish her undying love of K-dramas, superheroes, and everything romance. She hails from the far-off galaxy of the Chicago suburbs.

Find her online at ajpine.com, facebook.com/ajpineauthor, Instagram @aj_pine, Twitter @AJ_Pine, and TikTok @aj_pine.